HAND PICKED

MAY ARCHER

Cover Art: Cate Ashwood Designs

Cover Photo: Wander Aguiar

Cover Model: @caymancardiff

Editing: One Love Editing

Beta Reading: Lucy Lennox, Shay Haude, Leslie Copeland

Proofreading: Victoria Rothenberg, Lori Parks

Prologue

Dear Mr. Williams,

Congratulations! We are delighted to inform you that your submission, Weaving a Legacy, *has been chosen from the many entries in the* Craft a Better Life *contest.*

An elegant, centuries-old granite farmhouse full of quaint historical artifacts, set on forty idyllic acres of land with two enclosed livestock pastures in charming Little Pippin Hollow, *Vermont (estimated value: over 1 million dollars)* will be yours in perpetuity, and the ownership thereof will be transferred into your name as soon as is practicable. All fees have been paid by the contest-holder, Benjamin Pond, and all that remains is for you to sign ownership papers and collect your keys. As the property is currently vacant, you are free to take possession at your earliest convenience. We're excited for you to embark on your fairy-tale adventure!*

Sincerely,

James T. Kruk
Kruk, Dommer, and Fruit PLLC

. . .

*All claims in regards to the value, size, and substantive nature of the property are made in good faith based on information provided by the contest holder and have not been personally verified by our firm.

Chapter One

LUKE

Eight months later

"What, um—" I peered up through the giant gaping wound in the living room ceiling, through the second floor and the attic beyond, to where a few snowflakes leftover from last night's blizzard drifted across the twilight sky. "What happened here?"

The man-child beside me coughed lightly. "Well. I, ah... I think you've got a brand-new hole in your roof, Mr. Williams."

I nodded slowly. "Yup. Thank you, Murray. Yes. Now that you say it, I do believe it *is* a hole in the roof." I stared up some more. "Any insight into how it might have gotten there?"

"Oh. Well." Murray pulled his hat down more firmly over his ears and stuffed his hands in his pockets. He was tall—half a foot taller than my five-eight frame, at least—but still just nineteen and gawky as all heck. He craned his neck and peered up also, like the answer might be written in the heavens. "Uh, I figure... I figure it's 'cause this bit of roof ain't where it's s'posed to be?"

He kicked lightly at the large pile of snow, plaster dust, and rotten wood that stood like a miniature Matterhorn in the middle of the wide-planked hardwood floor.

Murray was not wrong. The plaster and lath were not where they were supposed to be. Nor where they'd been just the day before.

But then, many things seemed out of place in the postapocalyptic "fairy-tale adventure" I'd "embarked on" last summer… including, I sometimes thought, *me*.

"Uh-huh. *Uh-huh*," I agreed gravely, staring down at the pile of junk. "Murray, excellent observation."

He beamed. "Do you know, I'm kinda starting to maybe understand why old Ben Pond gave his house away in that essay contest last year?"

I chuckled ruefully. "Yup. Funny how that happens, huh?"

I hadn't understood it either when I'd first won. I'd been too excited at the prospect of living in a *historical treasure*, owning acres of land where I'd raise sheep and host fiber arts retreats, and having a whole town full of new friends, to really question why a man would just give away his family's property to a stranger and leave town.

My friends back in North Carolina had wrinkled their noses and said if things sounded too good to be true, they probably were… but I'd known better. Unexpected good things happened at least as often as unexpected bad things, especially if you worked hard and kept an eye out for them.

That was why, when I'd first parked my old hatchback out front last summer, I'd thought I'd found my own little slice of heaven. The building looked incredibly square and incredibly sturdy. Three stories of cream-and-gray stone were capped with a slate roof and four—*four!*—chimneys that stood like sentries looking over the yard. Ivy grew lazily up the columns that supported the portico over the mammoth front door.

The yard had been a bit overgrown, sure, but I wasn't foolish enough to expect perfection. In fact, I'd been gleeful at the idea of getting my hands dirty before school started in the fall—clipping the bushes, mowing the grass, getting the barn ready for the three rare breed Romeldale sheep that were due to arrive in just a few weeks' time.

I'd sent a picture to my mom, and she'd immediately replied, "You got your Happily Ever After, baby! Congratulations!" which was exactly how I'd felt.

I thought I'd found my place—the place where I could make a difference and have a purpose. The place where all my half-formed dreams were waiting for me. I'd found a ready-made *home*.

Then I'd unlocked the front door with the big skeleton key the lawyers had given me.

It had opened with a creak... and the entire doorframe had fallen into the front hall with a *thud*, startling a flock of birds that had flown out of the house and directly at my face, resulting in a manic do-si-do that had left me sunny-side-up in the yew bushes beside the front steps.

I'd gotten wise pretty quickly after that.

"Have you thought about maybe getting the roof... fixed?" Murray suggested tentatively.

Something about his hesitation made me smile. "I have, I promise. It's the next item on my list. But it's a very long list. But I'm a man with a short bank account."

"If you want, when I come take care of the sheep tomorrow, I can bring you over a big tarp, just in case it snows again," Murray offered. "Can't hurt, anyway."

"Yeah," I said tiredly. "That'd be great."

"I can try to put it up for you, too—"

"Oh, no. Heck, no. That's dangerous. I'll take care of it."

I wasn't sure how the fudge *I'd* get a tarp on a three-story-high roof either, especially on my own in the snow, but I was sure I could figure something out.

"And don't forget to tell me how much I owe you for the last two weeks, okay? I know you've got a tuition payment coming up."

"Yeah. Thanks, Mr. Williams."

I squeezed Murray's shoulder in acknowledgement. And since the front door still didn't have operational hinges, I steered him toward the back door through the ruins of the kitchen—a room which managed to pair cracked Formica and a crumbling, soot-stained brick fireplace in an aesthetic I was calling Early Eclectic Hovel, which was gonna become trendy any day now.

"You remember I said you should call me Luke, right?" I said once we'd stepped out into the cold night. "You've been taking care of my sheep and plowing my driveway for months now. And when you feed a man's ruminants, it bonds you, Murray. In many cultures, we'd be family."

Murray snickered. "You're really funny, Mr. Williams. I —" His face fell comically. "Oops! *Luke.* Forgot already. Sorry! It's just that all Olin ever says at home is 'Mr. Williams does' this and 'Mr. Williams said' that, so it's hard to remember. You're his favorite teacher, you know, and my parents are really happy with how much he's learning."

"Aw. That's nice to hear." I taught first grade, so I didn't have a lot of competition for the "favorite teacher" title, but it was nice to hear that people thought I was doing a good job… even though I was sure certain *other* parents would disagree.

I couldn't help glancing across the snowy fields that separated my property from Sunday Orchard and the family of sweet, gorgeous lumberjacky types who lived there. I quickly looked away before my thoughts could linger too long on one lumberjacky type in particular: Webb Sunday.

Not everybody has to like you, I reminded myself. *It's okay.*

Murray kept talking. "And for sure you're Aiden Sunday's favorite teacher… even if you did kind of lose him that one time and Webb got all upset."

I sighed. "I was doing my job," I mumbled in protest, though it didn't seem to matter how many times I repeated it since Webb didn't seem inclined to hear me, and neither did anyone else. "And I didn't *lose* him."

"Sure." Murray nodded sympathetically. "You just sort of… misplaced him."

I sighed again.

Murray wasn't *entirely* wrong.

I wasn't a person who had regrets—mistakes were just learning opportunities, after all—but I greatly, profoundly, completely, *entirely* regretted listening to Principal Oliver last fall when she'd told me to let Aiden Sunday leave school with his mother though I knew the boy lived with his dad.

In my defense, I'd only been in town a couple of months. I hadn't understood the contentious custody dispute brewing between Webb Sunday and his ex-wife. I definitely hadn't understood that Amanda Sunday was known in the Hollow for being thoughtless and irresponsible and that Principal Oliver was one of her only remaining local friends. I'd simply gone along with what my boss told me, despite an uncomfortable feeling in my gut.

But Webb hadn't cared about any of that when Aiden hadn't gotten off the bus that afternoon. He'd lost his mind. And roughly four months and eight attempts to explain myself later, Webb still crossed the street when he saw me coming, so he clearly still held me responsible.

The worst part was, Webb wasn't the only person in town who wasn't joining the Luke Williams fan club. I got the idea that the rest of the folks in the Hollow didn't quite know what to do with me either.

People were friendly, of course. Heck, I didn't think folks around here knew how to be *un*friendly. They always smiled and said hi. Waved back when I waved first. Chitchatted if I initiated it. Nobody was overtly unkind to me *ever*.

But also I definitely didn't feel like I was one of them. Not yet.

And being an outsider didn't just mean that my social calendar was absurdly empty, it also had a real impact on my ability to do... well, *anything* related to my house.

The renovation loan I'd tried to get from Pippin Hollow Credit Union had been denied due to a length-of-residency clause that no one had mentioned when I'd first applied.

I'd tried to sell off a portion of my newly acquired land to finance the repairs, and I'd been told I needed a "clean title"—which apparently meant getting someone to search through a billionty years of Ben Pond's family's history and mark out the lot lines.

The only lawyer in town, Curt Simons, had claimed a conflict of interest and referred me to a guy in Two Rivers, who'd taken my retainer and promptly stopped returning my calls for three months.

It had taken a minute for me to connect the dots, but then I'd understood. The Sundays *were* Little Pippin Hollow. Their family had lived on their land for centuries, and everyone in town—even someone as new as me— knew that if you wanted a person to coach kids' soccer, or contribute to your fundraiser, or help build your barn, Webb Sunday was the man to ask.

So if Webb didn't like me, it made a strange kind of sense that the rest of the town would keep me at arm's length, too. I couldn't even be mad about it, because it was the kind of small-town loyalty I'd craved to be a part of…

It just stank that I *wasn't* a part of it.

But I kept hoping that if I worked hard and stuck around long enough, things would change.

"So." I gave Murray a brilliant smile. "Exciting plans for tonight, Murray?"

"I'm heading over to the Sundays' place to pick up Aiden for a sleepover with Olin. Even though the roads are clear, they're saying they'll probably cancel school again tomorrow, 'cause it's not safe for kids to get to the bus stops. A second snow day will be really great, eh?"

"Oh. Yeah. That's…" I reflected on what I'd done that afternoon—sitting in the drafty, overcrowded camper trailer that had been Ben Pond's actual home, all by myself, frogging out the stitches of the crochet project I'd ruined. "…great."

If by "great" you meant "likely to end with me eating every carbohydrate in my camper, shaving my head just to see how it looks, and watching organizational TikToks while I ignore the utter chaos of my own living space."

"Hey, if you're heading to the Sundays', would you mind dropping something off for me? I've got a book I promised Aiden. Let me just grab it."

I trudged across the plowed driveway to the 1978 Coachman Cadet and pulled open the door with a spine-jarring yank. The rusty hinges squealed, and a few flakes drifted down to join their brethren in the snow below. The nineteen-foot travel trailer wasn't much to look at, but at least it didn't have snow falling *inside* of it. Plus, it had electricity, gas heat, running water, and my Wi-Fi hotspot. What else could anyone need?

I turned on the lights and let the somewhat warmer air loosen my shoulders. "Give me a minute to find it. It's hard to keep things organized in here."

I turned in a circle to remind myself where to begin. Picture books, chapter books, school supplies, and heaps of colorful yarn took up every available space in the trailer.

When I spotted the book I was looking for, I extracted it carefully from its cubby. A zipper pouch of Magic Markers tumbled to the table below, knocking a stack of math worksheets to the ground.

"Gracious gravy. Sorry! One of these days, I'll find the right organization system." I rolled my eyes. "Or, you know, manage to part with some of my teaching materials."

I'd done as much as I could to spruce up the camper with a gallon of paint and a bunch of bins and bags from the dollar store, but it was a constant fight to keep the place from looking like a refugee from Hoarders: School Supply Edition.

Murray's big body nearly knocked me sideways as he passed me in the narrow walkway between the sofa and banquette. "I recognize this. It's Olin's, right?"

"Yup!" I smiled at the stick drawing of Olin, Aiden, Olin's brothers and sisters, and the dog that was taller than all of them put together. "When I was out sick a few weeks ago, the substitute had the students draw me pictures to cheer me up. Olin said his dog always makes him smile. I told him now his dog would make me smile, too."

Murray hummed and took the offered book from my hands. "Must be working. You sure do smile a lot, Mr.... um, Luke."

I laughed. "Sometimes you've gotta smile, Murray, or

you'd cry your eyes out. In fact, the best time to smile is when things are at their roughest. Find something to be grateful for, and fake it until you make it."

"I s'pose. Or you could just… do something to make yourself happier, right? Like, I told Webb he oughta get a puppy for Aiden to cheer him up. Poor kid's had it rough, missing his mom and all."

Thinking about Webb Sunday again made my stomach flip over, a kind of painful yearning-frustrated ache that got worse when I tried to push it away.

"They already have a dog, though," I said without thinking.

"Yeah, but Sally Ann's getting up there. If they get a pup now, she can train him up, and it won't be so hard on Aiden when she passes." He shrugged. "But what do I know? Webb knows best."

I felt my smile slip before I caught it.

Webb didn't know everything.

He didn't know me, or how much I liked this town, or that I wanted to be a friend to him, if he'd let me…

Wow, yeah, great job of putting that situation behind you and staying positive, Williams.

"Anyway. I best get going so I can pick up Aiden and make it home in time to watch the boys while my folks go to the town meeting. You going? Aw, you should," he said when I shook my head. "Big developer wants to build a vacation resort up on Fogg Peak—" He pointed somewhere vaguely north of the barn where my sheep were nestled down for the night. "Dad says half the town's gonna lose their minds if Mayor York lets it happen, and the other half'll lose their minds if he doesn't. Gonna be a doozy."

"Wrestlemania, but Little Pippin Hollow style?"

Murray snicker-snorted. "Kinda. And afterward,

folks'll end up at the Bugle to drink Rusty Spikes and watch hockey."

"Rusty Spikes?"

"Mmm. They're whiskey and… something that tastes like fruit punch. My dad says they'll make you forget your troubles. My mom says they'll make you forget your name." He grinned. "You don't have to drink if you don't wanna, though. You can just go for the hockey. That's what my mom does."

"Ah, well, I don't know a thing about hockey either, so…"

"Wait. You mean you don't know how to play hockey? Or you… you don't follow the NHL?"

"Uh… both?"

"Oh, my God, Mr. Luke." Murray's eyes went round and shiny in the near-darkness. "You poor thing. Nobody ever taught you?"

I ran a hand over my mouth to hide my smile. Murray didn't seem to pity me for the bomb crater in my farmhouse living room, but the fact that I didn't understand the intricacies of strapping knives on your feet and heaving yourself around an ice field was enough to bring him to tears.

"I'm afraid it's not on the curriculum in North Carolina," I admitted.

"It's the best thing in the world, Mr. Williams," he said in a hushed voice. "You gotta get somebody to teach you."

I liked how he thought the streets were crowded with people just dying to teach a man hockey…

Although, for all I knew, maybe here in Vermont they were.

"I'll do that. One of these days."

"M'kay." Murray inched toward the door, a little reluctantly. "Really think about going to the meeting, you know?

Winter can be lonely if you don't get out and clear the cobwebs once in a while, and people would be glad to see you."

I wasn't sure why that simple sentence from him brought tears to my eyes—probably because I wished so much that it was true.

"Good advice!" I said with false cheer. "You drive safely, okay?"

I waved goodbye and closed the door behind him, then turned around and promptly tripped over a stack of books, crash-landing facedown on my bed.

After a beat, I let out a muffled scream.

I prided myself on seeing the silver lining of any situation, but I was having a really hard time at that precise moment.

My historic home was crumbling to dust even faster than I'd imagined. My trailer was barely warmer than the outdoors. And I was getting tired of my own company.

I wanted someone to pour out my troubles to. Someone who'd pat my head and remind me that things would look better in the morning. Heck, I wanted someone to help me *make* it better in the morning, ideally with hot sex, strong coffee, a degree in roof repair, and a winning smile.

But since none of that was likely to happen, I needed to stop my pity party in its tracks because seriously, *yuck*.

So what I needed was to do exactly what Murray said —to *make* myself happier, if only for a minute. What I needed… was a Rusty Spike.

I flipped onto my back and contemplated the ceiling.

Was this a safe, sane, and responsible idea? *Oooh*, hard no.

Was it better than the alternative of sitting here all night and again tomorrow?

The wind blew through some unseen crack in my camper home like the shrill whistle of a teakettle, and I felt like fate had spoken.

So I jumped up, washed my face, grabbed my keys, and headed for the Bugle to see what fate had in store.

Chapter Two

WEBB

"A vacation resort in Little Pippin Hollow!" my brother fumed. "Ridiculous. Everyone knows Jeremiah Fogg donated the land around Fogg Peak to the town! It's *bullshit!*"

As I followed Hawkins up the steps to Little Pippin Hollow's town hall, I came to the uncomfortable realization that somehow, without my knowledge or consent, I'd gotten fucking *old*.

I would swear to you that just yesterday, I'd been playing high school football and flirting with girls. Now, suddenly, I was That Guy, who needed to hold the railing while climbing the steps because I'd wrenched my back while shoveling snow, and who was trying really, really hard not to roll my eyes at all the exclamation points I could hear in Hawk's outraged tone, because I couldn't remember the last time I'd had enough surplus energy to feel that much emotion over any-damn-thing.

This was not what I imagined thirty-eight would look like.

"It's *total* bullshit," I agreed, though I was thinking

more about my aching back than the proposed development. "But let's go hear what the real estate people and the mayor have to say, okay? Let's not jump to conclusions."

Hawk nodded once, firmly. "Know thy enemy," he agreed, though that was not what I'd said at all. "Good call."

My youngest sibling, seventeen-year-old Emma, gave me a concerned look behind Hawk's back as he yanked open the door to the redbrick building. A look that said *Do something, Webb*. But the best I could do was shrug in response.

Was it strange that my sweet, shy youngest brother was suddenly quoting *The Art of War*?

Yup. Sure was.

And that was why I wasn't home watching SportsCenter. For whatever reason, this proposed development was important to Hawk, so here I was.

But I had other shit to worry about, too. Like meeting with my attorney the next day about my ex-wife's custody case. Like trying to gauge when I was supposed to start having birds-and-bees discussions with my very curious seven-year-old. Like figuring out the solution to an upcoming staffing issue at the orchard that would let me pay one of my part-timers for a nice, long maternity leave while also not leaving *me* doing all the maple sugaring demonstrations. Like brainstorming how to bribe or guilt my uncle Drew into going to the doctor about the persistent shortness of breath he'd been pooh-poohing, since throwing a grown adult over your shoulder and forcing him to do things was frowned upon, even when that adult acted like a toddler. And all that being the case, I couldn't see getting riled up over the fate of a little parcel of land the way Hawk was.

I knew that probably made me seem like a grumpy

hard-ass but, well… maybe I *was* a hard-ass about a lot of things. Somebody needed to be.

The last—the very, absolute fucking *last*—thing I needed was one more thing to be responsible for.

When we got inside, I quickly spotted my older brother Knox standing in the corner with his boyfriend, Gage, and our neighbor, Norm Avery. I nudged Emma and Hawk to follow me as I made my way through the crowd.

"Hey." Knox lifted his chin. "You get Aiden off to Olin's okay?"

"Yeah." I unzipped my parka and stuck my gloves in the pockets. "He's already messaging me play-by-plays of the hockey game and selfies of him with Olin's dog." I rolled my eyes. "Tomorrow, the New Puppy Campaign is gonna be dialed up to eleven, so brace yourselves."

"Oh, it's begun. He already told me Sally Ann doesn't like playing fetch anymore and needs a puppy friend to 'make her feel young again,' like I've done for Knox." Gage glanced soulfully up at my brother and batted his eyelashes. "I mean, he's not wrong. Just think how I've changed your life, baby."

"Jesus," Knox grumbled. "Poor mutt doesn't know what's coming." He grabbed Gage by the belt loop and hauled him closer, dropping an arm over his shoulder as Gage laughed.

"So, Webb." Gage chafed his hands together expectantly. "How are you gonna spend your Aiden-free evening? Drinking? Debauchery? Nonstop revelry?"

Gage's teasing was like sunshine—warm and light, the perfect counterpoint to my brother's heavy sarcasm—and not for the first time since the two of them got together last fall, I wished I'd married a woman who fit me as well as Gage fit Knox.

But my ex-wife and I hadn't been that way, even on our

best days… and I had less than zero desire to get involved with anyone else.

"Clearly," I agreed. "I mean, does it get more wild than the Little Pippin Hollow town meeting? And then later on…" I leaned in like I was imparting a secret. "I might really lose control and get a full eight hours of sleep, because no one will be standing by my bed at 2:00 a.m. to debate the existence of alien life in the universe." I pursed my lips. "It takes a lot of stamina to party like me."

Gage snickered. "You make getting older seem so… appealing."

"Ugh." Em shuddered. "And you make parenthood seem so… *long*. No breaks, even in the middle of the night. No, thank you. Not for me."

I shrugged. I didn't think about shit that way. Sure, this wasn't what I'd envisioned when Amanda had first told me she was expecting eight-ish years ago. I'd imagined there'd be two of us to divide the labor and share the worry and… well, to be honest, I hadn't really known just how much there'd be to worry about.

But I wasn't complaining. I had a great life and hardly anything to complain about.

Every day, I worked the same land my great-grandparents had worked, so I could leave that land for Aiden and my great-grandkids.

I had an awesome family, including the extra members we'd collected over the years.

And I had a son who was by far the smartest person I knew, even though he sometimes did incomprehensible things like dunking his french fries in maple syrup or insisting yet again that Mr. Williams—overly cheerful, ridiculously earnest, annoying-as-fuck Luke Williams—was the best teacher ever, despite all evidence to the contrary.

The poor kid had no taste, but I had hopes that he'd grow out of it.

"And what's it feel like to have a kidlet who's disappointed when he hears there's a second snow day?" Hawk's lips twitched in amusement, no doubt remembering the way Aiden had stomped around gloomily that afternoon.

Figured that the only kid in the Hollow who was sad for a day off was *mine*.

"He's a little scientist," Emma defended fondly. "I think it's cute."

"It's not cute. He's just overly attached to his beloved Mr. Williams," I scoffed. "He'll get over it."

Knox and Gage exchanged a look.

"Speaking of getting over things, isn't it beyond time that *you* got over this whole… thing you've got against Luke Williams?" Knox demanded, with that big-brother superiority I hated.

I folded my arms over my chest. "The whole *thing* that involved him letting my kid go home from school with my ex-wife, without informing anyone, so that we all searched frantically for him for hours? No," I shot back. "I don't feel over that."

"But you know it wasn't Luke's fault," Gage said reasonably. He ticked off his other *reasonable* arguments on his fingers, "The principal told him to do it. He had no legal reason to—"

"Yes, yes, I know." I huffed.

It turned out I still had the capacity to feel some of Hawk's overblown outrage after all… mine was just directed at my neighbor.

"So, then?" Gage prompted, tenacious as always. "What's the deal? Why pick on Luke when you're usually so… fair?"

I ran my tongue over my teeth and told myself to keep

quiet. I should have known better than to bring up Saint Luke's name in the first place, because as far as I was concerned, we'd talked the topic of Luke Williams to death around our kitchen table—although, like a *Walking Dead* extra, it kept popping back to life.

For months, my family had been telling me how *kind* our new neighbor was. How *smart* he was. What a great *teacher* he was.

I couldn't turn around without hearing, "Give him another chance, Webb!" or "You two could be friends, Webb!" or "Thomas Webb Sunday, you did not need to buy out all the ice cream in Little Pippin Hollow just so Luke can't find any!"

All that time, I'd tried to explain that Luke Williams might *seem* like a lost orphan with his overgrown dark hair, comically large blue eyes, and habit of talking like a *gosh-dang-freakity-forking* preschooler who worried he might get grounded for cussing, but he was actually a grown man.

A grown man who'd won a house and a shit-ton of land without having to work a day in his life for it.

A man who'd gotten all up in my business from the day he'd arrived in town last summer and systematically destroyed my peace of mind.

It wasn't just the outrageous mix-up with Aiden last fall that pissed me off either. Hell, no. It had started way before that. And the things he'd done to annoy me... well, okay, they admittedly didn't sound as logical as those arguments Gage had been ticking off... but they felt real, damn it.

Like, the way he'd turned my son's head so that all Aiden talked about anymore was "super cool" Mr. Williams—who had endless time to chat, and do craft projects, and read stories, and listen to Aiden's most drawn-out theories, and teach Aiden "literally everything,

Daddy" from astronomy to philosophy to computer science to meteorology to what color cows liked best.

Or how Luke always seemed to be *right there* whenever I turned around, getting coffee at Panini Jack's, or chitchatting with the woman who ran the feed store about his damn sheep, or grabbing the last container of Boston Cream Pie ice cream out of the freezer at Peebles', smooth as you please, when everyone knew I was the only person in town who liked that flavor and Chuck ordered that shit especially for me.

It was infuriating.

Every time I came face-to-face with the man, my chest went tight and my gut clenched, like my body was trying to give me a warning my brain didn't know how to interpret.

I didn't think Luke Williams was a *bad* person, but that didn't mean he wasn't dangerous. Dangerous to my equilibrium and dangerous to my peace of mind.

I had too many people counting on me to be okay with that.

"'Scuse me, are you Webb Sunday?" a wheezy male voice said.

I turned and saw a short, heavyset man smiling expectantly up at Knox.

"I'm Webb." My voice came out grumpier than I meant it to, since I was still thinking about Aiden's teacher, and I deliberately tried to soften it as I added, "What can I do for you?"

The little man smoothed down his wispy hair. "Stephen Fox, Esquire," he said, offering me a hand to shake, like I was supposed to recognize the name.

Knox and I exchanged a look. I wouldn't put it past Amanda to get a new attorney to represent her in our custody dispute and sic him on me in public.

"Nice to meet you." I shook his hand. "Mr. Fox, if this

has something to do with my custody agreement, my attorney has already filed our custody petition…"

"Your—? Oh, heavens no! No, nothing to do with that, I assure you. I'm representing Luke Williams, of course. Your neighbor."

What was that expression about saying the devil's name and he'd appear? I gave Knox a hard look because *he'd* caused this.

I folded my arms over my chest. "What's *he* want?"

Gage groaned, no doubt at my lack of manners.

"Er, well… Mr. Williams is trying to untangle a bit of a Gordian knot regarding the title to his land, as I'm sure you know—"

Nope. I made it my business to know as little about Luke as possible.

"—so I figured I'd come introduce myself since I was already here for the meeting. No reason we can't keep things friendly, is there?"

Yeah, there sure was. Luke and I were not friends. Just the idea made me all… twitchy.

"What's up with his title?" I asked. "Does he not own the land after all?"

I tried not to sound too excited, but Gage gave me another exasperated look, so apparently, I failed.

Mr. Fox shook his head. "Oh, no, he definitely owns the land right enough. The issue is that I'm not sure exactly how much he owns. He won it all in a contest, you know. Poor man."

Yeah, right. Tragic. My heart bled for him.

"Anyway," the lawyer said, fumbling for the battered messenger bag slung over one shoulder, "no need to waste your time chatting when you have things to do and I could be billing for my hours." He chuckled heartily. "But I wanted to give you some preliminary information on our claim… where is it… ah, here."

He pulled out a sheaf of papers and shoved them into my hand. I stared at him while nerves began slithering in my stomach.

"What is this?"

"A copy of my preliminary research into the portion of land in dispute. For our claim," he repeated.

"What land? What dispute?" I blinked at him. "What *claim*?"

"The Pond land that's currently in use as a Sunday orchard, of course." He sounded exasperated, as if he'd explained whatever the hell this was in exacting detail and I was still obtuse.

"There is no *Pond* land used by the orchard. There's the land that my mother inherited—"

"Oh, no, that acreage is not in dispute."

"And there's the Sunday land that runs along the border with Lu—*your client's*—land, which was transferred to my family a very long time ago as a wedding portion," I said, biting back my frustration at this unexpected—and entirely freaking unacceptable—interruption of my perfectly mediocre night. "That land's not in dispute either."

"Yes, well, you'll see from my notes that it remains to be seen whether that transfer was legal." Before I could argue with him, he rustled in his bag again and produced a business card, slapping it on top of the stack of papers in my hand. "The meeting's about to start, so I'd best be on my way. Give me a call, and we can talk about it. Enjoy your evening!" He gave an absentminded smile and tottered away.

My siblings and I stared after him in shock.

"Who was that guy?" Hawk asked. "He's not from the Hollow."

"What the fuck just happened?" Knox growled.

Emma frowned. "Is he talking about the Pond orchard where your heirloom varietals are?"

My stomach plummeted to the floor. "He'd better not be," I said in a low, angry voice.

I'd been single-handedly cultivating that orchard since I was Emma's age. Over the years, I'd researched and acquired scion wood from a wide variety of apple trees that had nearly gone extinct, patiently grafted them onto rootstock, and nurtured them to health. And while I loved every square inch of Sunday Orchard, from the U-pick fields to the commercial operation to the pumpkin patch, the Pond orchard was my pride and joy. My labor of love. My life's work.

I was going to kill Luke Williams, plain and simple.

Gage took the papers out of my hand. "Everyone stay calm. Jeez, it's like Sunday brothers live to get all alpha-angry over nonsense. Let me take a look... oh."

Hawk shoved his head over Gage's shoulder. "Oh, what?"

Gage let out a humming sound. "It says here... Hezekiah Pond drew up papers upon his sister's marriage to Benjamin Sunday. He divided his land 'from the mighty oak to the hedgerow.' But the lawyer's note says the oak got cut down a hundred years ago..."

Emma snorted. "Hedgerow. I thought that was a made-up word in those *Pride and Prejudice* fanfics Hawk reads."

"They're not all fanfic," Hawk muttered. "Some are retellings. There's a difference."

Knox was over Gage's other shoulder, reading under his breath. "Part of that land passed back to the Pond family on Esther Whistlebaum Pond Sunday's death, as a legacy to her nephew, but only so far as 'the line running due east from the bend in Pond Creek to the fence before the cider house.' And the creek dried up during the world-famous beaver overrun of 1872."

Now Hawk was the one snorting. "Beaver Overrun. Sounds like the name of a girl band."

Emma elbowed him out of the way before plucking one of the papers out of Gage's stack. "Wait. It says here the hedgerow was decimated in the Great Spongy Moth Plague of 1867. What does that even mean? I'm still not sure I understand what a hedgerow is, much less a spongy moth plague."

I shook my head and tried not to grind my teeth. "None of this matters. It's not his fucking land. The stone wall between our properties was erected before the Civil War, for God's sake!"

Gage muttered under his breath. "And people think Floridians are weird. What kind of language is this written in? Ye olde farmhande? Can anything this old still be legal? Can we get someone to translate this?"

Knox met my eyes over Gage's head. "Webb, the wall doesn't mean anything. You can build a wall... anywhere. Are you sure the property transfer is legit?"

My fingernails bit into my palms. "Of course it is! We've planted on that land for centuries. If Luke *fucking* Williams thinks he's going to dispute a land transfer that happened in the Revolutionary War era, he's got another think—ah, Mrs. Graber! So nice to see you. Yes, he's fine. Just sleeping over at a friend's house." I tried to smile at the librarian's kind inquiry, even though I knew it was just a nosy excuse for coming over here to see what had the Sunday siblings in a dither.

Once she was gone, I turned back to my family and noticed Hawk and Emma snickering. "What is it now?"

Emma was laughing too hard to speak, so Hawk said it. "Jebediah Sunday signed a 'friendship agreement' saying he could continue growing his crops on Abraham Pond's land for 'one hundred fruitful harvests,' with a certain percentage of the Sundays' 'yield from our friendship' to be paid to Abraham's heirs. That lawyer guy has a note here asking how many fruitful harvests there've been since 1836 and whether or not the Sundays have been delivering apples to the Ponds."

"I'm not giving Luke Williams my apples," I snapped, drawing way too much attention.

I felt fury boiling up inside me, coiling and kicking like a living thing, as if all the restless anger I felt about all the shit I couldn't control in my life had coalesced into something too enormous to ignore.

As it happened, Hawk had been right. It was possible to feel very, very angry over a tiny parcel of land.

Incensed, really.

Infuriated beyond the telling.

My face heated, and I realized I couldn't stay here for one of Little Pippin Hollow's interminable town meetings.

I needed to leave.

"He'd probably like our apples," Emma said, tapping a fingertip to her chin. "At least... he might like Gage and Knox's apples, if you catch my meaning."

"I don't," I spat, not wanting to hear about Luke Williams and anyone's apples.

Knox got a knowing look on his face. "I have the pickup line already ready."

I shot Knox a look. "Don't say it. Do. Not. Say. It."

"How do you like them apples?" Knox said dutifully

before all four of them lost their collective shit and I stormed out into the night.

There'd never been a clearer sign that tonight was the night for getting utterly and completely wasted.

And I knew just the place for it.

When I hit the cool night air, I stopped long enough to take a deep breath and try to calm the hell down so I didn't flash an angry scowl at all of the townspeople still filtering into the building. It was just long enough for Knox to catch up to me.

"I'm sorry. I was just trying to introduce a little levity to the situation. We don't know how serious this is yet, Webb, so take a breath."

"It's fine. I just need a drink. And I need to not sit through a bunch of bullshit about some ridiculous clause in some *other* dude's idiot ancestor's will, and how a developer wants to pave paradise and put up a… a vacation resort. I could give two shits about Fogg Peak when I'm busy worrying about Sunday Orchard, and I'm really fucking tired of random-ass documents from almost three hundred years ago determining the course of people's lives today."

"Fine, then let me go with you," Knox offered. "I'll tell Gage—"

"No." I shook my head and took a step toward the door. "Thanks, but I want to be alone."

Knox laid a restraining hand on my arm. "Webb, I know you're angry. I don't blame you. But you have family. You have an attorney. We have resources. We'll fight this. Please don't do anything that's gonna get you in trouble or hurt your custody chances. And sure as shit don't go anywhere near Luke Williams."

Until he said the words, the thought hadn't entered my mind. But as soon as he did, it was all I could think about.

My jaw worked side to side. Luke Williams could certainly use a piece of my mind right about now.

"Think of Aiden," he said softly.

Was he kidding?

I jabbed a finger toward him. "Fuck you, Knox. I only *ever* think of Aiden."

Aiden was the reason I was so damn angry. Angry because I worked my ass off to give him stability and a good home, despite his mother leaving us when he was four years old. Angry because I'd spent my life propagating varietals in that orchard so they could be enjoyed by Aiden and his kids and grandkids one day, and now someone was trying to snatch that stability away.

"I'm going to the Bugle," I said flatly, motioning across the empty town common to where the lights of the bar shone. "Come and get me when you're done."

A wall of welcome heat greeted me when I stepped inside, along with the usual sounds of a hockey game in progress on the big screen and a country music song playing over the speakers.

I hung my jacket on a hook, remembering to duck my head under the low doorframe and touch the brass Unity Bugle on the plaque by the door for good luck, then headed directly for the alcohol.

"Rusty Spike?" I greeted Van, who'd been tending bar there longer than I'd been old enough to order.

"Well, hey there, Van!" Van mocked as I slid onto a stool. "Have you lost weight, Van? Ain't seen you for the whole second half of football season, Van. How's the hockey going tonight, Van?" He leaned toward me. "I'll give you that one for free—Habs are losing, thank the bugle."

I snorted. "I'm betting they're losing because Montreal couldn't score a goal if they were the only ones on the ice, but sure. It's your good-luck bugle. *Now* can I have a—?"

"Hey!" Van slapped his towel against the bar near my hands. "Respect the bugle, Sunday. That fucker's been hanging there for two hundred years as a symbol of unity, good fortune, and friendship. It's our town's greatest treasure. It's the reason this bar exists!"

"I apologize," I said solemnly. "I'm in a shit mood, but I shouldn't take it out on…" I waited a beat before finishing. "The bugle."

"Hmph." Van filled a glass from a giant beverage dispenser filled with reddish-orange liquid that I knew contained whiskey… and an incredibly dangerous something that made the whiskey not taste like whiskey. "You folks are starting early tonight. You're lucky I made a triple batch for after the town meeting."

"Yep." I was already busily sucking down the tangy beverage. There was something apple-y about it. Maybe lemony too. "That's me. Lucky."

As I drank, I surveyed the bar. I couldn't remember the last time I'd been in here without my brothers or Jack, or even Amanda back in the day. What did people do in bars when they didn't have a friend to talk to?

There weren't many faces I recognized, which was probably good because it meant there were lots of tourists, but was also weird because I was used to knowing most people in town.

A table of women in the middle of the room cheered at something on the television, and one of them—a pretty blonde in a pink snow hat—gave me an up-down look and a flirty smile.

Oh, right. That was what people did in bars.

I licked my lips, and my cock perked up at the idea of getting some action that didn't involve my right hand for the first time since my divorce.

Her smile turned into a wink in my direction, and my palms went a little damp, nerves warring with anticipation. I hadn't flirted with anyone in a long time, and I forgot how this was supposed to go.

Or maybe I'd never really known.

"You know, Webb," Van continued, apropos of nothing. "The thing about the bugle is, it's misunderstood."

"Oh?" I murmured as Van refilled my glass. I hoped he didn't think I was listening.

The woman kept sneaking covert glances at me from under her lashes, making my blood fire for reasons that had nothing to do with fucking Luke fucking Williams and his ice-cream-robbing, land-thieving, apple-grubbing, son-stealing treachery, and I was very willing to let myself be distracted.

Her long, blonde hair looked really, really soft, and I'd bet anything it smelled like coconut shampoo.

My dick twitched in my pants. I apparently had good feelings about coconut shampoo.

"… so already it had a legendary past," Van was saying. "But the bugle truly became symbolic when Barnaby Sunday fell in love with Moriah Pond, the most beautiful girl in the Hollow. Her father wouldn't consent to the marriage, because Barnaby was but a lowly sheep-herder with only a small parcel of land—"

My attention was caught momentarily. "People who like sheep are *weird*," I pronounced.

And that was just a known fact, which had nothing to do with Luke Williams and his sheep, since I was very much not thinking about Luke Williams anymore, and especially not tonight.

I held out my glass for a refill.

"Yeah. Okay." Van filled it up. "Anyway, as I was saying, these star-crossed lovers were doomed by Moriah's father, who didn't trust Barnaby's motives for getting married and wanted to protect his daughter. The entire town's loyalty was divided. But there was a kindly preacher in town who wanted to help. He gave them the bugle—"

I darted another covert glance at the woman and caught her looking back at me. She seemed interested, but I had no idea what to do with that. Did she want me to make a move? And did that mean sending her a drink or something? Was that what people did? It all seemed like so much damn *effort*.

And I could imagine my siblings' old-age comments if they ever heard me say that.

I had never been more aware of the fact that nearly all my dating experience prior to this had been with Amanda, who I'd known since we were in elementary school. Things between us had just sort of... happened when we were in our twenties. And then kept happening.

"—and so, on account of the Unity Bugle, the law was handed down that two people who'd pledged their troth on the town green and proven their commitment to one another would be joined, no matter who had somethin' bad to say about it. Peace and unity were restored to the town. Moriah and Barnaby lived happily ever after. And the spirit of goodwill, good fortune, and good friendship remains in the bugle to this very day!" Van sniffed and wiped his cheek with the back of his hand.

"Uh." I peered at him. "Are you okay?"

"Yes. Fine," he choked. "It's just so beautiful, you know? The bugle story. Like a fairy tale."

"Right. Sure. So… question." I cleared my throat. "In your expert opinion, what's the best way to pick someone up at a bar?"

"Pick someone… Were you even listening?" Van huffed.

"Obviously. I heard every word," I lied. "It's about… unity. And… friendship."

Van appeared mollified. "Well, then. To answer your question, I'd say you buy a drink for the lady or *lad*… you have your eye on."

I raised an eyebrow. My brothers Knox, Porter, and Hawk were all gay, so folks figured I was, too, deep down, especially after Amanda and I divorced.

They kept providing me supportive opportunities to come out, which was sweet, in an ass-backwards way, and also excruciating. I felt like I constantly had to prove my straightness.

"Van, if I had my eye on a lad, I wouldn't keep it a secret," I informed him. "So you buy the drink… and then what?"

"And then… I dunno." Van scratched his chin thoughtfully. "What do you want to have happen from there? You looking for a fun night or something permanent?"

The reality of my situation crashed down on me like a bucket of cold water.

I was not a hookup guy. I never had been.

But I was also not a relationship guy. Not anymore.

And I couldn't imagine navigating the boundaries of a casual in-between thing, when I was already focused on Aiden's custody, and running my business, and taking care of my brothers and sister, and winning the Cold War with Luke Williams, who was trying to annex my fucking orchard like fucking Napoleon.

"Whoa," Van said. "You looked murder-y for a second there."

Probably because I was.

"Never mind," I told Van, grinding my teeth. Then I shook my empty glass. "Just keep 'em coming, okay?"

I watched the hockey for an entire period, sucking down more Rusty Spikes and ignoring Van's concerned eyeballs while the alcohol spread out from my stomach to all of my limbs in hot little tendrils. It wasn't unpleasant at all… but it also wasn't as distracting as I'd hoped, because now that Luke Williams was in my brain, every sip of my drink just seemed to cement his presence there.

Knox was super wrong, I realized. The last thing I needed was to *avoid* the man—I'd been trying to do that for months, and it hadn't worked. No, what I needed to do was confront him. Look into his weird, big eyes and tell him that I was not fooled by his pretty smile—

Pretty?

I scowled at the television. *Jesus fuck*, Luke Williams was literally making me lose my mind.

"Hey, Van?" I tapped my glass again.

Van looked at me closely. "You got a ride home, right?"

I rolled my eyes. Having people up in my business was the best-worst part of small-town life. "Yep. Knox, when the town meeting lets out."

He glanced over my shoulder. "Think you can give your neighbor a lift home, then? He's been tossing back the Rusty Spikes, too. Been talking to himself in the corner for the last thirty minutes at least."

I half laughed. Some fools just couldn't hold their liquor.

"Of course. Which neighbor?"

"The new teacher. Luke Williams." Van pointed toward a shadowed booth on the far side of the room.

"Wait." The whole world became a record scratch, and I turned my stool so quickly my head spun. "Wait, wait, wait. *That's* Luke Williams?"

My nemesis had been here in this bar all along?

"Yeah, he said he—Webb? Where ya goin'?" Van called as I pushed off the stool.

I didn't answer him. I'd gotten halfway across the floor before I noticed that I was walking, and once I'd thought the word *walking*, the whole process became trickier, especially when I tried to add talking into the mix.

When I saw that distinctive cow-lick-y hair and sweater vest, I lost control entirely.

"Hey! I have things to say to you—" I began.

Then I tripped over my own feet and stumbled, catching the edge of the booth and barely stopping myself from going ass-up in the center of the table like a Christmas roast.

Luke didn't seem nearly as startled as he should've been to have six-foot-three inches and two hundred pounds of irate Sunday practically land in his lap. In fact, when his big blue eyes finally managed to focus on my face, he *smiled*, like he'd been waiting for me to show up.

I frowned.

Really, who had eyes that color blue? It was an absurd color.

Insufferable.

Inexplicable.

"Oh, Webb," the man said happily, clasping a hand to his chest. "Thank goodness it's you!"

I sucked in a breath, and my nose caught the faint tang of woodsmoke clinging to his sweater vest and the sweet-rough scent of whiskey on his breath. I couldn't help inhaling deeply... and my cock stirred against my zipper, despite all the Rusty Spikes coursing through my bloodstream.

Huh. Turned out my feelings about woodsmoke and whiskey were at least as strong as my feelings about coconut shampoo.

Well, fuck.

Chapter Three

LUKE

Sitting alone in my booth, contemplating my night's work, I pondered exactly when my plan for the evening had gotten out of hand.

"I think it was with *you*," I told the first of the line of empty glasses on the table in front of me, repressing a tiny belch. "You were seductively delicious but ultimately not good for me, just like Mitchell back in college. 'Get your nipples pierced, Luke. It'll be hot, Luke.' *Bah.*"

I took another sip from my full glass and addressed the second and third empty glasses, lining them up behind the first like my students at lunch period. "You two promised to help me learn hockey, but did you? *Noooo*," I said severely. "You just made it all blurry."

"And you two." I prodded the fourth and fifth glasses into their places. "You were adorable. But now I'm not just sitting alone at a bar, I'm sitting alone at a bar while *talking to the glassware* like one of you might magically start singing at me in Angela Lansbury's voice, and that's just ridiculous." I paused, then whispered, "But, like, if you *were* gonna speak, now would be the time."

"Hey!" a deep voice replied. "I have things to say to you."

I gasped in shock.

But then a hand came down on the booth by my head, and suddenly, Webb Sunday was looming over me, all angry and gorgeous and *speaking directly to me.*

It was harder to believe than talking glassware, frankly, but much less concerning for my mental health.

"Oh, Webb." I pressed a hand to my chest. "Thank goodness it's you!"

Webb sucked in a deep breath and then scowled, like the very *smell* of me annoyed him.

"I hope you're happy now, you… you… *apple thief*!" he accused. I looked around me for apples but found none.

The man had probably been drinking and gotten mixed up, poor guy. Or maybe the glasses had been talking to him, too.

Either way, I saw this moment for what it was.

Fate had given me a chance to make Webb like me.

But when he braced one hand on the vinyl booth above my head and the other hand on the table and stared down at me all hot-eyed and breathy, it was hard to remember what I was trying to do.

"Erm. Can I buy you a drink?" I offered in lieu of apples. I held up my nearly full Rusty Spike. "These're yummy."

"I cannot be *bought*, Luke Williams," he informed me. He thumped his own glass onto the table beside mine. "I brought my own."

The way he said my name like it was all one word made my stomach feel floaty and nervous.

He was so handsome, and God, it had been *so long* since I'd had a real conversation with anyone but Murray or someone under the age of eight, I couldn't help smiling at him and wishing we could just... talk.

"Stop looking at me like that. You might've fooled my family, Williams, but the game is up. You're an orchard-thieving con artist. Admit it."

I shook my head sadly. I could maybe parse those words individually, but I wasn't sure what they meant together. "I'm trying to understand you, Webb, but frankly, I've already used up all my brain cells tonight trying to understand the hockey, and— Oh! Oh, wait! You could explain it to me. That would be awesome."

"Explain... hockey?" He sounded confused. "Like... all of it?"

"Yes! Exactly! I'm trying to follow along, but I need a hockey-teaching friend. I've been led to believe..." I licked a drop of alcohol off my lips. "...that Vermont has those."

"We are not friends."

"No, that's true," I agreed, and he frowned harder. "*Buuuuut...* we could be! You seem like the kind of knight in shining armor who'd pat my head if I asked him to. Or carry a man's sheep home over his shoulders."

My eyes widened. *Mother trucker.* Had I actually said that out loud? There wasn't enough alcohol in all the land to make *that* statement okay.

I started to open my mouth and explain that for Christmas my mom had gotten me this farmer calendar sponsored by one of her local charities. Every month had pictures of half-naked men cuddling adorable lambs and baby goats, and Webb Sunday looked very, *exactly* like Mr. May.

But before I could explain any of that, though, Webb said flatly, "I want nothing to do with carrying your sheep," which was fair enough... but kinda too late. I was already busy admiring the way his arm muscle, which was conveniently close to my eye holes, bulged against the worn fabric of his navy blue Henley.

He *could* lift a sheep. Possibly all three of my sheep at once.

I'd honestly never assessed a hot guy with that criteria, and I could see now that I'd been missing out. This was going to be a new personal fantasy.

Also, adding to the fantasy, his whole being smelled like Christmas trees and clean laundry, and I was pretty sure I'd just cracked some kind of secret code. Why were gay men out there buying Tom Ford cologne when we could rub ourselves with pine sap and a Tide pod and smell like a sex god?

Webb sucked in a breath and held it for a second, and my stomach plunged as I worried I'd said that out loud too.

He leaned in closer, threateningly close. "Stop it right now. I know what you're plotting."

"Oh, sugar." I felt my face go hot. "You do?"

"Yep. And it's never going to happen."

"No, of course, I know," I assured him. "Because you're straight."

"What? No." He scowled. "What does my sexuality have to do with my apples?"

"Wait, you're *not* straight?"

"No, I *am*. Of course I am. I—" His hand made a slicing motion through the air. "Stop trying to confuse me! I know all about your designs on my orchard. Questioning old deeds and lot lines that have been perfectly fine for centuries. And I'm here to tell you you're never going to win. I will never pay your apple tithe, no matter what the Friendship Agreement says, and that land is *mine*."

"Land?" I clung to this one comprehensible word. "Oh, gosh no. I have no designs on your land. I have plenty of land already. Too much."

"*Liar!*" he whisper-yelled.

"What, me?" I said, horrified. "N-no, I—"

"You've put on this act since you got to town where you're all *friendly* and *happy* and *competent*, when really butter wouldn't melt in your mouth. Just who do you think you're fooling, Luke Williams? How long do you think you can keep up this charade? How long?"

Something about his words hit me hard. I still didn't understand what he was accusing me of, but I was very afraid that he saw me, in that moment, more clearly than I saw myself.

He was right. *So* right.

I sucked in a breath, and my whole body trembled.

I *was* a happy, positive person, or at least I tried to be, but I'd been pushing back the tide for months and… it was hard. And competent? No. Heck, no. I was doing my best, but my beautiful, historical home was crumbling to literal dust.

I was lonely. I was tired. And I really, *really* didn't understand why Webb didn't like me.

Against my will, I burst into tears—and not the quiet, dignified kind, but chest-heaving, the kind of gut-wrenching sobs that had been building up for months. I freaking *hated* it but couldn't stop.

"I never lied to you!" I cried. "But I do lie. I lie all the time. To myself. To my mom. To everyone. I wanted to have a fairy-tale adventure for my mom's sake, but I'm not doing a very good job at adventuring, and now my horse is falling down… I mean *house*. I don't have a horse… and now I probably never will! And I'm destroying history, and I was so *cold*, and I don't think anyone in this town likes me very much."

"What? No." Webb scowled, his eyes a little panicky. "That's not true. *Hush.*"

I wanted to hush. I was trying to hush. But the harder I tried, the more difficult it became.

"It is true!" I blurted. "It really is. Everyone's polite and all, but… they're still mad at me for what happened with Aiden. Your family never says hi to me anymore, and n-nobody seems to know my name, and I don't *know* how to make pie like your uncle Drew, and tonight, my living room…" I broke off with a shake of my head.

Too pitiful. I was *not* telling that story.

"Look," I said. "I have no idea what you mean with deeds and con artists, and if you want my land, you can have it. All of it. Just… please go away and leave me alone, okay? I won't bother you anymore."

And I meant it, too. After this, I was done trying to convince him to like me. It was time to stop wishing things were different and direct my energy to good things instead.

No more attempting to explain myself.

No more daydreaming we were friends and staring across the fields.

No more sheep-carrying fantasies…

Or, like, hardly any.

"Ah, fuck." Webb stepped back from the table, and for a single beat of time, he looked horrified and helpless in the face of my tears. Then he resolutely grabbed a stack of slightly damp cocktail napkins from the table and began scrubbing my eyes.

"Okay, hush now," he murmured. "You're okay. I've got you. Let me do this."

The irony was not lost on me. I'd really wanted someone to say things like that to me tonight. I'd just imagined it being a good bit sexier.

And exponentially less awkward.

"Let go!" I tried to squirm away, but he cupped the

back of my head gently and force-dried me like I was a child.

"No, no, let me fix it. Everything's fine. Here, blow." He held the soggy napkins to my nose.

"No way." I whacked him in the stomach. "I am not going to blow you, ever." I mentally replayed my words and felt my face get hotter when I hadn't thought that was possible. "Just please go away, Webb."

Leave me to my humiliation.

"Y'okay over there?" the bartender yelled.

Webb waved him off. "Yeah, Van, we're good. We're excellent. Luke's just... upset about the game."

After a shocked beat, the bartender moaned, "Ah, shit. Luke's a Montreal fan?"

Someone behind Webb cheered. "Hell, yeah! You might be a flatlander, but I knew I liked the look of you, Willams! Olé!"

I pulled the cuffs of my sweater down over my hands, pressed them to my damp eyes, and wished the world would start making sense.

"I'm sorry," Webb said, sounding sincere. "I scared you, didn't I? I wasn't trying to bully you. I would never actually hurt you. I'm not... I was just..." He nodded at the seat across from me. "Can I sit down and explain?"

"Now you want to sit?" I sniffed. "The time to ask that was probably before you attacked my face with paper products." But after a beat, I relented. "Fine. Suit yourself."

He slid into the booth. "I'm sorry," he said again. "I may be a bit more inebriated than I thought. I'm not thinking... straight." He grimaced, then added darkly, "At *all*."

"My mother always says drinking just makes you more inclined to do things you secretly want to do when you're sober," I said primly. Then cautiously, I asked, "Is this about what happened last fall? With Aiden and your wife… I mean, *ex*-wife?"

"No. I… I know that wasn't… intentional," he admitted, not quite meeting my eyes. "This is about the bullshit I heard from your lawyer tonight. He showed me the papers about your claim on my land." His gaze swung back to me. "I love that land. I love that orchard in particular. And I know that's no excuse for…" I waved a hand. "For being threatening. I know a man my size should be more careful. So I'm sorry for that. But I'm not giving up my orchard."

I hadn't felt physically threatened by him at all, despite him being twice as big as I was. In fact, my only thoughts about his size were… erm… really, disconcertingly positive ones.

Fortunately, I managed not to blurt *that* out.

"Wait, when did you hear from Stephen?" My brain felt like a clogged filter, struggling to process. "What claim? Why would I want your orchard?"

"For money? For revenge? Why does anyone do anything? Don't pretend you don't know what I'm talking about."

"But I don't! I haven't spoken to Stephen Fox in weeks. He never calls, he never writes, he just… *bills*."

Webb stared at me for a long, long moment. His jaw worked side to side. His eyes flared. Then he dropped his head and raked both hands through his dark hair.

"Jesus fuck," he groaned succinctly. "You're telling the truth, aren't you?"

I nodded.

So while I kept my mouth occupied with my Rusty Spike, Webb told me what he could remember about papers and wills and hedgerows, spongy moths and Friendship Agreements, and centuries of apple tithes based on the size of his "fruitful harvests." By the end, I was horrified.

"I would *never* want your tithed apples," I assured him. "And you can have the orchard, if it turns out it's mine. I'll sell it to you for a dollar. Heck, you can have some of my land, too. Help yourself." I swept out an arm magnanimously.

"Fuck that. I don't need *pity*," Webb grumbled. "I'm just saying, you don't steal another man's legacy—"

"So. Let me understand." I dried my eyes with one hand and held up the other for silence. "You don't want my lawyer to claim the land for me."

"Hell no. It's my family's land. Always has been."

"M'kay. So you want me to ask Stephen to stop investigating?"

He hesitated. "No. You need a title so you can sell or whatever. I'm not asking you for any favors."

"Right. So if he finishes investigating and it turns out it *is* my land... you don't want me to give it to you for free either."

"No," he repeated for a third time. Then he hesitated again. "Wait. You're making it sound weird and unreasonable."

I propped my chin on my fist. "Are we sure *I'm* the one who's doing that?"

"It just would've been easier if no one had ever brought it up." Webb must've realized he sounded like a petulant kid because he sat up straighter and blew out a breath. "You make shit... complicated."

"But if we were friends..." I leaned across the table and grabbed Webb's hand impulsively. "When things got complicated, we could put our heads together," I slurred with drunken sincerity. "And *uncomplicate* 'em."

Webb snorted. "You're like a motivational poster with

44

arms and legs, Luke Williams. Don't you ever get tired of acting so fucking cheerful?"

"Freakin' exhausted!" I wiped away the last of my stupid tears and grinned at him. "But I can't help it!"

Then Webb laughed out loud. And for a single drunken minute, it felt like things between us were starting to calm down...

But they were just heating up.

Chapter Four

WEBB

Damn, Luke Williams was hard to dislike, once I got over hating him.

"Hockey... is like life," Luke informed me, sipping on a Rusty Spike with his dark hair standing on end and his cheeks flushed dark pink.

I nodded sagely. "Profound, yet true."

"There are many nets, obviously. Everyone has their own net." He gestured with his glass to encompass the entire world in his metaphor. "And some of us are red guys." He pointed at himself. "And we are just trying to do our *jobs* and run the puck down the... the..."

"Ice?" I suggested.

"*Yes*," Luke agreed gratefully. "We are trying to run it down the ice so we can smash it in the net with our hooks, because that's what we are born to do. And some people are blue men." He pointed at me. "And they're trying to stop us from smashing by smashing us instead. And that's annoying, Webb. It's annoying. But it's kinda *your* job. So I'll allow it. It's okay."

"Thank you," I said sincerely.

"But then there are the black-and-white stripey dudes, and they just… they blow their whistles and throw up roadblocks when good people are just trying to do their job. And all of a sudden, everything is stopped and nothing is fun anymore. It's like everyone is *fighting*. They restrain the men in the plastic boxes, and it's all so excessive and confusing. That's what I think anyway."

"Uh-huh." I nodded. "And I think you're drunk."

"Maybe so. *Maaaaybe* so. But I'm also not wrong." Luke sucked down more of his drink, and a tiny bit of liquid dribbled down his chin.

I wanted to lean over and wipe it off with my thumb, and it was getting harder to remember why I wasn't supposed to do that.

"Just let the men do their jobs!" he shouted, smacking the table with his palm. "No more plastic boxes!"

"Fuck yeah!" Alan Laroche pointed across the bar at Luke and grinned. "Exactly what I'm saying, Williams! The refs are *blind*, eh?"

Luke looked startled for a second, like he'd forgotten where he was. "So blind!" he told Alan. To me, he murmured, "What, um… did I miss?"

I ran a hand over my mouth to hide my smile. "Penalty for elbowing," I explained. "You can ram a player but not with your elbows out."

"Oh. Yeah, that sounds dangerous." He frowned like the elementary school teacher he was. "Okay, so maybe *sometimes* plastic boxes are necessary."

"Imagine that? The NHL will be grateful for your support," I said solemnly.

I'd stopped counting how many drinks I'd consumed after the third round Luke and I had ordered together, but it was safe to say I was far, far drunker than I'd been in two decades.

I was so drunk, I was listening to my nemesis neighbor expound on hockey as a metaphor for life, which was the highest level of drunk.

Luke grinned and knocked his booted foot into mine companionably, and I grinned back. When he turned his head to look at the TV, I noticed a tiny smudge of dried purple poster paint on his face, and a warm, affectionate kind of feeling came over me that I usually only got when Aiden, Hawk, or Gage did something sweet.

Okay, no, wait, correction. I was listening to my nemesis neighbor expound on hockey, and I was *enjoying it*. So much so that I wasn't sure it was remotely accurate to call him my nemesis anymore. *That's* how drunk I was.

I laughed lightly to myself and tried to hide it by sipping my drink.

From this close, I could see Luke had a smattering of freckles on his nose, and I felt the most bizarre need to count them. Then he wrinkled his nose and his freckles scattered, so I had to count again. I couldn't help but notice the way his sweater sleeves were still down over his wrists, like his hands were cold even in this sauna-hot bar.

I couldn't help but notice *him*…

And I realized in a flash that I was so drunk, I was thinking Luke Williams—a dude—was kind of… good-looking. Which was a level of drunk I'd literally never achieved before.

A level of drunk I hadn't known I *could* achieve.

And I wondered idly if I was going to be more surprised about it in the morning, but in the moment, it just felt *good*. Like flirting with the blonde at the bar but better, because I was never going to use a pickup line on the man, and Luke was already acquainted with the complexities of my life and didn't seem put off.

Hell, he *was* half the complexities of my life.

Maybe it was the Rusty Spikes talking, but being friends with Luke seemed way easier than hating him, and I felt stupid for not realizing it sooner.

In fact, I was having so much fun, I almost didn't care that my brother had abandoned me. It was, weirdly, exactly what I'd needed but hadn't known I'd needed that night.

"You," I proclaimed magnanimously, "are not awful."

"Oh. Wow." Luke blinked his attention away from the television. "Thank you?"

"In fact, I like you. I think we should be friends."

"Really?" His gaze narrowed. "Are you just saying that because I cried? Because that's gross."

"No!" I thought about it and admitted, "Okay, maybe a little. But only because it made me realize I was being a jerk. And you're wrong, you know. I don't know a soul in town who doesn't like you. I don't know why you say they don't talk *to* you, 'cause I can't get 'em to fucking shut up *about* you. But that's neither here nor there. The point is, I was unfair to you. For reasons."

"What reasons?"

"Well." I scrunched up my face. The reasons existed. I knew they did. Somewhere at the periphery of my brain. But damned if I could catch the slippery fuckers. "You make my stomach feel—" I made a vague motion to my abdomen.

"Nauseated?" Luke asked, wide-eyed. "Oh my God, is it my cologne? Wait, I don't wear cologne. Is it *me*?"

"—and you're a damn ice cream fiend."

He blinked. "Oh. Well, no, that's true," he admitted sorrowfully. "And that's… a deal breaker?"

I spread my hands. "I promise, it sounded more convincing in my brain."

"Ah." Luke nodded. "Happens to me all the time."

"So… friends?" I said again.

"Heck yeah! See, good things happen all the time, even when you least expect them!"

Luke's eyes, already glassy from the alcohol, almost *glowed* with excitement, and I had to look away. I couldn't remember the last time anyone had looked so happy with me for so little effort.

"I still don't want anything to do with your sheep, though," I muttered. "Especially if it involves me carrying them over my shoulders." My back twinged just thinking about it.

"No, no," he agreed quickly. "Promise. The ladies keep to themselves anyway. But you and I can be… neighbor friends. And maybe Drew can make me pie again." Luke hesitated. "So do we, like, shake hands now? Because it feels like we need to commemorate this? Or maybe—"

The most random idea occurred to me, and I burst out laughing at how perfect it was. Not only the perfect way to commemorate a new friendship, but also the perfect way to let the town know—if they really didn't know already—that Luke Williams was a good, friendship-worthy guy.

"Okay… okay… so Van was telling me this story earlier— *Shhhhh. Shhhhh*," I insisted, even though *I* was the one who kept interrupting myself with bouts of drunken giggles. "Did you ever hear the story of the Unity Bugle?"

Luke shook his head, looking mystified and intrigued.

"So, that bugle on the plaque by the door is the Unity Bugle." I pointed. "It's how the bar got its name. And according to Van, it's like… there was a pretty girl? And sheep, which is fitting. And… other things. A father, maybe? But then there was a preacher who came and brought goodwill. And… I'm honestly not sure how the bugle came into play, but then the spirit of friendship lives *inside* the bugle to this very day, and they lived happily ever after just like in a fairy tale."

"Just like in a…" Luke's eyes flashed like this meant something to him. "Wait, who lived happily ever after?"

"Uh." I frowned. "Unclear. The whole town, maybe? Or the pretty girl. Either way, *friendship*. Unity."

"Right! Yeah! Okay! Awesome! So…" Luke paused, and his face crumpled. "Wait, no, I don't understand at all. What do we do?"

"We blow the bugle on the town common," I explained patiently. "To show that we forgive each other, and we have unity now."

"Awwww. We have unity now." Luke pressed his hands to his cheeks. "We sure do!"

I pushed out of the booth and reached out a hand to help him out, and then the two of us ran for the entrance like we were Aiden's age. The place had mostly cleared out now that the game was over, and there were only a few folks sitting at the bar chatting with Van.

Luke and I got our jackets off the hooks.

"Is that the bugle?" he whispered, pointing to the plaque. "It looks old."

I looked at it—really looked—for the first time in years. It *did* look old, and the year 1767 etched below it confirmed this. It occurred to me that maybe, possibly Van wasn't going to want a couple of drunk guys to take the precious bugle out into the night, even if we had the best possible intentions.

"Where ya goin'?" Van demanded. "Thought Knox was taking you both home after the meeting. It ain't over yet."

It wasn't? Jesus. I was doubly glad I hadn't gone.

"Er. He is," I said. "But Luke and I just need to, um, do a quick thing first." I sounded about as suave as Aiden when he was trying to get away with something—the kid was the worst liar ever—and I gave Luke a helpless look.

Van braced both hands on the bar top and watched me suspiciously. "What quick thing?"

"A historical reenactment," Luke cut in, using his best, most official teacher voice. "Webb was telling me about the, ah… the inspiring bugle story you told him earlier—"

I nodded enthusiastically. It was funny how hearing him say my name in that uptight voice was actually kind of a thrill, now that we were on the same team.

"—and so he and I decided we would reenact the bugle blowing, to cement the change in our relationship."

Van's eyes were wide as saucers, and he looked at me. "You? You want to blow the bugle with… *him*? A *lad*?"

I was aware that I hadn't been very fair to Luke until about an hour before. I'd been stubborn and even a little immature. But I regretted that. And I resented the implication that I couldn't change my mind and offer the man friendship.

I threw my arm around Luke's shoulders, pulling him so he stumbled drunkenly against my side with his head against my neck. "Yes, with *him*. And he's not a lad, he's a grown man, thank you very much. I like him. And the whole town should know it."

There. That should take care of any lingering bad feelings. Not that I thought there actually *were* any.

"And that's why Webb and I want to be…" Luke broke off, like he was searching for the right word.

"United," I supplied. "Hence, the Unity Bugle."

"United," Luke repeated, taking the bugle off the wall. "You're so good at words, Webb."

"Aw. Thanks." I stood a little taller. Not a lot of people appreciated it, but I had a fucking great vocabulary.

Van's jaw dropped. "Holy shit. Hooooly shit." He held

out a hand toward a man on a stool. "Pinch me, Ravi. Webb's being sweet to someone who's not his kid."

I scowled. I could be sweet!

When it was warranted.

It just… was never warranted, that's all.

"And you two are sure you know how the bugle blowing works?" Van demanded.

Luke shot me a look of disbelief, and I snickered. How hard could it be? It was a *bugle*. You *blew* it. The instructions were right there in the action.

"Yeah. We know how it works," Luke assured him.

"Hot damn," Van breathed. "I have no idea what the protocol here is! I'm gonna have to tell the mayor, of course."

He made it sound like we were stealing the fucking thing.

"Jesus. We'll have it back to you in two minutes, Van. You're ruining the mood." I rolled my eyes and grabbed Luke's free hand. "Come on."

"Do you know the Unity Pledge?" Van called. "There's a ritual, you know! You have to hold up your hand and say 'I, Webb Sunday, pledge unity…'"

The door closed behind us as we ran out into the cold night, cutting him off.

We jogged as far as the gazebo in the center of the town common, when Luke turned to me, laughing so hard he was gasping for air. "This might be… the most ridiculous thing… I've ever done."

"I did some pretty ridiculous stuff as a kid, but it's been a while. This is *not* responsible dad behavior." But, shit, for once I didn't care. We weren't hurting anyone, or permanently tattooing our faces, or running off to Vegas—God forbid. We were two fully clothed men, having silly fun. And I felt lighter and younger than I had in years.

"M'kay." Luke held up his hand like he was taking an oath in court. "I, Luke Williams, pledge unity with you, Webb Sunday."

"Thomas Webb Sunday," I corrected. "To be official."

"Oh. Interesting. Okay, Thomas Webb Sunday," he repeated. Then he blew the bugle.

It sounded like I imagined a flatulent rhinoceros would, and the two of us laughed our asses off.

I held up my hand so we were palm to palm. Luke's hand was so small and chilly against mine that it was instinctive for me to wrap my fingers around his. "I, Thomas Webb Sunday, pledge unity with you, Luke Williams." Then I took the bugle and blew it also, long and loud enough folks probably heard it in Two Rivers.

And it might have been the alcohol talking—okay, it was definitely the alcohol talking—but the whole thing felt weirdly important. Momentous. Right.

At least it did until I noticed the town meeting had let out and the entire population of Little Pippin Hollow was standing around the town common, just *watching* us.

"Is that the Unity Bugle?" a woman's shocked voice demanded.

"Mother of God, is that Webb and the teacher? Are they holding hands? Have they blown it?"

"Did you say Webb blew the teacher?"

"They've recited the vows!" a man's voice exclaimed.

"They said they knew how it worked," Van confirmed. "They said they wanted to cement the change in their relationship."

"Did someone tell the mayor? Has the scroll been invoked?"

The scroll?

I snickered at the confusion on Luke's face, which perfectly reflected my own.

"Not a hundred percent sure what's happening right now," I whispered. "But I feel like we failed at uncomplicating things."

And that feeling was confirmed a moment later when my brother's voice rang out across the common.

"Webb Sunday, *what have you done?*"

Chapter Five

LUKE

I closed my car door gently and quietly outside of Panini Jack's diner and leaned against the cold metal for a second. Morning sunlight glinted off the snowdrifts and icicles, making kaleidoscopic strobe-light flashes against my closed eyelids, and I knew exactly how the Rusty Spike had come by its name because every flash of light did, indeed, make me feel like my skull was being impaled.

Hooray for truth in advertising.

Too bad every cell in my body was crying for mercy.

My phone dinged in my pocket several times in quick succession, and I flinched at the sound. I flinched again when I realized who was messaging.

Mom: *Morning, LukeyLou!! *sunshine emoji**

Mom: *I saw online you've got a high of 28* today and another day off!!! *snowflake emoji**

Mom: *Are you stuck at home with all the snow? Did you put dental floss in your survival kit, like in that article I sent you?*

Mom: *If you're stuck home, let's FaceTime later! I want to see your fairy-tale house and meet my grandchildren. *sheep emoji* It's been months and months already!*

Oh dear Lord.

I loved my mother so, so much. I loved her enthusiasm. I loved her positivity. I loved that she was invested in my life in Vermont. I even loved her stubbornness... sometimes.

But I was not going to show her the reality of my "fairy-tale house," no matter how often she asked, especially now that it had an unintentional skylight in the living room. And I was not gonna show her *me* when I was all puffy and bloodshot.

I typed a reply with one eye shut.

Me: *Morning! Signal's too weak to FT, remember? Busy now. Call me later. Love you!*

I couldn't say I regretted the previous evening, exactly... but that was only because I couldn't remember all of it. Trying to recall specific events was like trying to see through muddy water.

That was probably a good thing, because every once in a while, a crystal-clear memory would rise to the surface, and my entire body would flinch in mortification.

Had I actually begged Webb Sunday to teach me about hockey?

Had he *done* it?

Had he accused me of being a con artist before or after he said I was trying to steal his orchard?

At what point had I mentioned to him the thing about —dear God—*carrying my sheep?*

Had I actually licked his bulging biceps? I was pretty sure that had been a drunken fantasy. But what about me smiling at him like he was the best thing since blueberry pie and him—oh heavenly freak—smiling back?

And tiny newborn baby Jesus, had we really ended up blowing a bugle in the middle of the town square, where my bosses and the parents of my students could see me being drunk and disorderly? *Don't worry, townsfolk! Your impressionable youngsters are safe with me! Pay no attention to the minor incidents involving brass instruments and misplaced children.*

As of this morning, I was done with drinking for another decade at least.

I'd been sorely tempted to stay in bed and ignore reality for the rest of the day, but I knew from past experience that the best way to handle a challenge was to meet it head-on, with a smile and a can-do attitude.

Besides which, I couldn't stop worrying that I'd done something worse than the bugle blowing and the longing looks. There was a memory on the tip of my brain that kept taunting me. Had I danced the two-step around the gazebo naked? Or compared Webb's eyes to moss agate?

Better to know the worst.

Probably.

I took a deep, fortifying breath and pulled open the glass door to the diner. My stomach only revolted a tiny bit at the smell of cooking food, but the promise of life-giving coffee made it worthwhile.

I summoned a polite smile for the woman behind the hostess stand, which wasn't hard to do. Katey Valcourt was one of the only people in town who always had a friendly word for me.

"Morning, Katey. Could I please—"

"Full house today. You'll have to sit at the counter or join a table." She snapped a plastic menu out of the holder. "I suppose you'll want to sit with the *Sundays*."

"Uh…" My stomach flip-flopped. Sit with the Sundays? *Me?*

Did I?

Damn. Word of the bugle blowing must've spread quickly.

I looked over her head to the packed diner. Sure

enough, Webb was sitting at a horseshoe-shaped booth at the back along with his sister Emma, their uncle Drew, and a guy named Marco, who I was pretty sure was Drew's boyfriend.

Webb didn't look nearly as gravely injured by the Rusty Spike shenanigans as I felt. In fact, he looked… good. Really good. His hair was neatly combed, his Henley—a gray one this morning—strained across his muscular shoulders, and his eyes had lost a little of the tightness they usually carried in the corners. He grinned at something Emma said, then balled up his napkin and threw it across the table at her, and I couldn't help smiling dopily, remembering him looking at me like that the night before.

I wished I could remember how much of Webb's warm, friendly demeanor from the night before had been real. Given how long and heartily he'd disliked me, I figured it had mostly been the alcohol.

A memory surfaced of Knox driving us home in my car—with all the windows rolled down despite the subzero temperatures, just in case anyone felt sick—while Emma and Hawk followed behind us, driving Webb's truck. Webb had sung an unforgettably terrible, tuneless rendition of "Sweet Caroline" nearly the whole ride, while Gage and I did the *ba-ba-ba*'s in the back seat, and Knox muttered, "Jesus Christ, Webb," every time Webb attempted a high note… which was often.

I wanted that. That feeling of friendship. That feeling of *fitting*. Badly.

"M'kay, you're gonna need to ogle him on your own time," Katey snapped, which was rude and vaguely horrifying and not at all what I'd been doing… was it? "Let's go."

She stomped around the podium, clearly expecting me

to follow, so I did, trailing after her through the restaurant with all the speed of a reluctant, arthritic tortoise.

"Good morning, Luke!" a woman called from a nearby table.

I blinked and turned my head slightly to see if there was another, better-liked Luke standing behind me, but no.

"Uh. Morning?" I offered.

"Morning, Mr. Williams," a woman I recognized from the town hall permit office said... which was funny since I'd seen her at the store the other day and she'd walked right past me. "I meant to thank you for the book you sent home with Jasmine the other day. She loves it."

"Oh. Hey." I raised a tentative hand. "That's... great to hear."

"Luke, my brother!" A guy I recognized from the bar the night before stood, grabbed my hand, and pulled me into the kind of dude-bro handshakey-back-thumping-hug ritual I'd seen other guys perform my whole life but had never actually participated in. "Habs gonna beat the Pens tomorrow night or what?"

"Wow, okay, that's my lung. Yeah, we... we sure are," I agreed. I wasn't sure exactly what I was agreeing to, but the guy seemed to approve, judging by the way he set his hands on my shoulders and shook me like a maraca.

"Fuck yeah. See you at the Bugle tonight for the football?" he demanded. "Rusty Spikes on me!"

"Oh. Ha. Maybe not quite so soon? Gotta forget the last round first." I pressed a hand to my head, which was ready to explode like a shaken soda can from all the unexpected jostling.

"That's the damn truth! But you're a Hollowan, Williams," he said inexplicably. "You'll learn to love 'em." He lovingly thumped me twice more before I managed to extricate myself.

I was a Hollowan? *Was that actually what people here called themselves?* And was it the drinking that made me a citizen? Or the hockey?

This town was so weird.

By the time I caught up to Katey, she was already standing beside Webb's booth, twirling a lock of her blonde hair as she batted her eyelashes at him. Webb nodded and smiled along.

See that? He's perfectly friendly. This is gonna be fine, I chastised myself. *Get a grip, Luke.*

Except then Webb caught sight of me over Katey's shoulder as I sidled up to the table, and his green eyes darkened with some emotion I couldn't quite identify. Not anger, not at all, but for sure not let's-blow-a-bugle friendship either.

Awesome.

It was too late to turn back, though, so I put on a big smile and moved forward, because that was what I did.

"Hey," I greeted softly, directing the word to the condiment caddy in the center of the table.

I hated sounding so unsure. I hated *being* so unsure. I straightened my spine. "Is it okay if I sit here?"

"Luke!" Drew's genuine smile made his face crease beneath his tie-dyed headband. "What a treat."

"Of course you should come sit," Emma invited, pushing down around the horseshoe so I could take a spot on the end of the booth across from Webb. "You look like you need some coffee."

"You look like you might keel over," Marco corrected with a kind of waspish fondness. "Much like this one did a little while ago." He elbowed Webb, who grunted.

Webb lifted his eyes to mine. He looked... cautious, I decided. But that was fine. That was *great*. I could work with cautious. I was feeling pretty cautious myself.

Katey snagged an empty coffee mug from a nearby table and thumped it down in front of me. "Pot's there." She pointed toward the carafe in the middle of the table.

"Okay. Thank—"

"Everyone else already ordered. What can I getcha?"

"Well, I—" I darted a glance at my menu, which was still tucked under her arm.

"Pancakes?" She tapped her pen against her order pad like she was writing a period. "*Figures.*"

"I… I guess it'll be pancakes, then," I called after her. "Great! Thanks!"

Emma pushed the coffeepot toward me with a grin. "Don't mind her. Katey likes flirting with Webb," she explained. "She doesn't like that Webb doesn't flirt back."

"Em," Webb warned. "Leave it."

Emma grinned back, unrepentant. "Just sayin'. You could throw the woman a bone every now and then, for the sake of—"

"Emma. Carbury. Sunday. The breakfast table isn't the place to talk about your brother's bone-throwing," Drew scolded, nearly making me choke on my first sip of coffee. Then he added pointedly, "Or really long-standing lack thereof."

"Enough," Webb said firmly. "Katey's a great person, but there's no chemistry there. Also, she strikes me as the marrying type, and I am *never* getting married again. Been there, done that."

Hmm. Katey was pretty, if you were into sassy blondes. I wondered why there was no chemistry.

I wondered who he *did* find attractive.

And then I wondered why the hell I was wondering, 'cause it was sure as heck none of *my* business.

"Morning, Sundays." Jack Wyatt, the owner of the

diner, clapped Webb on the shoulder in greeting. His eyes sparkled with humor as he turned to me. "*Luke.*"

"Oh, God." Webb rolled his eyes grumpily. "Just say it."

"Say what?" Jack was a picture of innocence.

"Whatever the hell's got you wearing that constipated goldfish expression. Go on."

Jack spread his hands innocently. "It's called a *smile*, Webb. Can't a man just be happy? It's a bright, sunny morning. My friends and neighbors are gathered under my diner's roof. Helena Fortnum and her friends are staging a topless knit-in down at town hall today because they feel the mayor's not taking their concerns about the development seriously. *Topless octogenarian knitters*, Webb. So much to be happy about."

Webb lifted an eyebrow. "You're a strange, strange man."

Jack's grin widened. "Okay, I *also* might have just heard a rumor a little while ago that a pair of handsome gents— including my own best friend—were causing a ruckus on the common last night." He rocked back and forth on the balls of his feet like a little kid.

"Jesus, you're the worst gossip ever. Luke and I had a couple drinks and watched hockey. That's all," Webb scoffed.

"Together?" Drew looked between us delightedly. "So you two have buried the hatchet?"

"Better than that." Jack wiggled his eyebrows. "I heard they were blowing each other's bugles right on the town common."

"Don't be an ass," Webb scoffed.

"Don't be silly!" I said at the same time, inadvertently making our denials sound very… rehearsed.

Webb shot me a dark look, but the eye roll he directed

at Jack was light and easy. "Luke and I happened to be at the Bugle at the same time. We… talked."

"Resolved some misunderstandings," I elaborated.

"Yeah. Had a drink or two, possibly three—"

I nodded. "And watched the game. The Habs lost."

"In the end, we realized that there was no good reason for us not to be friends, so we… we declared our friendship. Didn't we?" Webb gave me a significant look.

"Yes, indeed. That's exactly how it happened. Precisely as I remember it," I confirmed.

"Declared your friendship?" Jack repeated slowly. He cocked his head. "What, like, verbally? In the bar?"

"Er, no. More like…" I cleared my throat softly. "Musically. On the common."

Webb huffed out a single breath of startled laughter, and his eyes regained a touch of the warmth they'd held the night before. "I only remember bits and pieces."

"Same!" I grinned, relieved. "I was worried there was something worse, but if you don't remember anything, then probably—"

I broke off as the diner door flew open and a group of chattering Hollowans—*I guess we're using this word now*—crowded inside, led by none other than Mayor York himself.

"They're over here, Ginny!" the mayor called excitedly, pointing at the back of the restaurant.

Pointing at… *me*.

"The fuck?" Webb seemed just as confused as I was and looked twice as scowly about it.

A thirty-something woman carrying an old-fashioned reporter microphone and a man with a video camera jostled through the crowd, and the mayor directed them to the area right in front of our table. He bumped a protesting Jack aside and took his spot.

"How's this?" he asked the cameraman. "Do you have a good angle of the happy couple? What about me?" He ran a hand over his hair.

The cameraman gave him a thumbs-up.

"Looking great, Uncle Ernie!" the reporter assured him. She turned to Webb and me and whispered, "You two. Try to look a little more besotted, okay?"

Besotted? *What?*

But she'd already turned back and smiled broadly at the camera. "Good morning. This is Genevieve York-Muller reporting from the town of Little Pippin Hollow, with a heartwarming story of true love and the charming practice of handfasting—"

I looked to Drew and Marco. "Oh my gosh! Did you guys get handfasted? Congratulations!"

Marco shook his head resolutely. "Hell no. I'm not into kinky stuff."

Webb poked the mayor in the back. "Mayor York, what's this about?"

The mayor slapped his hand away.

"It's fine, Uncle Ernie," the reporter told the mayor. "We'll cut the interruptions in editing." She shook her hair back, fixed her smile in place once again, and continued in a hushed-excited voice, "Handfasting, which can be a form of commitment prior to marriage, much like a betrothal or an engagement—"

"Ohhhh, *that* kind of handfasting," Marco said.

"—may have fallen out of practice in modern times throughout much of the world, but in this pristine hamlet, the tradition is alive and well, thanks to a law that was written nearly three hundred years ago and a very special brass bugle that dates back to the Revolutionary War!"

The reporter made a slicing motion across her throat.

"M'kay. That's where we'll shift to the B-roll. Your turn, Uncle Ernie. Go ahead."

"Right, yes." The mayor cleared his throat and gestured to a woman in the crowd. "Dora? Honey, where's my scroll?"

The mayor's wife hurried over, bearing a two-foot-wide scroll on a velvet pillow.

"I am proud to read the following proclamation, which was signed into our official town record just this very morning by me. Ernest York. Proud mayor of Little Pippin Hollow."

The mayor picked up the scroll with great ceremony and let it unfurl all the way to the floor. He cleared his throat, gave the camera a brilliant toothpaste smile, and began reading. "Whereas Thomas Webb Sunday—"

"Oh, no." Webb shook his head. "*Fuck* no. I want nothing to do with this shit, whatever it is."

"—has been a resident in good standing of Little Pippin Hollow, Vermont, for his entire life and is not only a prominent town leader, but also owner of the delightful, family-owned Sunday Orchard—" The mayor glanced directly at the camera again and added, "Where you'll find fine heirloom apple varietals and agricultural fun for the whole family! Check out www dot sundayorchard dot com for more information!"

"What in the *world*?" Em whispered.

He glanced down at the scroll again. "And whereas Luke Guilford Williams—"

"*Me*?" I squeaked. "Wait, how'd you get my middle name?"

"—who is a sheepherder by trade—"

"I think he prefers to call it *teaching*," Marco interrupted.

The mayor spoke louder. "—is an esteemed new resident to our town, who has become an integral part of our community—and enjoys shopping at Pippin Feed and Supply for all his animal needs! Stop by their location on Tree Wagon Turnpike and mention my name for a twenty percent discount!"

Webb began shaking his head… and continued shaking it like a metronome as anger tightened his features and tensed his shoulders.

Mayor York stood taller and continued. "And whereas love is love is love, and unions of all types are welcomed and encouraged in our inclusive, diverse community—which also happens to be home to Mattson's Sugar House, call 555-GO-MAPLE to reserve your spot at one of our maple sugar jamborees today!"

"What is happening?" I hiss-whispered over the table. "What is going on right now?" I was pretty sure I knew, but that didn't make it any easier to believe.

"And whereas both parties are of sound body and mind and were confirmed by multiple witnesses to fully understand the seriousness of the act they were undertaking—"

"Like fuck we did," Webb growled.

"And both parties are believed to have long harbored affectionate feelings for one another—"

"Affection?" I squawked. The man had barely tolerated me! "*Affection?*"

The mayor clapped Webb on the shoulder, and Webb stared up at him in horror. "—and have joined their hands on the town common, blown the revered Unity Bugle, and pledged their unity so that they might seal their troth—"

"Doesn't *troth* mean marriage?" Drew demanded of no one in particular.

"Oh my *God*, you got married?" Emma cried, way too loud. "Holy crap, Webb."

"No," I whispered, panicked. "No. We didn't. We're not. Absolutely not even a little bit. We... there was a legend of the bugle, and a pretty girl, and— Webb, *tell them the legend!*"

"And whereas both parties will have been furnished with a list of conditions they must complete within the eight-week handfast period in order to confirm their willingness to be declared lawful spouses under the terms of the Little Pippin Hollow Handfast Act of 1762—"

The mayor motioned to Dora, who hurried forward to hand us each a miniature scroll with a bow and a flourish.

I took mine, too stunned to refuse.

Webb made no move to take his, so she set it on the table in front of him.

"Now, therefore, I, as mayor, do formally declare that the aforementioned couple, Webb Sunday and Luke Williams, are hereby *handfasted*. What the bugle has joined together, let no man put asunder."

He sighed in satisfaction and rolled the scroll back up. "Gentlemen, on behalf of the town, I'd like to express our appreciation that you've chosen to unify your lives through this venerable tradition. I hope you know you can count on all of us to help and support you as you work to complete your confirmation tasks."

I was drunk. I had to be. There was no other explanation.

"Cut!" Ginny called happily. "Great job, Uncle Ernie. I'm thinking we can do a couple segments a week on this. Maybe first we'll interview the grooms—"

"Good idea!" the mayor agreed.

"Terrible idea. We are *not* grooms." Webb spoke for the first time in a long moment. "Jesus Christ, Ernest. I'm not even gay. What the hell is this about?"

"Hey." The mayor jabbed a finger at Webb. "I won't have you being homophobic."

"Homo—" Webb shook his head, bewildered. "I'm not! Jesus, Ernie, you *know* I'm not. I'm just saying—"

"Fascinating," Ginny breathed. She motioned to the cameraman and stuck her microphone in my face. "Mr. Williams, were you aware that your fiancé isn't gay?"

"Well, I—" I began.

"We're not *fiancés*!" Webb shouted over me.

"I apologize," Ginny said. "Do you prefer partner? Or... handfaster?"

I shook my head. "You've got it wrong. Webb and I are—"

"Are *nothing*," Webb said in a tone of finality that rang through the restaurant like a bullet to my heart. "Luke Williams is nothing to me."

My stomach pitched, and my hands went cold.

So much for *unity*.

Chapter Six

I was not marrying Luke Williams. For many, many reasons.

I brought my ax down on an unsuspecting log—*whack* —and the bisected halves fell into the snow—*thud*.

First and foremost, I was not gay.

I picked up half of a log and put it back on the chopping block.

Whack. Thud.

I was pretty sure I wasn't even bisexual.

Whack. Thud.

It wasn't that I would mind being bi, if I was. Not even a little.

Whack. Thud.

Or okay, maybe a *little*, but only because it would prove Van and certain other busybodies in town right, and that would be annoying.

Whack. Thud.

But not because I thought there was anything *wrong* with liking guys. I mean, once Knox finally stopped dicking around and asked Gage to marry him, I was gonna groomsman the hell out of one or both of them. And if Aiden came to me tomorrow and said he was marrying a man, I'd... well, okay, I'd tell him he was seven and to go do his fucking homework before he considered matrimony, but I'd be supportive.

Whack. Thud.

It was just that I would *know* if I were into guys, the same way I knew I had brown hair and loved ice cream and hated talking about my feelings. The same way I knew I was a Capricorn... or a Cancer, whichever was the January one. Because a person could hide a lot of things from himself, sure, but not something this enormous and monumental. Not if he already had three gay brothers, for fuck's sake, *and* a gay uncle and had grown up in an environment where lube preferences were sometimes discussed at the dinner table.

Whack. Thud.

And of all the guys in the world who could possibly unlock my latent bisexuality, was it really likely to be shy, slightly nerdy, golly-gosh-darn Luke Williams, with his Pollyanna manners, baggy khaki pants, and sweater vests, when I hadn't even liked the guy until our paths happened to collide at the Bugle the night before?

I tightened my grip on the ax and firmly did not think about his deep blue eyes or his swirling freckles, the way his smile got caught on his incisor sometimes when he laughed or the way my stomach writhed and dropped every time I caught sight of him.

Whack. Thud.

I did not think about where he was, right at that moment, or what he might be doing.

Whack. Thud.

I also did not think about the way my cock had

responded to the woodsmoke smell of him since that was entirely due to being drunk. Drunk and confused.

Some people's dicks stopped working when they were drunk, but clearly mine was the opposite.

Whack. Thud.

And, okay, even if I *was* bisexual—which the jury was still out on—*and* attracted to Luke Williams—which I super was not—it didn't matter at all, practically speaking, because I was not going to act on any of it.

Fuck no. Me and Luke Williams? *Pfft.* That was a complicated disaster waiting to happen.

We couldn't even get drunk without getting accidentally handfasted, for God's sake. Plus, he was my son's teacher, which seemed... weird.

And, most importantly, a guy like Luke Williams practically had the word *relationship* stamped on his forehead, which was a hard limit for me.

My previous relationship had drained me dry emotionally and financially three years ago when Amanda left me and our son to go off and chase rainbows.

And then, just when I'd started to think things might be okay, Amanda had reappeared and decided she wanted back in Aiden's life, first by freakin' *kidnapping* him after school one day—an incident she dismissed as an "oversight" but which still gave me nightmares—and then by taking me to court to challenge our previous custody agreement so she could see him more often.

And the trickiest part of all that was, I was going to have to set my fears aside and work with her, because even if it killed me, I would do what I had to for Aiden—

"I think it's learned its lesson."

"What?" I whirled around to face the house and found Knox leaning back against the pony-rail fence, booted feet crossed at the ankles, barn coat open, shading his eyes with his hand against the afternoon sunlight.

I'd been so lost in my head, I hadn't heard him leave the house or walk across the gravel driveway.

"The wood." He nodded at the chopping block. "It's safe to say you've asserted your dominance."

I turned back and surveyed my work.

Shit. I'd been chopping the same half log over and over without even noticing, and now it was nothing but wood chips in the snow.

"Doesn't really matter." I set the ax down and pulled my gloves on more firmly. "I already have three cords of firewood laid by. This was just…"

"Clearing your head like Dad used to do?" Knox guessed.

I nodded. "Olin's mom's bringing Aiden home in a little while. I need to get my head on straight by then." I picked up a new log and laid it on the block. "You need something?"

"No. Not really." Knox rubbed his lips together. He glanced back at the house, then at the sky, then at the tree line. He cleared his throat. "You, ah… you wanna talk about it?"

I shot him a deeply questioning look, and he shrugged. "Dude. You started it. I seem to remember someone forcing me to talk about my feelings more than once last fall."

Whack. Thud.

"That was different. When you were being an idiot with Gage, talking helped. But my shit…" I huffed out a half laugh. "No."

Whack. Thud.

"This is about Luke Williams, isn't it?"

Whack. CRUNCH. I overshot the log and impaled the

73

ax into the chopping block. The shock of it reverberated up my arms.

"*Fuck.*" I dropped the ax to the ground and rubbed at my biceps. "Why would you say that?"

"Webb, you ran out of the town meeting last night ready to declare war on the man—"

"Exaggeration. Besides, once he and I talked, I figured out it was all a misunderstanding. Luke said he didn't know what his lawyer was working on."

"And you believe him?"

"I…" I remembered him bursting into tears and felt my muscles tense in shame. "Yeah. I do. Although, I don't trust his attorney in the slightest, so I asked Curt to check into things, too." I picked up the ax once again. "And I decided I'd try to be friendlier. Set a good example for Aiden, you know?"

Knox hooted. "I found the two of you staring into each other's eyes, holding hands, and blowing a bugle. If you were any friendlier, you'd've been arrested for indecent exposure."

"That's not funny," I warned.

"Oh, I beg to differ." Knox grinned, the fucker. "I was there, and it was hilarious. In fact, I think Neil Diamond sang it best. *Hands… touching hands…*"

"You suck. And it's *not* funny, because the mayor's pretending that we're fucking engaged, and he's getting the whole town in on the act." I set another log on the block.

"Uh-huh. The way they were telling it at the Bugle today, you and Luke are already married. Apparently, handfasting means different things in some parts of the world than it does in the Hollow. And Chandra North and Joyce Chan were arguing over your ship name. Joyce says *Williday.*"

"Christ." Just what I needed. "Awful."

Hand Picked

"Right? I know. Gage and I much prefer *Lubbe*."

I gritted my teeth.

Whack. Thud.

"I also got an earful from Emma—who was *outraged*, by the by—that you were an asshole to your intended at breakfast." Knox poked his tongue into his cheek. "Tell me again how that newfound friendliness is going?"

A tendril of guilt coiled in my stomach as the memory of the hurt on Luke's face before he'd managed to blank his expression at the diner this morning, collided with the memory from last night, of Luke in tears saying no one liked him.

Whack. Thud.

"He's not my *intended*. Don't start with that stuff."

Knox cocked his head and studied me. "Wait, this handfasting is really bugging you, isn't it? *Why?*" He acted like of all the fucked-up aspects of this situation, it was my attitude that concerned him most. "It's just... the Hollow being the Hollow. They care about you and wanna see you happy. And you *know* they love matchmaking. This... it's matchmaking on steroids. Matchmaking as a spectator sport. But they can't actually make you marry the guy."

"I know!"

"So why do you care if they think you're handfasted? *You* know the truth, and so does Luke. *You* know you're not attracted to him—"

Whack. Thud.

"Wait, *are* you attracted to him?" Knox asked, sounding mildly shocked. "Because if you are, I—"

"Don't be ridiculous. I... That's... not the point."

"Oh my God, you can't lie for shit, and that was *not* a denial. You know, it's okay to be attracted to him. It's even okay to act on it and enjoy yourself. Sexuality is fluid, and you'd be setting a good example for—"

I set my jaw. "Knox, I know all that, okay? And none of that is relevant. I just feel bad for Luke, having to deal with people gossiping about us, that's all. Because they are, and that sucks when he already felt like people around here don't accept him. He's a good guy."

"Well, at least you'll cop to *that*."

"I knew it all along, I think," I admitted, blowing out a breath. "He gets under my skin, and I don't like that. I don't understand it—"

"I think I might."

"—but it's not his fault. And after talking to him last night, I know that my... unfairness was hurtful. So I'm trying to do better."

"Hmm. You might recall, I took an instant, irrational dislike to someone who got under *my* skin, once upon a time. And now I'm madly in love with him, except he stole my damn sweatshirt months ago and he won't give it—"

"Knox." I held up a hand. "I get that you're trying to be helpful or distracting or something, but I've got a lot on my mind. I met with my attorney about Aiden's custody right after breakfast—"

"Oh, shit." Knox straightened and got serious immediately. "I forgot that was today. Jesus, you *did* have a hell of a morning. No wonder you were cranky at the diner. What'd Curt say? How'd it go? Is the handfasting going to interfere with the custody situation?"

I set down the ax, grabbed the water bottle I'd left on top of the snow, and chugged it down. "It went okay, I guess? He said the best way to handle the handfasting is to just let it expire without completing the tasks. It's a random town bylaw with no legal significance as long as the terms aren't met, so it shouldn't affect the custody dispute." I took a deep breath. "But I decided to let Amanda start having additional visitation anyway."

"Wait, what? But Webb, you said…"

"She's flighty as fuck? She makes promises and flakes? She's always after the next shiny thing? She hurts Aiden's feelings again and again? Yeah." I took off one of my gloves to rub the back of my neck. "But she's stuck around a lot longer than I expected this time. She's been dating Roberta Oliver's brother for a few months. And Aiden… he loves his mom. No matter how flaky she is, he wants to see her. I feel like I'm hurting him just as much by keeping them apart as she does by disappointing him."

"*Shit*," Knox said with feeling. "So… what? She just… gets to visit him whenever? That doesn't sound right."

"No. Noo-ho-ho. No. We're starting out slowly. Curt and I drafted an agreement where she'd start out by taking him to hockey practice and helping out with Nature Scouts. Those are some of Aiden's favorite activities anyway, and he'd like to have her there. And I—"

"You'll feel better because there'll be supervision," he surmised.

"Exactly. If they don't show up to practice, his coach will let me know, and if he's not at Scouts, Maryanne will call me. But assuming Amanda sticks—which is kind of a big assumption—then in a few weeks, she'll take him for overnights." I shook my head. "I don't know why that makes me nervous when he spends half his nights at Olin's, and Olin spends the rest of the nights here, but it does."

"Yeah, it does," Knox said with feeling, and it helped to know he understood.

"Anyway. The judge signed off on it. I think it made a good impression on her that I offered to try this. And if Amanda doesn't follow the terms of the agreement—"

"Meaning, if she disappears with Aiden again?"

I nodded grimly, my hands tightening into fists. "That would be an end to it. The judge didn't look too favorably on Amanda's conduct last fall, and it made me feel better to know she took it seriously."

"No shit. So... you're good, then?"

"Yeah." I hesitated. "Or I will be. Eventually. Once I wrap my head around some things."

"Uh-huh. And you'll process your feelings by... chopping a block of wood into tiny splinters?"

"In the time-honored tradition of our ancestors, Knox." I rolled my eyes. "You know, the one that doesn't involve freakin'... *apple tithes* and bugle blowing."

He laughed. "Is the chopping working yet?"

I thought about it for a moment. "Kinda, yeah. I do feel better." It might have had as much to do with my brother's presence as it did with the wood chopping, but I wasn't going to tell him so. He'd only get *more* annoying.

"And how's *Luke* feeling about things?" Knox prompted.

I sighed. If I knew Luke—which I didn't... but was kinda starting to—he was probably at home, alone, wearing a sweater vest and thinking cheerful thoughts... and feeling unliked—*again*—for something that wasn't his fault.

God, I was such an asshole.

Knox lifted an eyebrow at me like he knew what I was thinking and agreed.

I grimaced. "*Fuck.* I should, ah... probably go apologize, huh?" I said fake-reluctantly, like I hadn't been waiting for an excuse to go find Luke and make sure he was okay.

As a *friend*. Clearly.

"Oh yeah," Knox advised. "Bring gifts."

Chapter Seven

LUKE

Have you ever tried to attach a plastic tarp to a slate roof five feet over your head while a stiff, cold Vermont wind whips your hair into your eyes and turns your fingers to icicles?

No?

As I lay sprawled on the roof of said portico, blinking up at the afternoon sun, I wanted very badly to say that I hadn't tried that either... and that the wind hadn't then gotten underneath the tarp, creating an inadvertent parasailing situation, which had then caused me to kick the ladder down to the ground and left me stranded twelve feet above the ground...

But that would be a lie.

"What the freak was I thinking?" I asked the puffy clouds drifting overhead.

The answer was that I hadn't been thinking. Not even a little.

I'd been hungover and hurt and desperate to get something done—to *fix* something, even if it was just putting a tarp on the roof—to make myself feel better.

Clearly, I had been wildly successful.

"Nothing says empowerment like being stranded on your own roof," I muttered, thinking of the phone I'd left safely in the camper to charge.

I peered over the edge of the roof at the giant snowbank where the ladder had landed and pondered whether the snow would break my fall... or just break me.

It was tempting to jump because I really did not want anyone to find me up there—*no, seriously, parents, other than the missing child, the drunken bugle blowing... oh, and that one hilarious time I threw a hissy fit and got stranded on my own portico, I'm the best role model ever!*—but if one of my students heard Mr. Williams had jumped off a roof and decided to try it, I'd never forgive myself.

So, instead, I resigned myself to being stuck until Murray came on sheep duty and decided I'd try to enjoy it.

Positive thinking for the win.

I leaned back against the roof, looked up at the sky, and started humming a tune when a deep, conversational voice from way too close below me yelled up.

"'Sweet Caroline'? You know, I'm beginning to associate that song with terrible decisions."

I startled so badly I nearly lost my perch.

"Holy shoot. Webb?" I peered over the edge of the roof again, and sure enough, there were the world's thickest forearms, folded in judgment over the world's broadest chest. My heart gave a little squeeze that had nothing to do with my situation and everything to do with the memory of Webb's stony face back at Panini Jack's. "What are you doing here?"

"*Me?*" He snorted. "You're on your roof without a ladder, Luke." There was a tremble of something in his voice, and I couldn't decide if it was anger or amusement.

God, why did all of my worst and most embarrassing moments happen around this guy?

"Am I?" I said airily. "I hadn't noticed. I'm enjoying the lovely view. So much... snow."

"And how are you planning to get down?"

I sniffed. "I'll figure something out. Eventually. Probably."

"Fair enough. And when you don't, I'll have them inscribe that on your tombstone. *Here lies Luke Williams, who would have figured something out... probably, eventually,*" he said dryly. "Now, move back from the edge so I can prop the ladder back up there."

"You know, I'm not certain I'm ready to get down, but thanks anyway." I stuck my chin in the air stubbornly, though I was pretty sure he couldn't see me. "I might stay up here a while longer. Doing yoga. Meditating. Expanding my consciousness."

"If you don't come down, you won't get to see what I brought you."

"You brought me something?" I peeped over the edge again, reluctantly curious. "Is it arsenic?"

He snorted. "No. Jeez."

"Another Rusty Spike?"

"Definitely not," he said with feeling. He shaded his eyes as he looked up at me. "I wouldn't do that to anyone ever again."

"Even though I'm *nothing* to you?" I shot back.

Dang it. I hadn't intended to bring up the scene at breakfast, but apparently I was spending all my shame pennies that afternoon.

Webb hesitated. "I didn't mean that the way it sounded earlier. I was blindsided by the scroll thing. I told you last night that I want to be friends, and I mean it. I just... wasn't a very good one to you earlier."

Hmph. "I was blindsided, too. And it's not like I *want* to be handfasted to you, you know. I barely knew what hand-fasting was before this morning. Heck, I'm still not sure I know. But if I were going to inadvertently betroth myself to a guy, my baseline minimum standard would be to pick a guy who could have the slightest inkling of attraction for me."

Webb opened his mouth to speak, hesitated, then shut it again. "Can you come down? I'm getting a crick in my neck talking to you."

I pondered how much I cared about his neck—*sadly, a lot*—and whether I was ready to face the further embarrassment of being on ground level with him—*nope.*

I lay back down against the shingles. "I appreciate your concern, but just leave the ladder propped up here, and I'll come down later. Also, it must be said, you are terrible at apologizing."

"I'll apologize when you come down. And... I brought ice cream."

I sat up and leaned forward again, eyes narrowed. "Ice cream?"

He held up a white plastic bag that had been lying on a snowbank. "Two pints of Boston Cream Pie."

"That's... that's my favorite," I said suspiciously.

"No kidding. You're always buying out Chuck's entire supply so there's none left for m—for anyone else who'd like to buy some."

I rolled my eyes, but I had to admit I was getting cold... and ice cream, even in the dead of winter, was my kryptonite. "Fine, then. Hoist the ladder."

Webb did more than hoist it—he kicked away the snow on the ground to find a stable place to set it, and when that didn't work to his satisfaction, he braced the ladder with both hands.

"Come on down," he directed. "Take it slow, okay?"

Once again, I rolled my eyes. "I know how to descend a ladder. I got up here, didn't I?" I swung myself carefully off the roof and onto the top rung and quickly clambered down. "I don't need your… h-help."

My hand brushed Webb's arm, and too late, I realized that the way he stood meant that I was essentially climbing backward into his embrace. My knees were on a level with his head, and if I kept going, my ass would be—

I swallowed hard, my face going hot. "I'm almost down. You can let go now."

"Nah. Go ahead and get all the way to the ground."

"I've got it from here," I insisted.

"You're too high," he shot back. "Three more steps. And quit rocking the ladder."

"I'm not rocking it! You're making me nervous. Step away!"

"Get down first!"

"For heaven's sake, I'm perfectly safe—" I tilted sideways to glare at him, and my foot slipped on the metal rung. I grabbed for the ladder and overbalanced, making the ladder tip precariously… with me on it.

"Jesus fuck, Luke," Webb cried. He pushed the ladder away with one hand and hauled me back against his muscled chest with the other. His beard tickled the exposed skin at the back of my neck, and suddenly, I was very aware that he was holding me. Hugging me. His free hand came around my waist, where my jacket had rucked up, and held me tighter, his bare fingers somehow hot against my skin.

It was not a big deal, but it also *was*. And an uncomfortable truth I'd been trying not to acknowledge for months bubbled up from my chest.

I was attracted to Webb Sunday.

And not attracted in a "yes, he's a handsome man of symmetrical features" sort of way, which anyone would have to admit about Webb, but in a "holy son of a beaver, I would like to lay myself out in the snow like a buffet and beg this man to lick me up" way.

Despite all the other mortifying things I'd done in Webb's presence, this one struck me as extra embarrassing. He was the father of my student. The *straight* father of my student. He'd actively disliked me until the night before, and I wasn't sure he liked me much better now for all that we were "friends"…

And yet, when his finger accidentally slid a millimeter below the waistband of my jeans to glance over my hip bone—my hip bone, of all places!—my dick twitched.

So much for my baseline minimum standards.

I was so screwed.

Mortified, I squirmed out of his grip and launched myself sideways into the snowbank—note to self, snow wasn't nearly as soft as it appeared—which would have made for an awkward move under the best of circumstances. But I'd somehow forgotten that Webb was still clinging to me, trying really hard not to let me fall, and since he was unaware that I'd been trying to get away since I'd failed to use words, I'd pulled him with me… then landed on top of him.

"*Hnn—ffff*," he groaned from beneath me.

"Sorry! Oh, shoot. *Shoot, shoot, shoot.* I'm so sorry!" I rolled off him, heedless of the ice pellets going up the bottom of my jacket and down the back of my jeans, especially when I saw he was lying in the snowdrift with his eyes closed, unmoving.

"Webb?" I ripped my glove off with my teeth and stroked a hand over his cheek. His beard was softer than it looked, which was really kinda…

Mother trucker. That was really not something I should have been noticing at that juncture.

Keep it together, Williams!

"Are you okay? Did you… are you injured? Speak to me." I pushed Webb flat on his back and knelt in the snow, running my hands over his hard, hard chest and equally hard abdomen.

Focus, Luke.

I couldn't feel a wound through his jacket, which was good. But when I gripped his wrist, I couldn't find his pulse, which was *bad.*

"Oh, God, don't die!" I glanced toward the house and the camper beyond it, where my phone was. It felt miles away. "Should I do CPR?"

I studied Webb's lips for a second. They were good lips. Plush and firm. Kissable.

Not the point! Sweet caramel corn, Luke, think!

I moved my hand over his nose to check if he was breathing—

"Planning to finish me off?" Webb asked, clearly teasing.

I glanced up in horror and found his green eyes wide open… and locked on me.

"No!" I snatched my hand back. "I…"

"Because I have to say, I might have been unkind earlier, but I didn't actively try to kill you."

"I'm not trying to—! Wait, were you just pretending—?"

He did some kind of full-body curl that let him stand without using his hands and began brushing the snow off himself. "I'm sorry for earlier," he said sincerely, "but now you're sharing the ice cream."

I forced myself to look away when he dusted both

hands over his sculpted rear and got to my own feet less gracefully.

"Son of a bunion," I muttered, knocking the worst of the snow off my knees. "Should've seen that coming."

"Let's get inside." He clomped up the stairs to the front door, swinging his ice cream bag. "We can go over the—"

"Wait!" I cried a second too late.

Webb pushed the front door open... and just like last summer, the entire frame collapsed into the front hall. This time, I saw particles of wood splinter off, and I winced.

"What... the fuck... just happened," Webb growled, eyes wide as he stared down at his hand, which had been clenched around a doorknob until seconds before.

"There's a slight problem with the door," I said apologetically. "I should have warned you, but no one actually comes in this door, because no one ever actually comes out here, and I—"

"This is a *huge* safety issue!" Webb exploded, turning on the top stoop to look at me, his teasing, lighthearted demeanor utterly evaporated. "If you'd been behind that door when someone tried to open it, you could have been crushed. Jesus Christ, Luke. I was trying not to bite your head off about climbing up on your portico without making sure the ground around your ladder was stable, but this—"

"Hey! The ladder was perfectly stable when I climbed onto the *portico*." I set my hands on my hips. "And it's none of your—"

"Facts are facts," he insisted, talking over me. "You were up on the portico, and the ladder was down on the ground, so clearly—"

"Because I had the ladder balanced on top of the portico so I could reach the roof, jerkface!"

I clapped both hands over my mouth and stared at him

with wide eyes. "I'm so sorry. Name-calling is never okay. Please accept my—" I babbled in horror.

At the same time, Webb exploded, "Are you fucking serious? The fucking roof? Are you fucking *insane*?"

Okay, so clearly Webb didn't share my concerns about insulting language.

"I wasn't doing it for *funsies*, Webb Sunday!" I said defensively. "I was trying to get a tarp up there before it snowed again and caused even more damage. I had no choice."

"Sure you did! You could have asked a professional!" he shot back. "You could have bought a decent-sized ladder."

"What professional? And how would I pay them? And how would I transport a ladder anywhere with my little car? Criminy, I'm doing my best!" I took a deep breath and tried to calm down.

I prided myself on my patience, but the second I was around this man, it seemed to evaporate.

"Besides," I said in a more moderate tone, "this whole place is a safety hazard. The roof and the door are just… a drop in the bucket."

Webb gave me a look of patent disbelief, and I sighed. "Go inside. You'll see."

With one last glare, Webb stepped over the remains of the door and into the entry hall. I watched his eyes track over the buckled stairs and ripped wallpaper before he stepped into the living room. He swore under his breath when he saw the small mountain of plaster and the hole in the ceiling, but I caught the sleeve of his jacket before he could go in and inspect it further.

"I don't think the living room's safe. That hole goes all the way to the roof, and more might fall any minute. That's why I was trying to get a tarp up there."

Webb blinked at me. He shook off my hand to brush past me in the other direction, through a second parlor, where he ran a hand over the deep cracks in the plaster walls. Finally, he stepped into the kitchen, where he made a strangled, distressed sort of noise.

Seeing the house through his eyes, I felt a creeping sense of shame, even though the condition wasn't remotely my fault.

"I, um… I reinforced the back steps," I informed him proudly. "Figured out how to pour the concrete and everything. And there were some floor joist issues in the basement that I got taken care of. Oh, and you should see the barn. I upgraded the electrical all by myself and got the water tank working for the sheep."

He ignored me and headed for the back staircase, but I grabbed his arm again to stop him. "The second floor was really weak in spots even back in July, and I haven't even tried to get to the attic."

"Fuck." Webb ran a hand over the blackened brick of the kitchen fireplace. "I had no idea. It wasn't remotely this bad last time I was inside here, but… that was a long time ago." He chewed the inside of his lip for a second, then sighed. "I keep telling myself I don't wanna hear this story, but I guess I probably do. How'd you get the land, then? Ben ran a contest, I know that much."

"He did," I agreed. "And I—oh, *lawsy.*" A cold draft blew down the chimney, and I shivered hard in my snow-covered clothes. "Sorry, what was I saying?"

"Jesus. Go change into something warm before you die of hypothermia and my family never speaks to me again," Webb ordered, sounding weary. Then he frowned. "Hang on, are you sleeping in this place?"

"In here? No way." It was on the tip of my tongue to ask if he thought I was an idiot, but I was pretty sure the answer was yes. "There's a perfectly fine trailer out there." I nodded toward the kitchen door and the yard beyond. "That's where Ben slept, too."

"Thank fuck for *that*, anyway," Webb muttered, grabbing my elbow. "Come on. Let's get out of here before anything else happens to you."

Chapter Eight

WEBB

"I can walk on my own," Luke protested, but once again, I ignored him. There was no way I was letting him go when this house was clearly a death trap.

I opened the back door and led him down the stairs with one hand clutching the bag of ice cream and the other locked around his arm.

We took several steps in the direction of a junk heap before I realized it wasn't a junk heap at all. It was Death Trap Junior, a clear case of tetanus if ever I'd seen one. The old travel trailer was a collection of rusted metal parts held together with dying vines.

My heart rate reached danger levels as I reared back. "*This* is your perfectly fine trailer?"

"Hey! Don't be rude. I know it's not the prettiest, but it's dry and mostly warm." Luke moved around me to open the door. "And at least I don't worry that it's going to collapse on me… much."

I climbed in behind him, trying my best to step lightly in case I caused a catastrophic collapse of the old tin box.

Luke scrambled to tidy up. He hung his coat on a hook

by the door, turned on the heater, and moved a towering stack of books and a shoebox full of kitchen sponges from one side of the camper's pleather dinette booth to the other before ushering me to sit.

I lifted an eyebrow and nodded at the sponges. "Planning to use those to repair the roof? Because I have a feeling they might not work."

His cheeks went adorably pink. "No. Obviously not. They're for an experiment to help teach the kids about hydroponics. Do you know, hydroponics can greatly increase plant yields *and* result in ninety percent more efficient use of water—?"

"I wouldn't say anything is *obvious* right now, Luke," I said, not meaning for it to come out as harsh as it did. "Not after seeing that fucking house. Not after seeing that you're living in this tiny trailer. Not after witnessing the tarp incident." I hesitated for a second but finally set the bag of ice cream on the kitchen counter next to his charging cell phone and hung my coat beside his.

"You didn't witness it," he pointed out. I could tell he was trying to keep calm. Maybe he was embarrassed by the situation. "You only caught the aftermath."

"The aftermath was plenty bad enough," I muttered. I wedged myself into the small spot he'd cleared and looked around at his tiny, hopefully temporary, home.

It actually didn't look that bad inside. Even though it was packed full of his possessions—including tons of school supplies, books, and crafts—it was somehow cozy. Colorful drawings were pinned up, and soft afghans lay over the back of the dinette bench and on the foot of the bed.

Seeing his little nest felt oddly intimate and a bit intrusive. But my eyes roamed over every detail hungrily. This was a side of the man I'd never expected to see.

Luke huffed. "Look, I'm doing the best I can with the house. And I haven't had a lot of time or money to work on the trailer, what with school and taking care of the animals." His words were defensive, borderline nervous babbling. "The best I could do was a fresh coat of paint and some accent blankets for now."

I hated that he felt like he had to defend himself from me. Clearly he was in a bad situation. I hadn't realized it before, but maybe I should have. Maybe I should have paid more attention to him and his situation, rather than only focusing on how it related to *me*.

The truth was becoming obvious. Someone—namely Ben Pond—had royally fucked this sweet man over. They'd put him in an impossibly difficult situation, and he seemed to be trying to hide it from everyone. Hell, we were his closest neighbors, yet none of us had even known he was in trouble.

I wanted to kick my own ass for being so selfish and oblivious.

"I know that," I snapped. I raked a hand through my hair. "I know," I repeated more calmly. "I didn't mean…" I fingered one of the crocheted afghans on the back of the bench. It was a shining example of his sunny personality. Despite living in Ben Pond's shithole, sweet Luke Williams had tried his best to make it a home. "It's nice, what you've done to it."

"Right," he snorted. "I can see how thrilled you are." A gust of wind hit the trailer and whistled through some invisible cracks, making Luke shiver again. "Look, I need to change. So… it was nice of you to drop by. I accept your apology for this morning. And the apology you should have given me for being a jerk just now, too. Now, go forth and be a jerkface no more." He gestured toward the door.

There was no way I was leaving yet. He was cold

and… and… I just… wasn't ready to leave yet. I cleared my throat. "Not so fast. You owe me a story, remember? A *fairy tale*."

"Oh, right." He sighed. "Fine. I'll get changed in the, ah…" He gestured toward the bed area that was located a few inches away from where I sat. It was separated from the main area by only a curtain.

Luke's face seemed to turn even redder as his eyes flitted around.

"But… here." He set a bowl and spoon from the dish rack on the table along with one pint of the ice cream before putting the second container in the freezer section of the minifridge. "Help yourself to a snack. I'll just…" He motioned at the curtain again.

"Okay." I nodded.

"Okay," he whispered back. Then he disappeared behind the curtain to change out of his wet clothes.

My heart was still thumping erratically for some reason, and my eyes remained glued to the curtain. The rustle of clothes and hiss of a zipper made me blink and squint as if that would somehow give me X-ray vision.

Why did I care? I didn't. But, well… I needed him to get dry and warm. Obviously.

You don't need to watch a curtain in order for that to happen.

I quickly scrambled up to spoon out the ice cream. Luke Williams was a grown man. He could get warm and dry on his own. It had nothing to do with me.

Except, of course, that I could hear every movement of fabric and body parts. I swallowed and focused on the ice cream, determinedly putting my eyes elsewhere in the room…

Which was when I saw the calendar.

What was it he'd babbled about the night before? Me carrying his sheep? I hadn't thought much of it at the time, but there was an entire calendar of images just like that tacked to one of the cabinets. I darted a look at the closed curtain and leafed through the calendar quickly. One half-naked, oily-chested man after another posed with adorable baby cows, and tiny chicks, and puppies, and pygmy goats, and… oh, *fuck*. Sheep.

Damn if Mr. May didn't look like a buffer, shinier, muscly-er… me.

Had Luke thought about…?

I mean, it wasn't possible he'd ever…

I adjusted my pants, squeezing my dick a little harder than necessary in warning, and kept my eyes on my ice cream bowl so I wouldn't think about Luke and any potential sexy thoughts.

That's when he started babbling again.

"Probably seems silly to spend so much time working on a place like this, but why be miserable if you don't have to? Might be a long while before the roof gets fixed. You've gotta take joy where you can get it, right? Oh, and speaking of the roof, *do* you know anyone who does slate? It's gonna be a while before I can afford it, but it'll be good to know how much that'll run me."

My eyes had snuck back to the moving lumps behind the curtain when Luke's phone squawked from the counter next to my elbow.

Luke poked his head out of the gap in the curtains and caught me spooning a clump of ice cream into my mouth.

"Shoot! I forgot my mom was supposed to call. You can ignore that."

"No, it's fine," I said, reaching for the phone and noticing it was a video call from his mom. I was grateful for the distraction. "I'll grab it."

"Wait—" Luke started to say, but I'd already slid my finger to accept.

"Oh my gosh, Lukey! FaceTime actually worked! And you… Oh. You're not Luke."

"No, ma'am," I agreed, smiling at her kind face. She had Luke's eyes and the same little crease Luke had on his nose that deepened when he got flustered.

"But you *are* a tall drink of gorgeous," she said with a grin. "What might your name be?"

"Er. I'm…" I glanced over at Luke to see what he wanted me to say, when I noticed he had the bottom of the curtain wrapped around his groin and *absolutely nothing else on*.

Suddenly, it was broiling hot in the tiny trailer.

I blinked at him, forgetting for a long, embarrassing moment that his mother was waiting for my answer. When she cleared her throat, I snapped back to attention. "I'm…Webb Sunday?" I said, squeaking it out like a question. "Webb Sunday. Luke's neighbor."

"Oh, yes! Webb! I'm so excited that I finally get to meet one of you boys! I've heard so much about you and your brothers."

I glanced over at Luke in surprise. He'd mentioned me to his mom? Me?

Luke groaned and ducked back behind the curtain to put some clothes on. When he emerged again, I noticed he hadn't bothered with a shirt.

As in, he was shirtless. He didn't have a shirt on. And also… I could see his bare chest… complete with *nipple rings*.

Who the fuck would've thought that Luke Williams would be hiding piercings under his baggy sweater vests? Not me. But now I was having a hard time thinking of anything else.

Maybe he'd turned the heat on too high when we'd

first come in, or maybe Ben Pond's stupid trailer's stupid heat was stupid broken. Either way, I was sweating.

Luke grabbed the phone out of my hand. "Mom! Hey!" he said breathlessly. "How are—"

His mom's voice snapped me out of my eyeballs' obsession with his bare skin.

"Luke Guilford Williams. Are you *naked?*"

Chapter Nine

LUKE

Was it possible to actually die of mortification? If so, I was enjoying my final moments, because *holy shoot*. In my whole life, I'd never felt as awkward and back-footed as I did with Webb Sunday.

I was used to being the person who took care of things —of my mom, of myself. I was used to being the authority figure in a room full of kids. But when Webb was in the vicinity, I seemed to morph into a bumbling fool, and I had only my own stupid, inconvenient attraction to blame.

"No, Mom! Of course not. I just… fell in a snowbank and got wet. Wow, you would not *believe* this weather we are having here—"

My mother would not be distracted. "You weren't doing anything dangerous, were you?"

"Me? Dangerous? *Pfft.*" I forced a laugh and shot a hard glance at Webb, a warning to keep his mouth shut. "Webb and I were just… playing in the snow."

He lifted an eyebrow, and I blushed even harder than I'd already been blushing.

"Awww. That's so sweet! Thank you so much for taking

care of my boy, Webb," she called. "You and your family have been so kind to adopt my Lukey!"

"Adopt?" Webb repeated in a voice too low for her to hear.

Mother trucker. I couldn't make myself look at Webb. "Mom, please—"

"Hush, Lukey, let me talk to Webb. I worry, you know, Webb?" she said breathlessly. "It's so wonderful that he won his beautiful house and all that land, but I worried that he might not be happy. Luke's always been shy except, as I'm sure you can imagine, when he's around kids—" She sucked in an unsteady breath.

"Mom, seriously. Webb gets it. You don't need to—"

"What I'm trying to say," she continued doggedly, "is that as soon as Luke explained to me that your family would be right next door, helping him whenever he needed it, it set my mind at ease. It really..." She broke off in a coughing spasm. "It really has."

"Mom," I cut in desperately. "Where's Aunt Sue? Is it time for one of your breathing treatments?"

"Sue's out for groceries, but I'm fine for now. Promise. I'm better and stronger every day, now that I don't have to worry about you, sweetheart."

"Yeah." I swallowed and forced myself to give Webb a pleading look, begging him to go along with my lie. "Mom, I—"

"Honey, just show me around your fairy-tale castle. You know I won't judge if it's not perfect! I fully expect that you've got dishes all over your sink and hideous wall-paper in the downstairs powder room."

"Actually, I, ah—"

"I know how you are, Sunshine," she said firmly. "You have no secrets from your mama."

"No, ma'am," I whispered miserably. "It's just that—"

"It's just that we're at my, uh… my camper," Webb blurted, snagging the phone back from my hand. "Sorry, Ms. Williams. I've been letting Luke use my camper as, you know, a… a workshop. For doing his… crochet?"

I scowled. *Who ever heard of a crochet camper?*

Webb widened his eyes significantly. *Like you had a better idea?*

"*Ohhhhh*, of course! Good Lord, Lukey, why didn't you say so?" she chided. "And here I am, rattling on like a ninny—"

"Not at all," Webb assured her. "You sound like a mother who loves her son very much. And it's pretty clear he loves you, too."

Over Webb's shoulder, I saw my mom beam. "You were right about him, Luke!" she croaked. "Webb Sunday is really the sweetest man—"

Aaaaand that was the moment when I melted right into a puddle of embarrassment, right there on the floor of the trailer. The End.

"I don't know if I said *that*, precisely," I protested… utterly unconvincingly, since that had been exactly what I'd said.

My mom ignored me. "Webb, honey, tell me—are you single?"

Would you look at that? Turned out I wasn't dead, because the universe had more mortification in store for me. *Yay*.

"Uh. Yes? I have a son, Aiden, who's in Luke's class—"

"Oh, that's right! The one with the drawings who's such a brilliant scientist. Did he ever lose his other front tooth? I know he was worried about it."

Webb gave me a look I didn't know how to interpret. "Yeah," he said softly. "A couple weeks back."

"Good, good." She lowered her voice. "Aiden's Luke's favorite student, but you didn't hear that from me."

"Oookay." I snatched the phone back. "That's enough of that. You know I don't have favorites," I said reprovingly. Not officially anyway.

She grinned, unrepentant, and a wave of homesickness crashed over me. Gosh, it was good to see her grin. And with so much color in her cheeks.

"You're looking really good. Aunt Sue taking good care of you?"

"Of course. You look wonderful, too, sweetheart. Maybe a little tired, though. Are you drinking enough?"

"Oh, plenty," I assured her, and Webb snorted. I knew without a doubt he was thinking of Rusty Spikes.

"Lukey, you're such a handsome boy, honey. With those freckles and those pretty eyes—"

"God, *stop*." My cheeks were on fire, and I could tell by her mischievous smile that she knew exactly what she was doing.

She tucked her tongue into her cheek, and her eyes danced. "Tell him, Webb! Doesn't he have the prettiest eyes?"

"Well, actually—"

"Don't you dare answer," I told him quickly. "Gotta go, Mom. I'll call you again soon."

She sighed. "Send me pictures of the sheep, or I'm gonna come up there and see them for myself. Love you, Lukey."

I assured her that I loved her, too, before we hung up... though I couldn't remember *why* at that moment.

"Wow." I cleared my throat and set the phone on the counter. "That was intensely mortifying."

"It's sweet," Webb corrected. "My mom died when I

was seven, but I like to think she'd've been like yours. You love her a lot."

It wasn't a question, but I answered anyway. "Yeah." My throat went tight. "I do."

"And she's… sick?"

"Her lungs, yeah. It was touch and go there for a minute. She's doing better now, but I still worry." I shrugged.

Webb nodded. He didn't ask me why I'd lied about my situation up here. He didn't assure me that she'd be fine or remind me to think positively. He just watched me silently. Patiently.

It was shockingly intimate, having someone study me that closely. And even though he wasn't saying a word and hadn't moved his behind from the bench seat the whole time he'd been in here, I couldn't help but feel… surrounded by him.

It was wonderful. Terrifyingly wonderful.

"So, the fairy tale?"

"Right." I dusted my hands on my sweatpants casually, trying to hide the way my heart was pounding. I sat on the bed while Webb leaned over to grab another spoon out of the dish drainer. He handed it to me along with the remainder of the ice cream.

"You want the long version of the fairy tale or the short?" I asked.

"The *whole* version." He twisted in his seat to face me. "The real version."

"Okay, then." I cleared my throat and stabbed at the ice cream. "Once upon a time, an overworked, underpaid elementary school teacher's mother encouraged him to enter an essay contest she'd found in the back of her fiber arts magazine—"

"Fiber arts magazine?"

"Yup." I licked my spoon. "The *Wool Gatherer Quarterly*. I only ever read it for the articles, but my mom reads it cover to cover——"

His lips twitched. "You? Read the *Wool Gatherer Quarterly*?"

"Not only read, I sometimes create patterns for them," I said, lifting my chin proudly. "Crochet, usually. I also knit, and spin, and weave… when I have a loom."

"Ah. That's cool." He fingered the blanket again.

"I think so. It's a creative outlet, and I get to enjoy the finished product. Teaching is awesome, but when you're dealing with kids, there's no immediate gratification——"

Webb nodded. "Like parenting."

He ran his big hand over the soft blanket once more. It did funny things to my stomach, and I filled my mouth with a huge spoonful of ice cream so I wouldn't be tempted to do something stupid, like beg him to touch me that way.

He is straight, Luke. And he's not meant for you.

"Anyway, as I was saying. The ad said something like, 'Craft a better life! What would you do with forty idyllic acres of rural, partially forested land, complete with enclosed pastures and an elegant farmhouse, nestled in the heart of New England? Tell us your fairy tale, and this castle could be *yours in perpetuity*!'"

"Sounds too good to be true."

I laughed. "So many people told me that. But, I dunno. My mom was so excited, and I wanted to believe it could be real, so… I did it. I poured out the dream of my heart."

"Which was…?" Webb prompted when I paused.

I took a deep breath. Was I really going to share this with him? "To find a place with an accepting community and friendly neighbors, as well as enough land to build a fiber arts studio where people from all over the world could come to learn the skills my mom tried to teach me over the years. I wanted her love and legacy to live on, even if lung disease stole her from me." I stared down at my hands. "Hokey, right?"

Webb stared at me for a long moment, then shook his head solemnly. "Not at all."

For some reason, his acceptance hit me harder than his earlier judgment had. Hot tears pricked my eyes.

Webb levered himself off the bench, and a second later, he sat beside me so he could bump his shoulder with mine.

"I live my great-grandfathers' legacy every day, remember? I work hard so I can pass that on to Aiden."

I lifted my gaze to his. "Oh." I hadn't thought of it that way.

"You said your mom's doing better?"

"Yeah. She had surgery and pretty intense pulmonary therapy, and it hasn't been easy, but she's a fighter. And when she learned I won the contest, she lost her mind with excitement. It was all gonna be a fairy tale, she said. An adventure. And she wanted me to live it for both of us. So..." I shrugged.

Webb nodded again, and I thought maybe he understood.

"She agreed to move in with her sister and follow her doctor's orders, so within a couple of months, I'd signed papers on my new property, googled teaching jobs and credentials in Vermont, packed up my stuff, and turned in my resignation at my school in North Carolina. It was all so easy, it felt like it was fate. And then I got here." I chuckled, then sighed.

"And you realized the dream was a nightmare."

I looked at him, startled. "Well, no. I mean... it's still a dream. But it's gonna require a lot more work than I initially thought." I huffed out a laugh. "Like, a *lot*."

"So, why not leave? Why not let the house sit here for a couple more centuries and go back to your old life?"

I frowned. "Just… give up? Would *you* do that?"

"Well, no, but…" He hesitated, then blew out a breath. "No. I wouldn't."

"Of course not. The house is mine now. Mine to take care of. Mine to complain about and sweat over and possibly fall off the roof of—"

"Not funny," he said gruffly. "It will *never* be funny."

I smiled softly. We'd have to agree to disagree about that, because when the mortification wore off—assuming it ever wore off—I was going to spend long private minutes remembering the feeling of his hands on me out in the snow.

"Anyway, I try to stay positive—"

He snorted. "Of course you do."

"—and focus on all I've accomplished so far. Like the back porch stairs, and—"

"And the barn for your sheep."

"Exactly. Those sheep live *well*," I told him proudly. "Though I still have some work to do on the supposedly enclosed pastures. My sheep see them as a personal challenge to hurdle."

Webb chuckled and gave me another friendly shoulder bump.

I was suddenly very aware that I was shirtless, and he was not, and he was really, *really* warm. I wanted to move much closer… which was why I scooted away and stuffed my mouth with more ice cream.

"And I'll get the rest of the repairs sorted, too. It'd definitely be easier to take care of things if I could get a loan, but when they said the place is mine 'in perpetuity,' they weren't kidding. I can't mortgage or sell off any of it to raise funds since I don't have a clear title on the place. And, according to my lawyer—"

"*Him.*" It was pretty clear what Webb's opinion of Stephen Fox was.

I snickered. "Yeah, him. He said it'd take months. And if he's talking about land surveys or whatever, it's gonna take even longer because I'm a man living on a teacher's salary with three hungry Romeldales to support… and a premium ice cream habit." I shook my empty carton at him.

"You might end up with more land after the surveys are done, though."

I cocked my head. "Seriously, what part of this story suggests that I want more land, Webb? Besides, I told you I'd happily give you—"

"Yeah, I know." He cleared his throat. "I believe you."

"Good." It was pathetic how good those words made me feel.

"But you can't keep trying to do the work yourself. It's fucking stupid. You're gonna get hurt, and—"

"I can handle it." I lifted my chin. "I'm looking into getting a personal loan. I haven't given up. Pippin Hollow Credit Union said I haven't lived here long enough to become a member, which sucks, and the other places I tried want me to put up collateral, but I don't have any except the land, which I can't use because—"

"Because you can't get a clear title, and round and round it goes."

"Yeah. It's complicated."

"Which is why you need a friend to help you 'uncomplicate' it?" He lifted an eyebrow.

I laughed. "No. This is no one's problem but mine, and I'll uncomplicate it myself. But it is sometimes frustrating. Which is why last night I needed to blow off some steam."

"And ended up blowing the Handfast Bugle instead."

"If only your townspeople called it that," I sighed. "You would have avoided it like the plague, Mr. Allergic to Relationships, and saved us all this trouble."

"Our townspeople. And I'm not sure that's true since I didn't know what handfasting *was* until after I'd already done it." He paused, then said in a rush, "You know it's not about you, right? The relationship thing. I just... I have no interest in getting married again. Ever."

I blinked at him. "Well, right, but even if you were, I wouldn't be the person you'd choose." I laughed lightly.

He frowned. "Don't say that. Look, I know we barely know each other, and after the way I've acted toward you, you have no reason to believe me, but you're a likable person, Luke. You're funny. A-and smart." His face darkened. "About everything except home repairs, anyway. And I'm sure any guy looking for a... a handfast partner would pick you. But I'm not—"

"That's..." I shook my head. Was Webb Sunday actually giving me the it's-not-you-it's-me speech? He was adorable. And so freakin' obtuse. "I meant because I'm a *man*, Webb. And you're straight?"

"Oh." Webb hesitated. "No, yeah, that's probably also a good point."

Probably?

I turned to eyeball him and found that Webb was already staring at me, green eyes intent on mine and lips parted just a tiny bit, his face so close that I could feel his breath on my cheek.

What... the...

Then Webb sucked in a breath and pushed to his feet so quickly I thought I must have imagined the whole thing.

"So! Speaking of the handfasting! We should, ah… talk about the, ah… the requirements. The… the 'confirmation tasks.' So we can avoid fulfilling them."

"Oh, right." I shook my head to clear it. "Yeah. Good idea."

"I had my attorney look it over earlier, and he chuckled a lot, but I haven't read it yet. I was a little bit… upset," he admitted. "Have you read it?"

I shook my head. I'd been waiting until I was calmer, too. I had a feeling I'd be waiting a while.

"Well, Curt—my attorney—said as long as we don't fulfill all twelve obligations within eight weeks, the hand-fasting process expires, the bylaw won't apply, and we'll be free."

"That easy?" I asked. "Awesome."

"Yup. But he also said Ernest York is gonna be publicizing the heck out of this thing. It's the kind of charming story that brings in tourists, *and* it deflects from the divisive clusterfuck of the resort development. You've heard about that, right?"

I nodded.

"And the people of this town…" He shook his head. "When they think there's matchmaking to be done, they get even more meddlesome than usual. And they're not gonna believe that you and I aren't actually… you know."

"Together?" I supplied.

"Exactly. So we're gonna want to be careful, otherwise we'll find out too late that eating pancakes together at Jack's somehow made our betrothal official because of the Little Pippin Hollow Breakfast Food Consumption Act of 1742."

I snorted. "Right. Lemme grab my copy. I put it up here." I stood on the mattress to reach the upper storage area.

"Where up there?"

I knew Webb was looking over my shoulder because I felt the heat of him against my naked back.

"Not sure. I may have chucked it up here in frustration before going out to deal with the tarp."

Webb chuckled, and a shiver moved down my spine.

This is a no-erection zone, Williams. Jesus, especially while I was wearing these pants.

"Got it!" I seized the scroll and jumped back down. "Okay, let's see." I threw on a sweatshirt, then moved a pace or three closer to the heater so I could no longer smell Webb's pine-and-cotton scent. "Here we go: 'At a general affembly... I mean, *assembly*, held at the Town Seat of Pippin Hollow on the tenth day of May, Anno Domini, One Thousand Seven Hundred, and Sixty Seven, be it here Enacted that Partners who may be disposed to Matrimony, where Sufficient Permission cannot—"

Webb sat down at the table again and let out a fake yawn. "I'm aging here, Luke. Skip to the confirmation tasks."

"Uh... Right. Part the First." I glanced at him over the scroll. "The bugle blowing. Too late to avoid that."

"Right."

"Part the Fecond... I mean *second*—"

"D'you need reading glasses?"

"No! Shush. It's just written with those *S*'s that look like *F*'s, and all kinds of weird capital letters. As I was saying... The Betrotheds must knowingly partake of Sweet Water drawn from the Pippin Well." I glanced up. "Water from Pippin Well? Is that a place? Or do they mean, like, ye olde municipal water supply? 'Cause if drinking tap water is enough, I'm halfway handfasted to this entire town."

Webb snickered. "You can be the one to tell Mayor York that we've become a handfasting *orgy*. The rules say knowingly, though. I bet it means you have to drink from the same glass I used or something."

"Ah, well, then that's easy enough to avoid." I arched an eyebrow. "You've probably got cooties anyway."

"Loaded with them," Webb agreed. He stroked a hand over his beard. "What else?"

"Part the Third, Betrotheds must Prepare a Matrimonial Domicile with their own Skillful Endeavors."

"Got it. No house building."

"More than enough houses between us already," I agreed. I looked back down. "Uh… Okay, Part the Fourth. Betrotheds must Layeth By a Store of Cloth, Salt, Tools, or other Provisions required of a Plentiful Union."

"Damn. Hey, Alexa," Webb called to my imaginary computer, "cancel the gift subscription to Salt of the Month that I purchased earlier."

Webb's teasing grin was back in place, doing funny things to my stomach, and I couldn't help grinning in response. "Agreed. You're salty enough already."

"Rude." Webb stood up and stole the scroll from my hand, then pushed me to sit on the opposite side of the table from where he'd been.

"Hey!"

"Part the Fifth," he read, leaning against my bright orange stove and making the thing look all kinds of sexy. "Betrotheds must Bestow Their Own Clothing or Footwear upon One Another." He looked up. "I can't foresee you borrowing anything of mine, and I cannot see me fitting into anything of yours."

"Accurate." I wondered how that worked back in the old days and had a brief mental image of some colonial guy wearing his future wife's dress.

"Part the Sixth says Betrotheds must Commingle their

Flocks of Livestock in Gracious Union, even as they will Join their Own Lives. Uh, how about no?"

"Nope. My sheep have better things to do."

"Sure. Part the Seventh, Betrotheds must Swear an Oath or Declaration of Intention to the Parents, Guardians, or Other Persons of Authority in the Life of their Betrothed." He pursed his lips. "If you were planning to confess your love for me to Uncle Drew, please refrain until after the eight weeks are up."

"I'm more likely to confess my love for Drew's blue-berry pie. My turn..." I reached for the scroll, but he set a hand on my chest to hold me back and held it out of my reach... which wasn't hard since he was half a foot taller than me.

"Nope. Part the Eighth," he went on. "Betrotheds must Attend Church or Town Assembly Together... Hmm. That one might actually happen. Does the Spring Fling count as a Town Assembly? Because we'll both be there."

"Maybe. Probably. Okay, so we'll already take the loss on that one. Now gimme." I tried to jump up and grab the paper, but he held me back easily and grinned down at me.

"Speaking of taking the loss... *Hush*. The tall people are reading."

"Hey!" I squawked, pretending I didn't like the feel of his hand on my chest and that his smile wasn't turning my brain into puree.

"Part the Ninth, Betrotheds must spend One Evening, from Moonrise to Sunrise, Bundled in the Betrothed's bed, and Greet the Morn Praising the Lord."

"Oh, wow." I wondered. "So not only do we have to get in bed together, I'm gonna have to pray? No way."

Webb wrinkled his nose in confusion. "I thought colo-nials were all prudish and shit. What's up with this kinky bed-sharing thing?"

"Bundling… that was the equivalent of a platonic sleepover, back in ye olde days. Potential betrotheds needed to chat in order to get to know each other, right? But in cold-weather places, it would be too chilly for them to stay up late talking without a fire—which was expensive—and it would be a b-i-t-c-h for the one betrothed to have to hitch up his horse and ride home in the snow. So instead, they'd put the betrotheds in bed, with a special bundling board running down the middle to prevent anyone getting handsy, and they'd tuck them in, and it would be really wholesome, and— What's funny?" I demanded when I saw him bite his lip against laughter.

"I dunno. Just…" He spread his hands. "Your… enthusiasm when you explain things. The way you spell out curse words. It's cute. Reminds me of Aiden."

Oh.

Well, then.

Awesome. I reminded him of his seven-year-old. Yep, that was a wet blanket to any potential sexy thoughts I'd been harboring.

I sat down. "Anyway, we'll avoid that one. What's the next part?"

"What's wrong?" Webb lowered the scroll to peer down at me. "Your mood just collapsed."

"Nothing. No. Just…" *I'm staring at your kissable lips, and you're thinking I'm cute like your child.* "It's been a heck of a day. Let's finish up and move on, okay?"

"Yeah. Of course. Here, if it means that much to you." He handed me the scroll.

"Part the Tenth," I read. "The Betrotheds must Simultaneously Immerse Themselves in a Publick Cleansing Font, River, Lake, Pond, or Stream."

"Public bathing? Please explain how *that* could be wholesome."

"I… I don't know," I admitted, mystified. "I've never heard of such a thing. Unless they were… clothed somehow? Anyway, not a situation we'll find ourselves in since it's *February*. Um… Part the Eleventh, the Betrotheds must have their Hands Bound Together by Rope—"

"We keep getting kinkier."

I snickered. "—in front of the Mayor, or Another Person of Authority within the Town—"

"Extra kinky."

"Shush. And then finally… oh! Oh, this is perfect." I couldn't help but smile at him in relief. "Part twelve. In order to seal our 'Blessed Union,' the Betrotheds must 'Appear on the Town Common by Sundown, on the Eighth Sunday of the betrothal period, *restate their oaths*, and blow the bugle again." I rolled up the scroll, set it on the table, and dusted my hands triumphantly. "There's no *way* we're going to check off everything on the list."

"Not planning to fall in love with me in the next eight weeks, then?" he teased.

"Please. About as likely as you are to fall in love with me," I scoffed.

Attraction was one thing. Love? No. I could hardly fall in love with someone who was so incredibly off-limits.

"There are not enough Rusty Spikes in all the land," Webb assured me. He held out a hand to shake, like we were making a deal, and I took it in mine, studiously ignoring how the slide of his callused fingers felt against my palm.

"So we agree," Webb said. "The easiest way to handle this handfasting is to ignore it as much as possible and let the whole thing blow over?"

"Absolutely. We may have stumbled into this handfasting thing, *but*," I said firmly, "there is obviously no way we could end up accidentally married."

Chapter Ten

WEBB

"Webb! I heard you're getting married, brother! *Mazel tov*."

"What?" I blinked away from a horrifying mental image of Luke trying to balance a ladder on his fucking roof to find my laptop screen had gone dark, the sun had fully set, and my brother Porter—the fourth Sunday sibling —was leaning against my office doorframe wearing a sly smile and a Hannabury College baseball cap.

"Hey." I ran a hand over my face. "When'd you get home, shit stirrer?"

"About an hour ago." Porter's face split into a playful grin that reminded me of our father. "And I think you meant to say, 'Porter, my favorite brother, I missed you! I'm so glad you chose to come home for the weekend.'"

"Did I?" I asked dryly, tilting my chair to stretch out my cramped back muscles.

"Yup. To which I would reply that I couldn't *not* come home when I heard that my favorite brother had such big news," he teased. "I'm surprised Reed didn't fly in from DC for the occasion so all us Sundays could be together!

Aiden's teacher's gonna make an honest man of you, eh? Is that what you were woolgathering about just now?"

"Please." I huffed out a breath. *Woolgathering* was spot-on, though.

I'd come home, got caught up with Aiden, hearing every detail of his sleepover and giving him the thrilling news that his mom would be taking him to hockey practice from now on, and then sat down to reply to an email from my accountant...

And instead, I'd googled slate roofs, Vermont inheritance laws, and Romeldale sheep before daydreaming about Luke.

But I was sure as fuck *not* telling my mischief-making brother any of that.

"You know, I swear I remember you telling Knox that *he* was your favorite brother back at Christmas," I said instead. "For, quote, 'giving you the gift of a brilliant brother-in-law named Gage.'"

"Oooh. You remember that, huh? *Awkward.* But a man can have more than one favorite, Webb," he said fake-solemnly. "And now *you're* giving me a brother-in-law, and I'm sure he's equally cool."

I thought about Luke, waxing rhapsodic about hydroponics, explaining bunk-boarding (or whatever the kinky colonials called it), and demanding that all hockey players be freed from the plastic boxes.

He *was* cool, in the un-coolest, most fascinating way possible.

But I didn't tell Porter about any of that either.

"Did you seriously come home just to give me shit?" I demanded.

"Nah. That's just a side benefit. I actually came home specifically so Gage can help me not fail my class. But when I got here, Uncle Drew filled me in on the whole

handfasting thing while I taste-tested his cinnamon rolls."
He leaned forward. "Ten out of ten, by the way. Porter-
approved."

I snorted. "I'm sure. What's up with your class?" I
demanded.

He rolled his eyes. "Of course that's the one part of
that statement you heard. Chill, Webb. It's nothing you
need to worry about. My professor is a pain in my ass, but
whatever." He brushed a hand through the air dismissively.
"I'm not Aiden, okay? I'm a big boy, and I've got it under
control."

"Yeah, I know." I ran my tongue over my molar and
forced myself not to reply further. The truth was, I sometimes felt more like a parent than a brother to Porter—and
to Hawk and Emma, too—which made sense since our
dad had died when Porter was just sixteen, and Uncle
Drew and I had been the ones who took care of them. But
I had to remind myself that I couldn't protect him from
everything... just like I couldn't protect Aiden from
everything.

Still, I couldn't help clarifying. "School's going okay,
then?"

"Yes. Fine. Mostly," Porter said impatiently. Then his
quicksilver grin reappeared, and he settled more comfort-
ably against the wall. "But enough about me. Let's talk
about *you* and what's going on in *your* world."

"My world," I mused. The leather of my chair creaked
as I got comfortable. "There's a lot, Porter. Do you want to
know what's *really* going on?"

"Fuck yeah. Tell me everything, especially about Lu—"

"Well, the good news," I said, speaking over him, "is
that I think my custody suit is going to be settled soon
because I agreed to Amanda having visitation, starting
next week."

"Oh," Porter said, sobering. "Shit."

"Mmm. Aiden lost his other front tooth finally, which is great, because Murray told me Aiden offered him five bucks to pull it with pliers."

"*Ooof.* That's something I would have tried."

"It *is* something you tried," I corrected him. "Muriel's calving in four weeks, which means sleepless nights in my future. Maple sugaring is starting next week, and I've got a Scout troop, a school class, and a group from the senior center in Two Rivers booked, but it looks like I'm gonna have to lead the demonstrations myself since Gwen's baby came early. Uncle Drew keeps saying his attacks of breathlessness are just because he's out of shape, but I'm not sure—"

"Christ, Webb—"

"I ordered scions of a dozen heirloom apple varietals that I want to start grafting up in the Pond orchard in a few weeks—" *Assuming the Pond orchard is still mine*, I thought but didn't say. "—and they're stuck on a truck in Wisconsin. Oh, and one of the gutters on the front of the house is sagging."

Porter's eyes had glazed over a little bit. "What I hear you not-saying is that you're not gonna give me any tea about the handfasting."

"No, what you hear me saying is that I have real shit to worry about... and so does Luke, believe me. This whole handfasting thing is just the Hollow being its usual wackadoo self, and Luke and I got caught up in it for a minute there. It'll all blow over soon... unless nosy folks keep spreading rumors." I gave him a significant look.

He sighed. "Disappointing. This means you *haven't* been harboring a secret attraction for Luke Williams, the guy you've been telling yourself you can't stand for months and months, huh?"

"What?" I scowled, my heart suddenly beating faster. "No! I never… Who told you that?"

Porter blinked in surprise. "Dude. No one told me anything. I was just giving you shit. But…" His eyes widened. "Wait, *are* you attracted to him?"

Why did people keep asking me that?

"Dinner, Sundays!" Drew shouted from the kitchen down the hall. "Aiden, come feed Sally Ann first, please."

"No!" I told Porter fiercely. "I…" I made a frustrated noise and stood up. I didn't want to lie, but I also didn't want to have to explain something I couldn't wrap my own head around. "Don't make this into something it's not, okay? Luke and I cleared the air last night. We're friends. We should have been friends all along. But it's nothing more than that. And for fuck's sake, don't mention the handfasting in front of Aiden. Clearly even adults are starting to believe it's real, and the last thing I need is for him to believe it, too."

Porter shrugged uneasily. "I'll keep my mouth shut, but it's not like he's not gonna hear about it over the next eight weeks, Webb. Not the way people are in this town. Hell, not the way people are in this *family*."

Fuck. I hadn't considered that. I'd have to find a way to explain it.

I followed Porter out to the kitchen. Emma and Gage were already deep in conversation about colleges, while Knox helped Drew bring the food to the table and Marco poured everyone water from a pitcher. Hawk walked in a few minutes late and quietly took his seat. Aiden raced around the island from the back hall, where our golden retriever was chewing her kibble, and headed for the long farmhouse table.

"Hey! Hands, mister," I reminded him, heading to the sink myself, and he rolled his eyes but complied.

As we sat down a moment later, I looked around the table and felt profound gratitude for all that I had.

My supportive family. Plenty of food and a snug house to eat it in. A son who was my whole world. Honest work I loved and a legacy to protect. All the things, I realized with a pang that Luke was working hard to get but hadn't.

I didn't want to take them for granted even for a minute.

Then Gage grinned at me across the table. "So. Webb. Anything *newsworthy* happen today? Did you happen to see anything while you were... *scrolling?*"

Drew guffawed.

Marco choked on a sip of water, and Knox had to lean over to thump him on the back.

"Not a thing," I said mildly while shooting him a fiery look and tilting my head toward Aiden.

"Well, I had lots of exciting stuff happen today," Aiden said importantly, scooping a giant helping of mashed potatoes on his plate. "I'm going to see my mom next week, because she's gonna take me to hockey *and* stay for pizza after. And I learned how to make snow cream at Olin's and stayed up until midnight, and I played with Olin's dog. *His* dog sits up on his hind legs on a kitchen chair while Olin eats breakfast." He paused for dramatic effect. "Dad, wouldn't it be awesome if we had a puppy we could—"

"We're not getting another dog right now," I informed him. "Try again in the spring. Drew, would you pass me that platter?"

"And *also*," Aiden went on, "Murray told Olin who told me that Mr. Williams doesn't even know about hockey. Can you imagine, Dad? Like, he's never even skated. It's, like, the only thing he doesn't know how to do."

"Oh, I'm not sure that's true," I said tartly. "Luke

doesn't know jack about ladder safety either. Pass the peas, Knox?"

Silence fell around the table, and I looked up to find the entire family trading glances.

"Ladders? How d'you know that?" Aiden demanded.

"Oh. We, ah… we discussed it. Earlier today. I went out to his house to… visit."

"*You?* Visited Mr. Williams?"

"Sure. I believe it's important to be fair and open-minded and friendly with your neighbors, and Lu—I mean, Mr. Williams—is our neighbor. So." I shrugged like it was as simple as that, though it hadn't been that simple at all… and even my seven-year-old knew it.

"Amazing. Would you say this is a *new* belief?" Knox asked brightly.

"I would say that as I've matured, I've come to certain realizations, that's all," I replied. I smiled at him sweetly. "Someday maybe *you'll* mature, Knox, and then you'll understand." Before he could snap back, I added, "Drew, I'm not sure what these chicken pocket things are, but they smell delicious."

"Thank you," Drew said after a moment. "They're called… *hand* pies. They just seemed… appropriate for today."

"Oh." I ground my teeth together. "Great."

"Bet those *hand* pies whipped up… *fast*," Em commented.

"So *fast*. I thought they'd go well with these *hand*-mashed potatoes," Drew went on with false innocence.

"And these peas!" Gage exclaimed. "Did you shell them by *hand*? I can always tell."

"I'm glad you made plenty, honey," Marco interjected. "I feel like I've been *fasting* all day."

MAY ARCHER

Drew snickered and patted Marco's hand. "You're lucky I'm so *handy* in the kitchen."

My family was a bunch of assholes, and I was going to sell every last one of them except Aiden on eBay.

I broadcasted a glare around the table, then proceeded to ignore them all and focus on my dinner.

Drew was a good all-around cook but an amazing baker, and the chicken pies—I was officially shortening the name—were delicious. I hadn't gotten three bites in, though, before my thoughts strayed back across the field and orchard to Luke.

I wondered if he was sitting in his trailer still and what he was eating. He'd better not be anywhere near that damned roof.

All these months, I'd assumed he was living happily in a house he hadn't earned, with no responsibilities. I'd even, maybe, envied him a little for being able to do whatever he wanted, including pick up and move to Vermont on a whim. The reality had been so, so different. And I should have known better. I *did* know better. Everyone had their own mess to deal with, and Luke had more than most.

He'd been trying to carve out a place for himself in the Hollow—even painting that rusted-out trailer with fresh cream paint and decorating it with those beautiful blankets, making the best of the shit hand he'd been dealt—and I'd begrudged him every last inch of space.

And even after we'd supposedly been *friends* and gotten ourselves locked into this ridiculous handfasting thing, I'd been more focused on making sure nobody thought the handfasting was real than on making sure Luke was supported.

But Knox had been right. Since when did I care what other people thought? Luke needed a friend, and I could be that for him.

"Food okay, Webb?" Drew asked. "You've eaten less than Hawk."

I realized I'd paused with my fork halfway to my lips, staring into space for fuck knew how long. "Oh. Yeah. Sorry. I'm…"

Porter gave me a knowing look across the table that said, *Woolgathering again?*

"I'm *fine*." I scooped up more potatoes.

"Daddy, I finished. Can I go upstairs? I'm watching a video on hydrapraetonic plants since that's what we're learning about next week in science."

"You mean hydroponic," I corrected. "That's when you grow plants in water. Do you know, it's a ninety percent more efficient way of using water?"

Aiden frowned, his little nose scrunching up and his Sunday-green eyes narrowing. "No, this is different," he informed me. "You probably just don't know about it. Mr. Williams does. He also knows about black-capped chickadees. We're going on a field trip to see them next week in their winter habitats."

"Oh, I see." It took serious effort not to laugh. I wished I had Luke's number in my phone so I could text him about this conversation, because I was pretty sure he'd find it hilarious, too.

And probably embarrassing. I imagined his cheeks flushing pink.

How weird was it that I was supposedly *betrothed* to the man but didn't have his cell number stored in my phone? Only in Little Pippin Hollow. I realized I needed to fix that.

"Homework done? Then go ahead and watch your video," I told Aiden. "You can teach me about *hydrapraetonics* later."

"Sick!" Aiden said, running off. "Thanks, Dad!"

I snickered to myself as I watched him leave, then resumed eating, only to find the whole family staring at me again.

"Wut?" I demanded, mouth full of chicken. I swallowed. "What's up?"

"Oh, nothing," Gage said airily. "Not a thing. Just… noting that someone mentioned Luke Williams's name, and you didn't turn green or bust out of your clothes or Hulk-smash the table."

"Or tell everyone he's *nothing* to you," Em said with a judgmental sniff. "Which was very shitty, B-T-W."

"Seriously," Hawk agreed.

"It's a momentous day, indeed. In fact… I think I need to make a proclamation about it." Drew stood up, grabbed the roll of paper towels from the counter, and began unrolling them like a scroll. He pretended to read, "Whereas Thomas Webb Sunday has managed, for the first time in recent memory, not to stick his size-thirteen boot in his mouth where Luke Williams is concerned, and listen to reason for ten seconds…"

I shook my head impatiently. "Alright, alright, enough. How long can I expect this teasing to continue just so I can plan my meals accordingly?"

"Oh, I'd say a solid week," Drew said happily.

"I vote a month," Em countered. "Minimum."

"Pfft. I'm planning to mix up 'whereas' jokes with randomly bursting into 'Sweet Caroline' until the end of my days." Knox leaned back in his chair and draped an arm over Gage's shoulders.

"That's gonna be sooner than you expect if you keep this up," I informed him. But then I sighed. "Look, I admit that Luke is… nice." To put it mildly. He was maybe the sweetest man I'd ever met. "I misjudged him. I'm the asshole."

"Finally. I've been telling you that for years," Knox agreed.

"Well, Jesus," Marco interrupted. "Don't be all dramatic about it, kiddo. You'll be nicer from now on."

"I will. I definitely will." The legacy I wanted to leave for Aiden was about more than orchards full of apples; it was about being a decent person. Living your life the right way. Showing up for the people who needed you.

"Hey, Drew?" I wiped my mouth with a napkin. "Does Norm's brother-in-law still have a roofing business?"

"Yeah. Jerry Walcott. Walcott Roofing. Why?"

"Like I said, I was at old Ben's place today." To Em, I added, "Apologizing for what I said at the diner earlier."

"Good," she said with a firm nod. "And you should find a way to make it right, too."

"I'm trying. The house needs some major work. It—" I hesitated. Luke had been so proud of the work he'd done, and he'd seemed so embarrassed about how much was left to do. I wasn't sure how much to share about the actual condition of the place. "I thought it would be good to get him the name of a roofer he can trust."

More like, I was thinking about calling Jerry myself and having him go out to quote the job. I knew Luke couldn't pay, but I also remembered that Jerry had a thing for refurbishing old farm equipment, and I just happened to have a rare model 1913 Case tractor in one of the outbuildings that I'd been thinking to fix up at some point.

Luke's roof was more important.

Making up for the way I'd treated him for *months* was more important.

"Well, I think that's great," Hawk said, his brown eyes misty. "I think, when a person's been an asshole, it's important to own up to it. People are more important than money or things." He swallowed hard and choked out, "Excuse me," before fleeing the table.

"Uh." I looked at Drew and then at Knox. "What's his deal?"

"Not a clue," Knox said.

"I just got here." Porter held up his hands.

"He's upset at Jack," Gage said. "*Clearly*."

"Jack? My best friend Jack?" I demanded.

"His boss Jack, the owner of Panini Jack's Jack. Yes, that Jack." Gage leaned over the table and lowered his voice. "I was over helping Helena Fortnum update the guest booking system at the Apple of My Eye when Mary Duarte from the Hair Lair came in—because, you know, Mary and Helena are in the same knitting group, and they go way back—"

"Baby, you terrify me," Knox interrupted. "How the fuck do you know this shit?"

"I love you, too." Gage patted his leg distractedly. "Anyway. I overheard Helena telling Mary that Hawk and Jack had a fight at the diner earlier. I guess Helena was trying to get people to sign a petition against the development, and she got up on the table and started singing 'Do You Hear the People Sing,' you know?"

"From *Les Mis*?" Marco demanded.

Gage nodded. "Mary said it was very moving."

"Dear God," I muttered.

"And then Jack made Helena get down, for safety reasons—"

"No shit," Porter exclaimed. "The woman is, like, a hundred and twelve."

"—and he told her she's not allowed to campaign for signatures to save the Peak inside the diner and he's not even sure which way he wants to vote. Hawk got really upset."

"Not surprising. Hawk's got years' worth of pent-up emotions that have to come out sometime," Drew said.

The others nodded, but I frowned. "I think you mean *months*. They only started talking about the development recently."

Marco gave me a pitying look I didn't understand.

"It'll blow over," Knox predicted. "Hawk's not one to hold a grudge, especially with Jack."

"I dunno." Gage sounded troubled. "Sometimes you can only push a person so far before they start coming to some important realizations."

I felt like I was missing some subtext in the conversation, and normally I would have insisted on knowing all the details so I could manage shit for everyone… but I couldn't bring myself to ask for more information. My brain had officially reached maximum capacity, and I told myself I'd think about it later.

When later came, though, Hawk and Jack were the furthest thing from my mind.

Instead, as I lay in my antique four-poster bed, staring out the window at the dark sky, all I could think about was the same damn thing I'd been thinking about all day—Luke *fucking* Williams.

The heart-stopping feeling of seeing him in danger.

The sweetness of his smile when it got caught up at one corner of his mouth.

The pulse-pounding feeling of seeing him almost *naked*, clutching that stupid curtain around him back in his RV, and wondering what he'd look like without it.

I felt my dick throb in my loose cotton sleep pants, and I pushed the heel of my hand against it.

Fuck.

I groaned softly and turned onto my back, shoving off

the quilt and pushing my pants down to my thighs so I could stroke myself more firmly.

I was definitely not going to jerk off thinking of Luke Williams because that would be fucking weird.

Or, okay, it would be fucking *hot*, at least in the moment. The weird part was sure to follow, though, probably when I spontaneously chubbed up at the next parent-teacher conference or couldn't meet Luke's eyes during a neighborly conversation because my brain was chanting a guilty chorus of *I jerked off to you.*

But fuck, there was something about Luke Williams.

Like the little smile that hovered around his lips like he always found something to be happy about. Or the way he ate ice cream like he was savoring every individual flavor, in a way that turned out to be weirdly erotic. Or the chaotic paint-spatter freckles on his shoulders that I was always, from this day forward, gonna know were hiding under his button-down shirts and sweater vests. Or the startled expression on his face when he'd caught me staring at him earlier today, and the way the surprise had morphed, for one quick second, into curious hunger that had me checking the front of his sweatpants for a dick print like a horny teenager...

And finding one.

Shit. My cock was harder than it had been in... God, way too long. Fucking *aching*, with precum already beading at the tip. And it was thoughts of Luke Williams that had gotten me here.

But as I ran my thumb over the head, collecting the wetness there and using it to ease my way as I pumped myself with my fist, I let myself go with it, because... well, because the man was seriously fucking hot, and I was tired of denying or overthinking that. Maybe Porter had stumbled on the truth earlier when he said I'd been harboring a secret attraction for Luke for longer than I wanted to admit.

"*Nfff.*" I couldn't stop the low moan that rose up from my throat as I imagined Luke right there in the cool quiet of my bedroom, watching me jack off for him. I imagined the way he'd look at me, his eyes wide and hot with lust.

I imagined pushing him into that snowbank earlier, in front of God and anybody who might come by, and kissing the fuck out of him… then warning him in dirty, explicit detail about exactly what I'd do to his ass if he ever did something so dangerous again.

I imagined ripping his clothes off in that tiny trailer, holding him down on those soft blankets he'd made, and touching his body until he screamed my name and his head was full of all the curse words he'd never let himself say.

My balls tightened until they were snug against the base of my dick, and I bit my lip as I threw my head back into the pillow, fighting to stay quiet.

But if I was going to commit to my first bisexual jerk session, I wanted to see exactly how much stuff I might be into and what I might have been missing out on.

I couldn't say I hadn't touched my ass before—not with three gay brothers tossing around intriguing phrases like "Tony came hands-free" and "a prostate orgasm lights you up like a roman candle." But I hadn't liked it when I'd tried it as a teen. And I *really* hadn't liked it when Amanda had tried it after reading about it in some article online.

But then, hell, I'd gone my whole life being positive that I didn't find guys attractive either, and now I had incontrovertible evidence to the contrary, so who knew what else might have changed? I braced my foot on the bed, spread my knees wide, and used my free hand to finger the skin behind my balls… and the puckered hole further back.

Shit, shit, shit. My entire body broke out in a cold sweat, and more slickness coated my fist as my cock showed it was definitely on board to try new things.

Who fucking knew? How long had my dick been keeping these secrets?

I gathered some wetness on my fingertip and stroked it over my hole, wishing I was the kind of guy who had a nightstand full of lube to experiment with. I slid the tip of my finger inside and… *Huh.* I mean, it wasn't awful. I just wasn't sure I understood what the fuss was about. Maybe I just wasn't wired that way.

And that was fine—more than fine—because I didn't need any extra stimulation. Fondling my balls while wondering what Luke would actually say if he could see me like this, naked and breathless, dick covered in my own fluid, was hotter than I could ever have believed.

I imagined him reaching out a hand to touch me and stroked myself faster, my toes curling and balls tingling as I felt my release getting closer. Christ, I wanted that. Wanted his hands on me. His mouth. His gaze…

I cried out as I came and quickly stuffed my fist in my mouth to muffle the noise as I stroked myself through my orgasm. *Holy. Shit.* I couldn't remember ever coming that hard. My legs literally shook, like all the energy in my body had been expelled along with the rapidly cooling puddle on my stomach.

I lay there for a minute, gasping, feeling simultaneously proud and nervous and not really wanting to consider either of those things too closely.

A knock at my bedroom door made me jump like a guilty teenager.

"Daddy?" Aiden's voice was a sleepy croak. "I need

you. I'm thirsty, and I forgot to get water before bed. And also, it's very dark downstairs." He hesitated. "So, c'you get some for me?"

Fuck.

"Yeah." My voice was hoarser than Aiden's. "Gimme two minutes. Go back to bed, and I'll bring you some, okay?"

"Thanks, Daddy."

I went into my little en suite bathroom and flipped on the light to clean myself up with a damp towel. I looked exactly the same as I had when I'd brushed my teeth before bed, even though it felt like a lot had changed.

It hasn't, I reminded myself. *Fantasy is fantasy.*

In reality, I was going to help Luke Williams get his roof fixed before he hurt himself, because that was what a good neighbor would do. I was going to focus on taking care of my son and not let anything else distract me.

Including this crazy attraction to my own betrothed.

Chapter Eleven

LUKE

"U-N-L-I-K-E-L-Y, unlikely," Aiden Sunday recited the following Thursday, kicking the back of his sneaker against the edge of the cafetorium's stage to punctuate each letter.

All of the other children who'd stayed after school for extra spelling bee practice had already been picked up, and Aiden and I had the whole room to ourselves.

"You got it!" I held up my hand for a high five, and Aiden smacked it enthusiastically. "That's twelve words in a row. Keep up the practice for the next few weeks, and you're gonna kill it at the spelling bee."

"C'you give me one more practice word? Please, Mr. Williams?" His gap-toothed grin was infectious and seriously hard to resist, so I usually didn't. But...

"That's what you said ten words ago." I folded my legs beneath me and sat beside him. "How about if you start working on your journal entry for Monday while we wait for your uncle Drew to get here?"

Aiden agreed but dragged his composition book out of his backpack with the enthusiasm of a sedated sloth. "Hey, Mr. Williams? Do you think my mom will come to the

Spring Fling? 'Cause the mayor gives out prizes for the spelling bee at the Spring Fling, and maybe if I can win one, she can see me get it."

I glanced up from the lesson plan I'd been working on. "I… I don't know. The Spring Fling is open to the whole town, so I don't see why not."

He nodded and tapped his pencil against his closed notebook for a few moments, then said fake-casually, "You know, Mom took me to hockey practice this week."

"Did she?" I'd heard about this… but only briefly. "Was it fun?"

He nodded enthusiastically… then stopped. "She came on Monday afternoon."

I frowned. "Okay? That's good, right?"

"Practice is Tuesday."

"Ohhh. Well, it was the first week, wasn't it? She probably got confused. Did she come back on Tuesday and take you?"

"Yeah! Totally!" He hesitated for a second. "Dad was annoyed, though. She… she forgets things a lot. She forgets *me* a lot."

My heart squeezed. "I am almost positive that's not true, bud. You're basically unforgettable. Some people just aren't great at remembering dates and times and take longer to adjust to new routines. Be patient. And remember your dad probably gets annoyed because he loves you, and he doesn't want *you* to be upset."

He cocked his head. "D'you think?"

"I do."

He looked relieved. "Because Mom's also gonna take me to Nature Scouts, 'cause I want her to meet Olin, and I was thinking, maybe she could pick me up after spelling bee practice sometimes, too, so she could meet *you*. Maybe you could ask my dad. Or ask Principal Oliver—"

"Why don't you wait," I suggested. "See how she does with next week's pickup. Then *you* can ask your dad. I'm sure I'll meet her sometime soon."

Under no circumstances would I be asking Principal Oliver to intervene, though, thank you very much. The woman had made no secret of her feelings for Webb Sunday and, by extension, our betrothal.

By Monday morning, word had gotten out about the handfasting—because this was Little Pippin Hollow, where every week was a slow news week and dogs having puppies was sometimes the lead story on the local cable news. When I'd walked into the teachers' lounge, I'd been greeted with celebratory donuts and hugs from nearly everyone, along with a dozen voices clamoring for every detail. *How long have you been dating?* Ohmigosh, *I can't believe you managed to keep it under the gossip radar so well that everyone thought you two disliked each other! Whose idea was the handfasting? Do you get a ring?*

I'd flushed hot and opened my mouth to explain that it had all been a huge misunderstanding... when Principal Oliver had cut in.

"You're going to find out pretty soon that Webb Sunday's no prize, Mr. Williams," she'd said, staring down her bifocals at me like a mousy, off-brand version of Cruella de Vil. "He's making his ex-wife jump through hoops to see her own son, and now he's inveigled one of my teachers into a handfasting before the custody is officially decided? Seems a little too good to be true, if you ask me."

I really hated when people said that.

Immediately, I'd stood a little straighter, hands clenched into fists, because our handfasting had been utterly ridiculous... but it hadn't been deliberate, that much I *knew*.

"Webb hasn't inveigled me into anything," I said firmly. Though damn, I wished he would. "And our relationship is no one's business but ours."

Then I'd left the room with my head held high, only remembering after I'd stalked back to my classroom that a man with bills to pay probably should not be deliberately antagonizing his boss.

It was hard, though, when it involved Webb and Aiden. Webb was a devoted father, and even when we hadn't been friends, I'd never doubted that.

I was sure Amanda loved Aiden, too. But, well, if I was being honest, it was hard to understand how a person could walk away from Webb Sunday if he wanted them in his life and in his bed, and that was the dang truth.

The man made a terrible enemy, but as a friend... *ugh*. He was amazing. Too amazing. Irresistibly amazing.

Case in point: I'd woken up on Saturday morning to an adorable text from him about Aiden and "hydropraetonic" plants. And the text had been signed "(This is Webb Sunday)" like I might not realize, which was ten times adorable-r.

I'd texted back a picture of my sheep clamoring around me while I fed them with the caption, "Popular!"

And it had somehow morphed into a whole *thing* where we'd texted back and forth every couple of hours for days.

Webb: (picture of an orchard full of bare trees) *So... about those apple tithes. I have bad news.* *sad emoji*

Me: (picture of Aiden, tongue sticking out of his mouth as he affixed grass seeds to pink sponges) *Hydropraetonic experi-*

ments underway. You wouldn't know about those, Webb, but Mr. Williams does because he's smart. *devil emoji*

Webb: *My brother Porter is a HUSTLER. He just went sledding with Aiden and Olin… and he's conned THE CHILDREN into carting HIM up the damn hill. I feel like I've failed as a parent on many levels.*

Me: *I just asked Liz at the library if they had any "books on tape" so I could listen while I crochet, and OMG I have become my grandmother, SEND HELP.*

Webb: *Would love to, but I had to ask Drew to explain why your text was funny since it looked fine to me.*

Me: *I love teaching, but good gosh, the bureaucracy.*

Me: *Principal Oliver is making me fill out permission slips to have kids participate in Pick-a-Book.*

Me: *A permission slip… to have a free book sent home with them!!! And these are not controversial books. We're talking… The Boy Who Loved Words.*

Me: *Sorry. I don't mean to be a downer.*

Webb: *Missed your texts because my kid was just reading out loud to me.*

Webb: *How does it feel to teach kids maybe the most important thing they'll ever learn how to do?*

Webb: *Don't let the bastards get you down.*

Webb: *And you couldn't be a downer if you tried. (I dare you. Try.)*

Me: **cry emoji* Thanks, Webb.*

.   .   .

Webb: *Aiden's mom is picking him up for hockey practice in ten minutes.*

    Webb: *Scale of 1-10, how bad is it that I want to follow them to the rink?*

    Me: *Wanting to do it? 1*

    Me: *Doing it? 7.5*

    Me: *But I'm at Peebles' and if I happen to drive past the rink on my way home, I think that's a 4, tops.*

I wasn't sure if this was what Webb Sunday was like with all his friends, but it was working for me in the best, worst way.

As in, every time my phone dinged and I saw his name, I got a thrill in my stomach, like I was back in middle school having my first crush on a boy. It felt lighthearted and fun and… well, I was really trying to focus on the good, but I couldn't deny that it felt precarious.

My attraction was now a full-blown crush.

"Mr. Williams, who's the best superhero?"

"Huh?" I blinked and found that I'd been staring at a blank page for a long moment. "Oh. Is this for your journal entry?"

"Yeah. You said to write four or five sentences about our favorite hero. So I'm trying to figure out who's most powerful. Like, Thor has a hammer. But also, Superman doesn't need a hammer because he's strong. And then there's Green Lantern—"

"Or there are real-life heroes," I pointed out. "Firefighters, nurses, lifeguards. You could write about those."

He wrinkled his nose. "I mean, yeah. But… that's kinda boring."

I pushed my lips together and tried, like I did a million times a day, not to laugh at the unfiltered stuff that came out of my students' mouths. "Hmm. Well, if you're asking *my* favorite superhero, it's Spider-Man."

Aiden cocked his head to one side. "That's… nice," he said dubiously.

I bit my lip. "He might not have the strongest powers, but he uses them wisely. He cares about people and looks out for them. People can rely on him. That's why he's my favorite." I paused. "And the webs. I love the webs."

Aiden grinned. "Yeah, okay. I mean, still not as good as Thor, though."

I grinned back. "Well—"

"Sorry, boys!" Drew Sunday hurried into the cafetorium wearing tie-dye leggings, a hoodie, and Crocs, though it couldn't have been more than fifteen degrees outside. His blood had to be as thick as cement. "I was working in the sugar house and lost all track of time. The sap is really running this week. Nice warm days and cool nights, you know?"

I shook my head. I had no clue. "I understand only the basics of syrup making, I'm afraid. One day, I'll learn."

"Come out to the orchard this weekend," Drew offered. "Webb and I are hosting Aiden's Nature Scout troop on Saturday for maple sugaring in the morning and skating in the afternoon. You're more than welcome."

"Oh, that's nice of you, but—"

"Please, Mr. Williams," Aiden begged. "Please, please, please? Dad and I can show you how to skate. Then once you know how, we can play hockey. Murray said your parents never taught you." He said this like it was the saddest turn of events he could imagine.

Drew and I exchanged a laughing look over Aiden's head.

"That's true," I agreed. "But I don't think—"

"My dad says the best way to learn something is by

doing it. And we have skates. Like a billion pairs. And you can borrow some."

I hesitated.

"My dad said it's important to be friendly with your neighbors," Aiden said pointedly. "So you really kinda *have* to come."

I huffed out a laugh as he hoisted his backpack and ran off to get his coat.

"He's right," Drew said gently. "You really should."

"Webb doesn't want to spend his afternoon teaching me to skate," I argued. "He's busy."

"Too busy sometimes," Drew agreed. "He's responsible for everyone and everything—it's just his way. Which is why the man needs to remember to take an afternoon to go skating every once in a while. And he'll be more likely to do it if you're there."

Would he, though? We might be friends—neighbor friends who texted, even—and we might be accidentally handfasted, but I highly doubted that he wanted me all up in his business.

"I'll think about it," I promised before packing up my own belongings and heading home.

As I turned off the main road and onto my driveway, I slowed way down. The long, gravel surface had become a sort of obstacle course over the past week thanks to the confusing Hokey-Pokey dance that Mother Nature was doing. By day, bright sunshine forced the snow to melt into springtime mud puddles, but then at night, winter bounced back, freezing the mud into solid ruts.

No judgment on Mother Nature, though, since my feelings for Webb were doing the same kind of dance. During the day, I reminded myself we were friends, and that was fine. That he was *straight, straight, straight*, not attracted to me at all, and that getting involved with a student's parent was never smart.

But at night?

When I was alone in the trailer, shivering under a bunch of afghans?

All my good intentions fell away, and I kept myself warm with fantasies of Webb's big, callused hands roaming my body, and the hard, muscled wall of his chest against my back—

My fantasy replay cut off when I pulled around the house and found the driveway next to my camper was already occupied by not one but *two* giant pickup trucks, in addition to Murray's. I recognized one of them—and that recognition made my heart rate pick up—but I'd never seen the other before.

What the heck?

I stepped out of the car just as Murray emerged from the barn, his red hair glinting in the sun.

"Murray? What's going on here?" I demanded.

"Hey, Mr. Luke! Oh, that's just the guys taking some measurements." He grinned broadly as he ambled in my direction. "It'll be nice to have that roof done, eh?"

"The roof?" I repeated. "How? I mean… *who?*"

"Oh, Jerry Walcott—you know, Walcott Roofing?—got one of his guys up there to see the condition so they could maybe repair it."

"But he can't!"

"No, he can't," Murray agreed sadly. "I heard 'em say it's in real bad shape and needs to be totally replaced. But they might be able to get it done next week. Won't that be great?"

I shook my head, speechless.

For months and months, I'd felt like a total outsider in the Hollow. Then I blew a bugle with the town's favorite son just *once*… and suddenly I was the target of nonconsensual home repairs?

I knew who'd been the driving force behind this, of course. I would have known even if I hadn't seen his truck. And when I spotted him coming around the corner of the house, looking way more sexy in his work boots and flannel than anyone had a right to, I was tempted to give the man a piece of my mind.

I folded my arms over my chest and walked toward him, and his eyes widened when he saw me.

"Uh. Hey, Luke! You're… here." Webb smiled winningly.

"Yes." I narrowed my eyes. "I live here."

His grin warmed with true amusement. "So, funny thing. Jerry Walcott—you know, Walcott Roofing?—is going to replace your roof. Surprise! Happy birthday."

"That *is* a surprise," I shot back. "Since my birthday is in September and you know perfectly well I don't have the money to pay for—"

"Webb!" A gruff, heavyset man with white hair and concerningly pink cheeks toddled around the corner of the house. When he saw me, his face split into a broad grin, and he immediately extended his hand. "Luke! Well, hey there. We've never been properly introduced. I'm Jerry Walcott—"

"Of Walcott Roofing?" I asked, deadpan.

"You've heard of us!" Jerry's smile grew even wider. "Real sorry to hear about your roof, son. You know, hard slate'll last you a century, but this one's seen that and more. Don't you worry, though, we'll get you sorted. You shoulda called me sooner!"

I rubbed my forehead. "Mr. Walcott, I—"

"Jerry!" he boomed. "After all, you're neighbors with my brother-in-law Norm Avery, and that makes us family."

It did? That was ridiculous, but also… kinda great.

I wasn't sure what my face was doing, but Webb ran a hand over his mouth like he was trying not to laugh at me.

"The thing is, Jerry," I began again, "you seem delightful, and I would love for you to do the work, but I'm short on funds at the moment. I tried getting a loan at the credit union, but I haven't lived in town long enough——"

"*Bup bup bup.*" Jerry waved my objections aside. "Your man here's sorted it all out. Convenient thing about marriage, eh?" He winked happily. "Two oars row better than one."

"But," I reminded him, "we're not actually married. We——"

"Oh, well, not yet, sure," he allowed. "But it's the next best thing, now that you're handfasted." He leaned toward me eagerly. "The wife and I caught the whole story on the news. Never heard of such a thing before, but I wouldn't be surprised to see other young folks like yourselves revive it. My Ellie cried, Lord love 'er. She's a sap for tradition, and she's a sap for love, and when you put the two together? The waterworks start up." Jerry sniffled, showing that Ellie wasn't the only sap. "She thought it was so romantical that you two kept it hidden so well for so long, too, just to avoid the gossips. You know, I don't hold with gossip a'tall."

I nodded slowly. "Right, no, of course you don't. But actually——"

"Why, I heard from Miguel, who heard from Evie, who heard from Katey at the diner," Jerry said avidly, "that you were even denying it after the fact, just to throw people off, which was smart." He tapped the side of his nose and winked. "But the cat's out of the bag now!"

"Actually, Jerry, the thing is, Webb and I——"

"——are so relieved that we don't have to keep up the

pretense anymore," Webb interrupted loudly, pulling me against his side so firmly I let out a little *ooof.* "And we're so grateful for all you've done. Really. We owe you one."

Pretense? What in the heckity?

And since when did we hug?

"You weren't kidding about the surprise," I muttered.

"Don't give it another thought," Jerry said with a wave of his hand. "Ellie would have my hide if she heard I could help you two out and didn't. 'Sides, I'm makin' out on the deal." He rocked up on his toes excitedly. "I'll come by for the Case early next week, alright? Gotta get home tonight."

Webb nodded.

"The case?" I glanced up at Webb, but Jerry was the one who explained.

"Webb's old Case tractor. We're bartering. It's the way we do things around here. You'll learn soon enough, Luke." The man patted my shoulder affectionately and made a move toward his truck, only to stop and snap his fingers. "Oh, and if you're still in the market for a loan, you might check with the credit union again. I've got a feelin' they'll waive that residency requirement now that you're making a home here permanently."

I blinked. "But—"

Webb's grip on me tightened. "Ellie still working at the credit union, is she?"

"Yep. Twenty-seven years come March."

Oh. I shut my mouth quickly.

"Congratulations again," Jerry called as he and his assistant got in his truck, and I nodded, because it seemed impolite not to, even though I hadn't the foggiest idea what was actually happening.

"Webb? Is there anything you might like to explain to me?" I asked out the side of my mouth.

"You mad?" Webb asked, still smiling in Jerry's direction.

"Depends. What did I just agree to?"

Jerry started his truck, and Webb and I each gave him a cheery wave.

"Look, you need your roof fixed, right?" Webb said reasonably.

"You know I do. But—"

"You were gonna do it yourself. I know. Once you figured out how to repair a slate roof—which many roofers don't even know how to do—and had the time to do it and learned how to safely climb a ladder."

"Hey!" I protested. "I know how."

Even if I didn't always put what I knew into practice.

"If there were ever a job to leave to the professionals, Luke, it's this one. It's dangerous."

I blew out a breath because I knew he was correct. But that didn't make him *right*.

"You can't pay for my roof," I insisted. "It's not fair." I didn't want to be a burden to Webb or anyone.

"I didn't, though," Webb said quickly. "No cash will exchange hands, I promise. For one thing, Jerry was so moved by the whole handfasting spectacle that he quoted us—I mean *you*—a really good price. And then it so happens I have an old machine he wants to restore, so we're bartering my tractor for this job. You'd be doing me a favor, honestly, by letting me do this, since it's, you know, giving me an excuse to clear out old junk."

I peered up at him suspiciously, and his green eyes blinked down at me, all innocence. "Good gravy. You fib about as well as your son does, which is to say, really, really badly."

His eyes crinkled at the corners when he smiled back—a *real* smile this time, and wasn't it a crazy thing that I knew the difference? "Then look at it this way: you offered to sell me the Pond orchard for peanuts, right? Well, maybe I'll let you. Maybe this is me doing something nice for you, too."

"But… we don't even know for sure if the land's mine in the first place. I called Stephen, and he hasn't called me back. What if it's yours already?"

I hated taking things from people. I'd much rather be the one helping.

"Then that's even easier, so who cares? Friends don't keep score," Webb informed me. "You do nice things for me because I'm your friend, and I do nice things for you because you're mine."

I ran my tongue over my front teeth, considering. I knew I was being stubborn, but… gosh, it made me feel weird to accept his help.

"Let me do this, Luke," he pleaded. "You don't know how many times I've replayed your mom's call in my head. When she talked about how she felt better knowing my family would be there for you… That's what it should have been like. It's my fault that it wasn't."

"But… why wasn't it?" I still didn't understand why he'd held a grudge against me for so long.

He blushed red. "I don't know. I was… wrong. About a lot of things. And it would mean a lot if you'd let me do this, in the name of friendship."

"*Ugh.*" I rolled my eyes. "Porter is not the only snake charmer in your family," I informed him.

"Does that mean yes?"

"Yes, it means… yes. Thank you, Webb. I can't believe you're doing this." I huffed out a breath. "Please tell me you negotiate better when it comes to your apple prices, or else I'm gonna seriously worry about your profit margins."

His deep laughter rang around the empty yard. "Trust

me, I'm a shark when it comes to my apples. You're getting the friends and family deal because the idea of you getting hurt…" He broke off with a head shake. "Not okay."

I melted. I really, really liked the idea of being his friends and family, and I wanted to bask in his protectiveness for as long as it lasted.

"It's been a week," I blurted.

"Hmm?"

"A week today since we were at the Bugle. That means there's only seven weeks left of our, you know, handfasting."

"Oh, wow. Right. Feels like longer. Seven more weeks of making a concerted effort not to go swimming together. It's been rough." Webb toed a line through the icy sludge of my driveway pointedly. "In seven weeks, we can go 'drink sweet water' side by side and celebrate not being betrothed."

"Having a drink side by side was what got us into this mess," I reminded him mock-severely.

Webb laughed out loud again. "Fuck, you're funny."

He pulled me against him more tightly… which was the precise moment when I realized that we'd remained standing, stock-still, with his arm holding me firmly to his side, even though Jerry had to be halfway back to town.

My heart stuttered. I doubted Webb even noticed he was doing it, and it was probably taking advantage or something for me to let it go on now that I *had*, but… God, it was so nice to be held like that. To feel someone's arm around me. To be close enough to see the corners of Webb's eyes crinkle when he laughed and to notice the little spot at the base of his jaw where he hadn't shaved very closely. To feel… cherished.

But despite how badly I wanted to stay right where I was for as long as possible—or maybe *because* I wanted it so badly—I stepped away. There were certain things a positive attitude could not bring about, and Webb Sunday returning my feelings was one of them.

"Come meet Eliza and her sisters," I said, pointing toward the rock wall where the sheep stood staring at us. "Webb, meet Eliza. Eliza, this is Webb. He's taken an irrational dislike to sheep, but don't lose hope. He might decide to be friends with you yet."

"I changed my mind," Webb said wryly. "You're not nearly as funny as you think you are." But he stood beside me and scratched Eliza under her chin. "And I'll have you know that I have no problem with sheep under normal circumstances. I just don't want to get all slicked up, sling them over my naked shoulders like a feather boa, and parade them through a sun-drenched field while giving you a come-hither look."

I turned and gaped at him, slack-jawed. "That's... incredibly specific, Thomas Webb Sunday."

Beneath his beard, his cheeks turned red. "I... I may have seen your calendar the other day. Back in your trailer. The Barnyard Beefcake one."

It was my turn to blush. "It's called Farmers and Friends," I said in a strangled voice. "It was a gift from my *mother*. Proceeds benefited the county animal adoption organization. And there was no... come-hithering. There was no hithering of any kind."

"Oh, there was hithering," he said decisively. "I felt very, very... hithered."

By the big, sweaty men? And what had he thought about that?

I opened my mouth to ask, then shut it quickly.

"Okay, then." I cleared my throat and tried desperately to turn the subject. "So. Wow. How about this weather, huh? Brr."

Suave. So suave.

Webb made a sound of disagreement. "This is down-right mild. And you're gonna miss these temperatures when your car gets stuck on your own driveway come mud season," he promised.

I laughed. "Great."

"But first comes maple sugaring season. Warmer days, chilly nights."

"Drew mentioned that when he picked Aiden up from spelling bee practice. He said you're taking the Nature Scouts out this weekend."

Webb rolled his eyes. "Murray and Olin's mom, Maryanne, is one of the Nature Scout Herd Leaders, and she asked me as a favor, so I couldn't say no. Besides, now that Amanda is taking Aiden to Nature Scouts, I haven't gotten to be involved as much, and I miss it. Aiden begged me to take them all skating afterward on Pond Pond, too." He pointed toward the water at the edge of his land. I'd never known the name of it before.

"It's called Pond Pond?" I asked, amused. "Like, the Pond family's… pond?"

"I come from a long line of very literal people, Luke." He raised an eyebrow in mock challenge.

I grinned back at him. I couldn't help it. He was bossy and sometimes surly, but goodness he was *fun*.

"You should come," he said suddenly, and I felt my smile falter.

"Oh, I don't know. Me on skates…" I winced. I would take suave to entirely new levels if I got out on the ice.

"You might like it. Skating is always fun, but skating outside is just… better. Aiden would love it."

"Yeah, he maybe invited me," I admitted. "After school. He volunteered you to teach me."

Webb grinned. "He's probably hoping you'll be on

Team New Puppy and can convince me." He pondered this for a second, then frowned. "Actually, you'd probably have some kind of convincing argument at your fingertips, complete with scientific research to back it up. So you're Team No Puppy Until Spring, got it?"

I could tell you his words didn't make my chest squeeze and my fingertips tingle… but that would be a lie. "Got it."

"And come on Saturday. Really. Aiden needs caring, responsible adults in his life."

I hesitated. "How is the visitation thing with Amanda going?"

"It's going." He shrugged.

"If you need to talk…"

"Thanks. I appreciate the offer. " He gave me a half-smile. "There are worse people I could have to pretend to be in love with for the next seven weeks."

"In… l-love?" I sputtered. "What?"

Webb shrugged. "Well, if we want that discount, we have to make a good show, at least in front of Jerry Walcott."

I groaned. I hadn't thought that through all the way. *Crap.* "But aren't you worried we'll confuse Aiden?" *Or me?* "We can't exactly claim it was an accident if we're going along with it. Are we just going to wait until the end of the eight weeks and say, 'Psych!'"

"I was thinking more like, 'Things didn't work out.' And then we'll stun everyone with our incredible maturity by managing to stay friends."

I huffed out a laugh.

"And as for Aiden… I'm gonna have to explain this to him anyway before he hears rumors."

"True. Do you want me to help? I could—"

"No, I'll take care of it," Webb said with such finality I

knew better than to argue. "But will you come on Saturday?"

Ughhhh. "I'm afraid you're greatly underestimating my lack of coordination," I warned him. "The maple sugaring part sounds great, but maybe I can cheer you on from the sidelines during the skating part."

"I'll take care of you," he promised. "Trust me."

I did trust him, I realized. At least, with ice skating.

"Okay," I agreed, forcing a smile. "I'll give it a try." Though I firmly believed it would end in disaster.

"Saturday's going to be the most fun ever," he promised.

As it turned out... we were both right.

Chapter Twelve

WEBB

By the midpoint of Saturday afternoon's Nature Scout Skate on Pond Pond, I was ready to admit that I'd been wrong about today being fun.

It was not.

It had nothing to do with the dozen six-, seven-, and eight-year-olds sliding around on the ice, starting random snowball fights, and whooping so loudly the trees rang with the sound, because Maryanne and the other Herd Leader were in charge of them.

And it had nothing to do with the weather either. Though it was overcast and I could smell an impending snowstorm in the air, the temperature had finally dropped back below freezing the day before, and after drilling the ice in a few strategic locations to check its thickness, the Herd Leaders and I had decided most of the pond was safe for skating.

No, the issue was Luke Williams—insatiably curious, constantly smiling, adorable Luke Williams, with his borrowed ice skates and all the natural grace of a shaky newborn calf—and the fact that every time I looked at the man, the churning in my gut ratcheted up a little tighter.

This wasn't fun—it was torture.

"Like this?" Luke asked, looking up at me with hopeful excitement on his face. He balanced on his skates while I pulled him along from the front and Aiden propelled us from behind, and together we formed the world's weirdest, slowest ice locomotive.

"You got it, Mr. Williams," Aiden encouraged. "You're doing great."

"I'm not sure about that, bud. You and your dad are good teachers, though. *Whoa!* Crap—" he began, then glanced over his shoulder at Aiden. "Uh, I mean, *crapulent toads.*"

Aiden snickered, and I shook my head briefly, trying not to laugh. I was usually pretty good about not swearing much in front of my son, but he'd definitely heard the word *crap* a time or ten... probably just that morning alone.

"Um. Hey, Dad? I'm gonna skate off *real* fast and just check if Grace and Alix are okay... okay?"

I glanced over at his friends, who were playing a fast-paced game of ice tag. "Hmm. They seem okay to me."

Luke looked up at me, eyes dancing with humor under his thick wool hat. "It's nice of you to want to go check, though, Aiden. Very thoughtful."

"Sure it is." I rolled my eyes. "Yeah, go ahead. Have fun."

"Thanks! Hey, call me if you need me, Mr. Williams!" Aiden yelled belatedly as he skated away.

"Sure will," Luke shouted back. To me, he whispered, "I'm not positive, but I think I may have lost cool points today." He seemed resigned.

I snorted. "It's not possible for you to have lost more

than me. Remember I told you I had to sit the kid down this morning and tell him a highly sanitized story about the bugle blowing?"

"Oh, I remember." Luke chuckled sympathetically. "Was explaining handfasting better or worse than discussing the birds and the bees?"

"Infinitely worse. At least sex makes *sense*."

I might have put off the conversation even longer if Jerry and Ellie Walcott hadn't sat down for an interview with the mayor's reporter niece the day before to express their support for me and Luke, but they had.

And then Genevieve had turned that interview into a news segment called "Hand-Fast Watch!" complete with a giant graphic of the mayor's scroll showing how many tasks had been completed and which were predicted to be completed, with a countdown clock in the upper corner of the screen as if Luke and I were a bomb that might explode at any moment.

And then someone had started making T-shirts with our ship name on them, and other folks had come up to me on the street and told me they'd always suspected Luke and I were meant to be together.

It was ridiculous, but as I'd told Luke last week, if there was one thing the Hollow loved, it was *love*.

And clearly Curt had been wrong about this thing blowing over, because this town was just getting started.

Because of all that, I'd woken Aiden up for breakfast a few minutes early this morning and sat him down at the kitchen table to explain the unexplainable… and I was pretty sure the embarrassment of that moment would become one of my core memories.

"So, you and Mr. Williams are, like, half-married?" Aiden had demanded excitedly, eyes shining. "And you're gonna get whole-married later?"

"No, no. That's what I'm telling you, kiddo. The bugle blowing was an accident because we didn't know what it meant." My face had gone feverishly hot. "We were just having fun and didn't intend to get handfasted."

"So…" His face had scrunched up. "So, you're *not* handfasted to Mr. Williams."

"Uh…Well. No. Technically, I am. But as long as we don't finish the steps, it won't be legal. We'll stay *friends*, though," I'd assured him. "Good friends. That part won't change."

Aiden had sighed. "Unless Mr. Williams decides he doesn't wanna be friends with you."

"That won't happen. Why would it?"

"Oh, Dad," Aiden had said sadly, placing his hand on my arm. "You're kinda boring. But it'll be okay. I'll still hang out with you. Sometimes."

"It could have been worse," Luke teased, like he knew exactly which part of the story I was dwelling on. "At least he said he'd hang out with you."

"He said *sometimes*," I grumbled, making Luke laugh harder. I steered him left, around a couple of kids practicing pirouettes. "Let's go this way. We wanna stay over here where the ice is nice and thick. Nice job."

"Oh, yeah. I'm incredibly talented at letting you pull me around, huh?" Luke clung to my arm and grinned up at me, his pink cheeks making his freckles stand out.

Jesus fuck, he was gorgeous.

There, I said it.

Luke Williams was the most delectable thing I'd ever seen, and my very confused, formerly straight self wanted to haul him in my arms and kiss him right there in the middle of the frozen pond and not give a single shit who saw us.

But I couldn't do that. I *wouldn't*.

Not when it would start a whole fresh crop of rumors and news segments.

Not when I had nothing to offer Luke but a bonfire of lust, a bunch of half-baked fantasies, and a severe allergy to relationships.

So, why the fuck had I insisted Luke come along today? I didn't have a damn clue.

And why had I texted him a dozen times a day, every day, all week long, when I hardly ever texted *anyone*? Also a good question.

And why had I practically elbowed Mark Burns, the second Nature Scout Herd Leader, out of the way when he'd offered to teach Luke how to skate? Once again, I—

Okay, no, actually, I knew the answer to that one. Mark was annoying as hell, and he'd practically talked Luke's ear off the whole time I'd been explaining the maple sugaring process that morning, even though I'd seen Luke gently shushing him more than once, which was fucking rude. And, frankly, I didn't like the look in his eye when he smiled at Luke, all overly friendly and eager to *help*.

The man was married, for fuck's sake, and Luke was my betrothed—I mean, my *fake*-betrothed, obviously, but Mark didn't know that—and yet Mark had still been trying to get his *helpful* fingers all over Luke. Luke didn't need a person like that in his life, so I was teaching him to skate myself.

"Son of a goose," Luke said as he lost his footing. "Sorry."

I grabbed both his hands in mine and forced him to look at me. "Don't be sorry. You really *are* doing great."

Luke looked over his shoulder at all the little kids skating circles around us. "Pretty sure this is Georgia's first time, too, and she seems to be skating on her own already."

"She's a kid," I said patiently. "It's not as easy picking

up something new when you're older. You start to focus too much on how much you don't know and get embarrassed. But when you get distracted and let yourself have fun, you do way better. Have you noticed that?"

"I hadn't." Luke smiled up at me. "Wow. That's really profound, Webb."

My breath caught in my chest at the sight of that smile, and just like that I couldn't pretend I didn't know exactly why I'd invited Luke today. Because I wanted any excuse to stand next to him, just for a little while.

"Yeah, that's me. Profound." I moved around to the other side and held on to Luke's jacket so he could get used to using his arms. "There you go. Awesome. You'll be playing hockey for the Habs in no time."

"Yeah, right. I'll settle for just staying upright."

"If you manage that, you'll be doing better than a couple of their wingmen."

"Shush." Luke smacked me lightly in the stomach and nearly lost his footing again in the process. "They're my team now, okay? Stop hating on my dudes."

"Your dudes? You didn't even know them until that night at the Bugle, and they're only your team because Alan Laroche misunderstood—"

"Doesn't matter," he insisted stubbornly. "They're mine now."

I laughed. "And you don't know the rules of the game and you don't know the players—"

"Yet. But you're teaching me. Besides, I like their jersey colors, and I like backing an underdog—"

I stared at him in horror. "The Canadiens are *not* an under—"

"And Alan Laroche taught me their cheer, and it's quite catchy." He lifted his chin. "So in my heart, they're mine. You can mock me all you like, but I figure people have made more important decisions based on worse things."

Good God, he was adorable.

"I'm afraid we can't be friends anymore, then," I sighed sadly. "I'm a Bruins fan."

"And you'll be sad to see your team lose, and the sight of me will just make it worse? Aww."

"Those," I told him, "are fighting words. I'm gonna go skate with Aiden."

He grabbed at my hand. "You can't, or I'll fall."

"Nope. I haven't been holding you for the last two minutes," I said smugly. "Ever since you got fired up about your dudes."

"Holy shoot," he whispered. "I'm doing it. I'm really doing it."

"You're doing it," I agreed, my chest squeezing with pride and happiness and other things that made my stomach fucking tremble like I was a teenager, not a grown man who knew better.

Like I didn't know that stomach trembling was likely to end in life-shattering disaster.

Like I didn't know that there was no such thing as a happily ever after in real life.

"Let me see if I can do the push-off part."

"Yeah," I said hoarsely. "Do it."

Luke pushed off and kept going—one foot and then the other, keeping his weight over his heels exactly like I'd taught him.

"Holy smokes! Webb! Look! I... Oh, shoot!"

The moment Luke went down was one of the scariest moments I'd ever experienced that didn't involve Aiden. His skate caught in a divot in the ice, and I winced as he fell forward onto his hands and knees, thinking he was gonna bruise. I'd already started skating in his direction to help him up when the ice made a booming, cracking noise… and Luke disappeared into the icy water with a splash.

Holy fucking shit.

My brothers and I had skated out here all the time as kids, and I knew there was no such thing as total safety, no matter how cautious you tried to be. Back when I was a kid, Reed and one of his friends had fallen in, and after my dad had dragged them out, he'd insisted that we all learn basic ice lifesaving techniques. I'd made sure my younger brothers had learned it, too.

But I'd be damned if I could recall any of that knowledge in the moment. My vision flickered at the corners, my heart pounded in my throat, and though I was skating fast, I felt like I was moving through concrete.

Luke's head popped up, and he gasped in a breath.

Thank fuck he wasn't trapped beneath the surface.

Somewhere behind me, the kids began screaming.

"Call for help," I yelled over my shoulder at Mark. "And keep them back!"

I didn't turn my head to see if he obeyed. My entire focus was on the man in front of me.

I dropped to my knees several feet away from the hole where Luke had disappeared and laid out flat. "Luke," I called as calmly as I could. "I'm right here. I'm gonna get you out."

"W-*webb*," Luke managed to get out. "Oh, f-f-f-fudge, it's cold."

"I know. I know it is. But listen to me. Control your breathing as much as you can, okay? Focus on your breathing."

"Y-yeah."

"Now lay out flat. Stretch your arms toward me. No! No, no. Don't try to lift out. Just stretch out your arms like you're swimming. Yeah, good! Now kick your feet and wiggle. Kick and wiggle. Yes. Yes! Yes. That's it. You're doing it."

Thank fuck, thank fuck, thank fuck.

"Just a little more. A little closer," I coaxed. "Small movements."

The second he was in grabbing distance, I grasped his hands and pulled him toward me while wriggling backward myself. When we'd gotten a good distance away, I pulled his soaking, shivering form against me and held him there tightly, needing to convince myself he was really okay.

"Don't try to stand up," I warned. "We're gonna roll, okay? I've got you, and you're doing so good, baby." I rolled us until we were within a few feet of the shore. "Okay. Okay, now I think we can try to stand. Let me help you."

Luke nodded, his teeth chattering, and let me pull him to stand up. With an arm around his waist, I half carried him to the shore where the kids were waiting.

"Mr. Williams!" a little girl shouted, clearly concerned. "Are you okay?"

Luke managed to lift a hand and give an approximation of a smile. "F-f-f-f—" he started to say.

"He's gonna be fine," I interpreted. "He did exactly the right things: he listened to me, and he stayed calm. So now we just need to get him warm."

"Hey!" Mark the helpful Herd Leader hurried down the shore with a load of emergency blankets, panting like he'd run all the way back to his truck to get them. He helped me strip Luke's parka, along with his gloves, hat, and skates, then wrapped several of the blankets around him. "I got my kit, and I radioed dispatch. If we need an ambulance, I can have one here in three minutes."

Oh. Right. I belatedly remembered that Mark was a paramedic and felt marginally more okay with his helpfulness.

Maryanne managed to keep most of the kids back, but Aiden broke free and ran forward to throw his arms around Luke. "I'm so sorry! I shouldn't have left you."

"Oh, g-gosh no. I am *so* g-glad you weren't with me, so you didn't f-fall in."

"Aiden." I tugged at his arm. "Move back, or you're gonna get all wet, too. He's gonna be okay, kiddo."

"You promise?"

"I swear," I said firmly. I would make sure of it.

Aiden nodded, his eyes shining.

"Luke, do you want to go to the hospital?" Mark asked. "Your core temperature's fine. I don't think you were in there long enough to get hypothermia, but we can take you to the hospital over in Keltyville and get you checked out—"

"N-no." Luke shook his head vehemently. "No hospital. Just s-so c-cold."

"I know. Let's get you home," Mark said. "My truck's parked up on the hill."

Luke's panicked eyes met mine. I imagined he didn't want the whole town to descend on his run-down house.

"I'll take him back to his place," I said gruffly. "It's only a quarter mile if I cut through the orchard on the 4x4."

What I was *not* going to do was stand around talking about it anymore.

I leaned down and grabbed Luke under his knees to hold him against my chest and started walking up the bank.

I was only vaguely aware of Mark squawking in protest, but I heard Maryanne say, "They're handfasted. Remember?"

"Get him warm as quick as you can, Webb!" he yelled after me. "Dry clothes. Warm drinks. *Share body heat.*"

My arms tightened involuntarily at the idea.

"Aiden," I called, "come on with us."

"No need," Maryanne said. "I'll make sure Aiden gets home. In fact, I'll take him back to my place, and he and Olin can warm up there. Focus on Luke."

I turned at that and looked at her, then at Aiden. Aiden nodded at me. "I'm okay. Feel better, Mr. Williams!"

Luke didn't respond, which was worrying. He huddled against me and let me carry him up to the 4x4.

When I'd gotten him seated, I decided he'd be better off without his wet shirt and sweater, so I stripped them off…

Which was when I remembered that sweet, buttoned-up, little Luke Williams had *pierced fucking nipples*, and a wholly inappropriate burst of lust speared through me like wildfire.

I quickly stripped off my own jacket and put it on him instead.

"Hang on," I said hoarsely as I buckled him in. "Just… hold on."

I drove up the hill to the orchard and then cut down a hill toward Luke's place. In my haste, I'd forgotten about the retaining wall that separated our properties—except the wall was so crumbled and sunken in spots that I was able to get around it without a problem.

It wasn't until we got inside Luke's trailer that I remembered why bringing Luke back to his trailer was actually a terrible idea. The place was only maybe five degrees warmer than the outside air.

I half carried him to the bed area, and he stood, still and docile, while I stripped him down to his boxer briefs, and then I hesitated. My fingers itched to strip him bare,

159

but that idea was *too* tempting. So instead, I got him out a pair of dry underwear, closed the curtain, and made him a cup of tea while he put them on and crawled into bed.

When I opened the curtain a few moments later, Luke was still shivering with cold despite being covered by a mound of afghans, and I had a moment of fear that maybe I *should* have taken him to the hospital.

"I'm s-sorry," Luke said softly. "G-good G-god. It's r-ridiculous. My body won't st-stop." He shuddered out a laugh. "I'll be f-fine in a minute."

I wasn't sure that was true, though. And I knew that the best way to help him was precisely what Mark had said —sharing body heat.

I didn't want to… specifically because I wanted to *so fucking badly*, and that felt incredibly dangerous. But then my mind helpfully replayed the footage of Luke plunging into the water, and I didn't care anymore about what was the safest for me.

I pulled off my sweater and undershirt and threw them on the table.

"W-what are you doing?" Luke demanded.

I contemplated my jeans. I really should leave them on, but the cuffs were soaked through and the knees weren't much better, and the last thing I wanted was to make Luke colder, so I stripped those off, too.

"*What are you doing?*" Luke repeated, shocked and panicked.

I pulled back the blankets. "Hush. I'm just warming you up." I climbed in beside him, gathered him in my arms, and drew the blankets back into place.

Luke held himself stiffly for a moment. "You sh-shouldn't…" he protested. "You… Oh my Godddddd." His whole body relaxed against me, and he melted into a puddle of Luke-scented goo, nestling his nose into my neck. "You are the warmest human in the universe."

I grunted in response. His nose was fucking freezing against my neck, his feet were blocks of ice against my calves, and his hands, which were trapped between us, were snow-cold.

Still, within minutes of his skin touching mine, I felt like I was being roasted alive from the inside out, and my brain short-circuited.

I began rubbing his back—my palm coasting up and down the long, smooth length of it—because I simply couldn't help myself. It felt like we were in a cocoon together in that tiny trailer. A step out of time. One secure minute in an incredibly unsafe world.

"T-talk to me," Luke said softly.

"Talk?" I repeated warily. "About what?"

"I don't c-care. Tell me a story. Or tell me what you ate for breakfast. Your voice is so deep and rumbly. It warms me up," he said blearily.

My heart, which hadn't recovered from the sight of him falling, lurched again at that. It reminded me of that night at the Bugle, when Luke had looked so happy to see me, even though we hadn't been friends yet… and all the times since then when he'd shown me the same expression, even when I hadn't deserved it.

In my life, a lot of people needed things from me, but very few of them simply wanted *me*—my presence, my voice. Things that cost me nothing but meant something to them.

"Okay," I said gruffly. "Uh… How much do you know about heirloom apple varietals?"

"N-nothing? I know there are red ones and green ones, though?"

"Jesus. That's a freakin' tragedy, Williams. We're gonna have to fix that."

His cold fingers twitched against my pecs, and I took one of his hands in mine, threading our fingers together. His breath hitched, but I pretended not to notice.

Luke laughed shakily. "Okay."

"There used to be thousands of apple varieties around here," I said into the quiet. "See, when the first European settlers brought apples over, those apples didn't thrive because they weren't used to this climate—"

"I feel their pain."

I snorted. "But the apple seeds that stuck it out and grew anyway, they cross-pollinated with the other apples that had stuck it out. They adapted," I said pointedly. "And what they became was something really amazing. There were tons of different flavors and textures and appearances. Every landholder had a different type of apple in their backyard."

"So what happened?" Luke asked softly.

"Economics. Food became more commercial, distributors cared most about whether the fruit was pretty and durable so they could make a profit. So apple growers focused on the apples that would sell. Nothing too different. Nothing too... soft."

"O-oh." His throat clacked as he swallowed.

"Which was a shame," I whispered, my mouth up against his ear so that my breath made him shiver. "Because sometimes the soft things are the sweetest..."

The air between us became tense. *Expectant.*

God, I knew what the objectively right thing to do in this situation was, but my hand wouldn't listen to what my brain was trying to tell it. I ran my hand down his back from his head to his waist again, and when he shivered, he moved even closer against me.

"… and sometimes different is… is *good*," I concluded, tilting my chin and pressing my lips to his.

He inhaled a shocked breath that exactly mimicked how I felt.

Had I really done that? Holy shit, I'd really done that. How fucking amazing.

Then he groaned low in his throat, wrapped his arms around my neck, and launched himself at me.

The sexy man in my arms was nothing like the sweet, shy guy who'd let me guide him around the pond earlier. This man kissed like he was ravenous and I was his favorite meal, devouring my mouth, and rubbing his tongue against mine. The kiss went on and on until I'd lost track of time, lost track of what we'd been saying, lost track of any reason I shouldn't want this. All I could do was *feel*.

And shit, there was a lot to feel—the lean muscles of his ass as I pulled him against me, the slight bristle of his beard against my palm as I held his cheek, and the… *oh, fuck*. The hardness of his dick as it pressed against my leg, inches from my own erection.

"Fuck, Luke. I—" I broke off as he moved his mouth lower, running his tongue over the side of my neck in a way that made my brain incapable of communicating with my mouth.

"Do you want me to stop?" he asked softly.

"No. God, no." The words were torn from the deepest part of me. "I need—"

"What? Tell me what you need."

"*More*." I pulled him against me and maneuvered so that I was flat on the bed with him straddling me, with my hard cock trapped below his ass.

"Oh, freaking heck," he moaned, grinding down against me, our bodies only separated by two thin layers of underwear. "Your body is…" He broke off with a head shake and coasted his hands down my chest with reverent hands, and the look on his face made it clear that he'd thought about this before.

Just like I had.

How hot was that?

His thumbs flicked my nipples—the perfect combination of pleasure and pain—and I gasped.

"Take these off," I demanded roughly, coasting my hands up the light hair on his thighs to tug at the hem of his boxer briefs.

He hesitated for a second, like maybe that had made things a little too real for him, but then I cupped his erection through the thin fabric, and he thrust against me helplessly.

"Luke, please." I could see the questions swirling in his eyes, but I didn't have any answers, only desire pounding through my blood like a drum beat. "*Please?*"

He bit his lip, then stepped off the bed and stripped off his underwear.

My breath caught in my throat. His cock was flushed and fully hard—so much so that it bobbed against his stomach—and I was clearly no cock connoisseur, but I could say for sure that the sight of it, especially combined with his wild hair and wild eyes and those fucking *nipple rings*, made my own dick twitch with the need to be free.

Luke put a knee on the bed, but he paused as I tore down my boxer briefs. He stared down at my length and licked his lips, and my dick pulsed in response.

"Come here," I demanded, missing the weight of him against me. I propped a bunch of his pillows behind me so I could watch him better.

"Don't rush me. I'm making plans. I need to look my fill."

"I already have plans," I informed him. "They involve *this*."

I used our size difference to my advantage, lifting him bodily until he was on top of me, straddling me again.

He laughed and sputtered—then closed his eyes and groaned unabashedly as my erection rubbed against the cleft of his ass again, this time with no barriers in place. Seeing him so lost, feeling his skin against my cock for the first time, was the single hottest sexual moment of my entire existence, and I didn't think twice before reaching a hand down to grasp his length in my fist and tug.

"*Oh God*," Luke whimpered.

"You like that?"

"*Uh-huh*. Your hands are so big and so perfect."

"You sound like you're drunk again," I said, and he looked it, too, his eyes glassy and his hair down over his forehead. I reached up a hand to brush his hair back.

"I *feel* like I'm drunk again. What do you want here?"

I blinked. What *did* I want? "I don't know. I… I can't do a relationship. Aiden needs someone to put him first, and I—"

"No." Luke smiled gently. "I meant what do you want to happen right now, Webb? What do you want me to do to you? What do you *not* want?"

"Oh." I swallowed. That was both easier and harder to answer. I knew my own face was bright red, but I forced myself to tell the truth, "I don't want to stop. I want to… I want to touch you. I want you to touch me." In demonstration, I planted both of my hands on his waist and pulled him down at the same time I thrust up.

A high-pitched whimper tore from Luke's throat, and my embarrassment fled—there was no room for anything in my brain except *want*. I wasn't sure what I was doing at all, but clearly my instincts were okay.

"Webb. Oh, *God*."

His cheeks were totally flushed, and he still looked dazed. I needed to kiss him like I needed my next breath, so I jackknifed myself up, bracing my hands behind Luke's back to hold him in place, and fit my lips against his. The kiss made my head spin but also was strangely calming, taking all the thoughts and worries in my brain and distilling them down to the single most important one in that moment. *Luke*.

"Fuck, baby—" I groaned.

"You called me that back at the pond, too," he said breathlessly.

"Did I?" I hadn't realized.

"I thought I hallucinated it. I hadn't thought that you... I hadn't imagined... *this*."

"I did," I admitted in a gravelly voice. I tugged gently on his nipple rings, and he gave a shuddery groan. "Some parts were a surprise, though."

His cock, which was trapped between our bodies, jerked at this admission, and I felt the slickness of his precum coating my stomach. I pulled away and lay back against the pillows so I could look down at the thick, engorged length of him.

The only sound in the trailer was the harsh sound of our breathing as I reached between us and gripped him again, more firmly this time, my palm encompassing the heat of him while I rubbed my thumb over his damp slit, spreading the sticky fluid there. Part of me couldn't believe I was doing this. Another part couldn't believe I'd waited so long. It felt *right*. And so fucking good.

"Wait, like this," he whispered. He moved back slightly, freeing my dick so it rose up between us, nestling against his.

"*Holy shit*. That's..."

"Good?"

"Mmpfh."

"Wait and see," he promised in a whisper.

He wrapped his hand around both of our cocks at the same time, then moved my larger hand to do the same. The heat of his dick against mine, in the warm vise of our hands, made my brain short-circuit.

Good Christ. There was no way this could get better…

And then suddenly, it *did* because he canted his hips, driving his cock through our combined fists, adding friction to the mix, and faster than I would have believed possible, I was balancing on the edge, my balls tightening up and my toes curling.

"God, Luke. *Fuck.* Like that. Just like that."

"You gonna come for me?" he demanded. "God, please do it. I wanted this so bad. Wanted you for—" He broke off with a high, keening moan. "For forever, it feels like. And I wanted to suck you off. And lick you all over. And to feel you inside me. But now… Now I want you to come for me."

"That clean little mouth can get so fucking dirty, Luke Williams," I gritted out, and then I couldn't say another goddamn thing because his fingers tightened around me, and just like that, my orgasm barreled over me, bowing my back with its force, making me cry out to the ceiling with the pleasure of it.

Luke kept going, stroking me through it, his own breaths coming faster, his hand sliding through the hot mess of my cum.

"Let me," I murmured, knocking his hand out of the way when my dick became too sensitive and jerking him the way I would jerk myself.

I watched emotions play on his face, one after another, as he writhed over me—wanting and lust and desperation and a kind of vulnerability that squeezed my heart.

"Webb. Oh, God. That's… please. I can't… I'm so close. I…"

"Come on, baby," I urged, and something about those three words—maybe the lust in my voice or the unconscious *baby*—worked like a magic incantation, because he came all over me, his release coating my abs and even my chest.

Luke groaned and collapsed against me bonelessly, heedless of the mess, tucking his face into the crook of my neck with a sigh, and even though I could feel the weight of a hundred different responsibilities pressing against me again, I pushed them back and let myself enjoy that one perfect moment.

"Well," he said, voice crisp and businesslike a moment later. "I… I certainly feel warm. So, thank you for that." The fact that his voice was still muffled against my skin sort of ruined the effect, though, and I laughed out loud.

From the protective circle of my arms, Luke laughed with me.

Despite just coming harder than I had in years, I wanted him again. And nearly as much as I wanted him, I wanted to keep him warm and satisfied. To keep him happy… which was scary as fuck.

But it was way too late to put the genie back in the bottle, just like it was impossible to un-blow the damn Unity Bugle, so I thought maybe, just maybe, I'd try to hold on to it for a little while…

Even though I knew it could only be temporary.

Chapter Thirteen

LUKE

It was funny how the smallest decisions could profoundly change your life.

Like answering an ad in a fiber arts magazine, for example.

Or blowing a bugle with your hot, grumpy lumberjackish neighbor on a cold, drunken winter's night.

Or spending an entire afternoon frotting with that grumpy neighbor after he helped you drag yourself out of a freezing cold pond and saved you from hypothermia.

Because once you made any (or all) of those tiny, slightly crazy decisions, you might find yourself living a life where your lonely Sunday morning got interrupted by two truckloads of Sundays—including that gorgeous, grumpy savior—who dragged you out of your camper wearing your baggiest jeans and rattiest sweatshirt and demanded you join them for breakfast at Panini Jack's.

"Morning, Katey. Table for eight," Webb said as Gage, Knox, Emma, Marco, Drew, Aiden, and I piled into Panini Jack's after him one Sunday morning, about a week after my fall into Pond Pond.

I still wasn't quite sure what was happening here. Why had they included me in the Sundays' Sunday breakfast outing? Was it a friendly neighbor thing, a "we're glad you didn't die in our pond" thing, or a "you touched my penis and I'd like you to do it again" thing?

All of those were fine, but if asked, I'd definitely be able to state a preference for which I hoped it was.

"Eight?" Katey repeated, frowning. "But Hawk's not with you all, and... Oh, I see." She pursed her lips when she spotted me but grudgingly asked, "You doing alright, Luke?"

"Yeah, heard you took a nasty plunge last week." Norm Avery turned on his stool at the counter to look me over, and his bushy mustache twitched. "Happened to me a time or two when I was younger."

"Same," an older lady agreed. "Not pleasant at all."

I gave them all a bright smile. I wasn't used to being the center of so much attention, but I didn't want to seem rude and awkward. "True! No harm done, though. Webb took care of me. But thanks for asking."

As well-meaning as the inquiries were, it was over-whelming to be the center of attention for the whole town. I could see the townsfolk, not to mention Webb's family, wondering why I was the only non-Sunday there. If only I had the answer myself.

"Glad to hear it." Norm reached over and thumped Webb on the shoulder. "Take care of yourself, because this one needs someone around to keep him in line."

"That's the damn truth," Knox said wryly.

Webb gave me a look that was part amusement, part... something hotter, and my palms went damp.

I wished I could read whatever thought was running through the man's mind. He hadn't seemed regretful or weird about us hooking up last weekend—on the contrary.

He'd given me a long, thorough, really *promising* kiss before he'd climbed back into his 4x4 to drive home across the dark orchard. He'd texted me sweet, silly things every day since then. He'd been his usual—well, the *new* usual—friendly self when he'd picked up Aiden on Thursday from spelling bee practice, shooting me a hot, sexy wink and a smile.

But…

I wanted more.

More of his warmth and his scent. More of his arms around me. More *talking*, since his voice was the most soothing thing on the planet… and also since I could not bring myself to text the actual questions I wanted to ask, like "Hey, so, was that the hottest sexy time in your personal history of sexy times, and if so, would you be amenable to repeating it?"

I knew he was busy, though. Maple sugar season had already peaked, and he'd been running tours all week, in addition to managing the orchard. I didn't want to be demanding… but I also wanted him to know I was very, very interested.

Today, I promised myself. *You'll ask him to come over later.*

Katey grabbed menus and started chatting to Em about softball tryouts—Katey, apparently, was the best pitcher the Hollow Swingers had ever had, and she wanted Em to join the team also.

But as she led us through the restaurant to a table in the back, with me at the front of the group, Alan Laroche waved me over.

"Luke! D'you see the game last night? Close call, eh?"

"Oh. Yeah. A heartbreaker of a game," I agreed.

"Refs missed a dozen penalties against Toronto," he said mournfully.

I sensed Webb behind me without turning around, and

he spoke over my shoulder. "Wasn't the refs' fault. Neutral zone trap killed you." He prodded my back and added teasingly, "Wouldn't you say, Luke?"

I lifted my chin. "Actually, I think we would've been fine if we'd had our goalie back, but we just don't have the depth on defense that we had a couple seasons ago." I hoped I'd gotten all of that lingo right.

"True," Alan sighed. "But we can keep hoping." He offered me a fist, and I bumped it.

"What the hell was that?" Webb's deep whisper curled around the nape of my neck as we walked on, making me shiver.

"That's called... I streamed the game last night while I crocheted," I said a little smugly, glancing over my shoulder. "And I maybe also swan dived down an internet rabbit hole of editorials for an entire afternoon. They're my *dudes*, Webb. When I commit, I commit."

"I thought I was supposed to be teaching you hockey," he teased, and my breathing hitched.

I tried to focus, but it wasn't easy with him that close. "I knew you were busy, and once I get obsessed with a new subject, I want to learn everything about it, so..."

"Interesting," he purred. "I was introduced to a new subject last week, too. And I have an internet connection also."

Could he be serious? My face heated, and I tried my best not to stammer. I failed. "I... I think we should compare notes."

He passed in front of me, and as he did, he slid his pinky finger along the edge of my hand, where no one could see it. The sensation traveled directly to my balls. "I agree."

Holy freaking mackerel. I was going to pop wood in the middle of a family breakfast.

No, really, parents. Despite the child misplacement, the drunken carousing, the massive hangover, the incident with the roof, and my incredibly inappropriate breakfast shenanigans, I'm incredibly trustworthy.

In desperation, I stopped at Maryanne's table to thank her for the soup she'd sent over the day after my dunking. I should have known I'd get sucked into a brief conversation with her and her friend Penny about the Spring Fling, but it at least helped me gather my wits before I reached the Sundays' table.

Until I realized the only empty seat at the table was on the end, directly beside Aiden and across from Webb.

Aiden patted the chair excitedly, and I slid into it just as Katey started rattling off the specials.

"We've got eggs Florentine, raspberry cheesecake pancakes, and the french toast of the day is banana bread french toast. What'll it be?"

I'd barely opened my menu when Drew started rattling off his order, quickly followed by everyone else.

I sighed. One of these days, I'd actually get to look at the menu at this place, but apparently not that day. "I-I guess I'll have the ras—"

"The eggs," Katey said. "*Fine.*" She tapped the tip of her pen against her order form and departed.

I closed my eyes briefly and huffed out a breath. It *was* fine. Eggs were better for me anyway.

Webb eyed me across the table. "Ask her to come back. Tell her you changed your mind."

I shook my head. If Katey being annoyed at me was the price I had to pay for having Webb in my life, I was more than willing to pay it. Besides, I knew she'd come around.

"If you want, you can have a bite of mine," Aiden offered. He leaned across the space between our chairs and into my side so I had to put my arm over his shoulders. "Chocolate pancakes with chocolate chips and M&Ms and peanut butter sauce."

"Good gravy. I feel a sugar rush just thinking about it."

He giggled, and I held him tighter. He'd been a little clingy with me all week after the pond incident but in a sweet way, sitting with me after spelling bee practice and asking me questions about my mom and what it was like growing up in North Carolina. And his journal entry last Monday had been so good, I'd encouraged him to share it with Webb.

"Did you tell your dad about what you wrote for your assignment?" I murmured.

Aiden shook his head and blushed. "No."

"What assignment?" Webb asked.

Katey delivered a pot of coffee, and Webb poured me a cup.

"Aiden wrote a journal entry about his favorite hero last Monday."

"Oh… Did you pick Thor?" Webb surmised. "He's got that hammer."

"See?" Aiden gave me a speaking glance.

I huffed. Sundays bred true, anyway.

"No, he chose a real-life hero," I corrected.

Aiden squirmed in his seat. "I maybe wrote about you saving Mr. Williams from the pond. How you knew just what to do and made us all feel safe. It was kinda awesome."

I had never seen Webb look so poleaxed. Not when the mayor had read the scroll to us. Not when he'd had sex with a man for the first time last weekend.

"Wow. That's… Thanks, Aiden. I don't know what to say."

"He's a very talented writer," I said softly. "And he sees a lot of things clearly."

"What are we talking about here? I used to be a good writer," Knox said, only hearing the last part of the conversation. "Wrote some poetry. Back in the day."

"*Shut it*," Webb said darkly. "Your poetry is not family-friendly."

Knox took a sip of his coffee. "There once was a man who liked apple picking…"

Webb groaned.

Knox grinned. "Who was in need of a really deep dic—"

"Oookay." Gage clamped a hand over Knox's mouth as Marco and Drew snort-laughed. "I think we'll save your poetry for later, baby."

I covered my mouth with my hand to hide my giggle. "So, where's Hawk this morning?" I ventured, trying to change the subject.

Webb shrugged. "Mayor York is assembling a committee to study the site plan, and Hawk signed up. He stayed home to study up."

"Maybe you should sign up, Luke," Marco suggested.

"Me?" I shook my head. The last thing I wanted to do was upset the delicate new reputation I seemed to have earned in Little Pippin Hollow. "Nah. I don't know enough about it."

"Which is why you'd actually be great," Drew said consideringly as Katey set out our food. "You're objective, and not a lot of people around here can say that."

"But you'd have to speak your mind," Webb challenged softly.

I bristled. "Hey. I speak my mind just fine when it matters."

Of course Katey set my platter of spinach and eggs in front of me at that exact moment.

I stared at the plate of contradiction.

After a beat, I forced myself to smile hugely. "This looks *wonderful*, Katey. Exactly what I wanted and didn't know I wanted! Thank you so much!"

Webb rolled his eyes and hid his smile behind his coffee cup. He seemed relaxed and happy, so I relaxed, too, enjoying my breakfast and letting the merry sounds of the Sundays' conversation wash over me.

"Found them, Uncle Ernie!" an eager voice cried. "The handfasters are here!"

I looked at Webb in panic. Was this déjà vu? Was I doomed to forever associate breakfast with the horror of being attacked by colonial-era bylaws? Both of us turned simultaneously to find Mayor York and his reporter hurrying toward us, cameraman in tow.

Genevieve appeared beside our table first. "You two are impossible to track down," she told me and Webb, half joke and half accusation. "I had to run a lame backstory piece on this week's Hand-Fast Watch where I interviewed a professor at Hannabury about colonial marriages. Snooze-fest! I could feel my ratings nosediving. But this week will be more exciting."

It would?

"Ernie," Webb said gruffly. "For God's sake, man, we're just trying to eat breakfast——"

The mayor hesitated momentarily, but when Genevieve gave him a thumbs-up and the camera began rolling, he smoothed his jacket and tried to look professional.

"I'm Genevieve York-Muller, and *this*… is Hand-Fast Watch!"

Aiden poked me. "What's a Hand-Fast Watch?" he whispered.

I exchanged a look with Webb and responded in the same soft voice. "Remember your dad told you about us blowing the bugle without knowing what it meant? Well, a bunch of people would like to make us finish all the silly steps. But don't worry, they can't actually make us do anything, okay?"

"Yeah." Aiden looked speculatively at Genevieve and the mayor. "Yeah, okay."

I turned back in time to hear Ernest York say, "… it is my solemn duty as mayor to see that our bylaws are upheld here in historic Little Pippin Hollow—where you can find both colonial artifacts *and* a genuine colonial interpreter at the Feeny Museum on Friend Street, not to mention agricultural tourism that harkens back to yesteryear at many of our local farms! Email Julia at Little Pippin Hollow dot gov for more details!"

Webb gritted his teeth, and I knew why. It was one thing for the two of us to have to deal with this stuff, and even to pretend it was real… but a whole other thing for it to happen in front of the other Sundays, especially Aiden.

"And now," Mayor York continued, "without further ado… it's time for the ceremonial ticking of the scroll."

"If this is about the roof thing," Webb began crossly, "you're barking up the wrong tree. The work hasn't even been done yet."

The mayor ignored him. "Whereas Thomas Webb Sunday and Luke Guilford Williams were seen immersing themselves together in a pond during their second handfast week, with over a dozen Hollowans as witnesses, I declare the Tenth Confirmation Task *complete.*"

I gasped. "Are you kidding? The public bathing requirement? I *fell* in and almost got hypothermia."

"But it was really romantic the way Webb carried you

out," a voice that sounded like Mark the Herd Leader argued.

"You two make me believe in fate," another man called.

"I knew you were in love way back last fall. Didn't I say, Irma? I said, those two are in love!" a third person gushed.

"I hope someday *I* get rescued from an icy pond," a woman's voice sighed.

"I don't suppose you two would be interested in doing a dramatic re-enactment of the near drowning?" Genevieve ventured hopefully. "For our viewers to—?"

"*No*," Webb snapped.

"Ah, well." Undaunted, Genevieve turned her attention to Aiden. "What do you think of all this, young man? Your father being handfasted to your teacher and taking part in this amazing town tradition? Isn't it wonderful?" She thrust a microphone across me and into Aiden's face.

I was so outraged, it took me a minute to access my powers of speech.

"W-well," Aiden began, looking tentatively from Webb to me. "Mr. Williams is awesome, so uh—"

"No, ma'am." I stood up, pushed the microphone aside, and gave Genevieve a defiant look. "No. This hand-fasting thing is cute and heartwarming. Y'all are in love with love. I get it. But you don't get to ask a *minor child* interview questions without asking his father's permission first. He's *seven*. Seven! He has no comment whatsoever, and if I hear that you've tried to ask him for one, I will... I will *consult my attorney*."

They didn't need to know that it might take him a decade to get back to me since freakin' Stephen Fox never returned my calls.

I swallowed nervously once the first burst of emotion burned off, but a voice called from a nearby table, "That's my kid's teacher right there! Hot dang. We need more like Luke Williams!" and I stood straighter.

So much for pushing the emotion away. Feeling the support of the community was punching all my feels buttons and leaving me a little too raw.

"We would have had a parental release signed before his interview aired," Genevieve grumbled. "Obviously."

"What's going on here?" Jack stalked out of the back, pulling on a sweatshirt. It looked like he hadn't slept all night.

"Official town business!" Mayor York said happily.

"Handfasting business," Genevieve confirmed with a nod.

Jack looked at Webb's furious face, then at me, standing in front of Aiden like a human shield, and he scowled. "Right, this has gone far enough. Do your handfasting business on your own time, Ernie. Not in my diner."

"But, Jack—"

Jack's usual friendly demeanor was nowhere to be found. "Let the Sundays eat their meals in peace. Call it family values," he suggested. He clapped the mayor on the shoulder while I tried not to chin-wobble in response to being inadvertently included in the Sunday family.

Ernie nodded. "You're right. I'm sorry. My office definitely cares about families enjoying breakfast uninterrupted. From now on, Genevieve and I will catch up to the happy couple elsewhere. Have a good day, everyone."

I imagined them pounding on the door to my camper and wished I could take back my outburst.

"Or you could give up this whole Hand-Fast Watch thing!" Webb called.

The mayor pretended not to hear him as he and Genevieve hustled out the door.

As I sat back down, I could feel all of the Sundays—

heck, maybe everyone in the restaurant—staring at me, but I couldn't meet their gazes. I felt weirdly embarrassed, like *I'd* been the one to cause the scene.

I forced a smile. "Aiden, how are those pancakes? I—"

Webb pushed his chair back from the table with a screech and stood. He took a single step in my direction, and before I'd had a chance to process what he was doing, let alone protest, he'd grabbed me by the back of the neck, hauled me against him, and kissed me quickly but soundly, right there in front of everyone.

"Thank you for standing up for my boy," he murmured against my lips before he pulled back a second later.

"Oh," I said articulately. My heart fluttered against my chest, and my cheeks *burned*. "That's… I… oh."

I was maybe a teeny bit going to need a fainting couch. I looked around just in case Panini Jack's had a heretofore unseen historical theme that might lend itself to a purpose-built chaise.

No luck. I tried to catch my breath and find some chill.

No luck with that either.

My emotions were riding a roller coaster, and there seemed to be no end to the ride.

Webb had just kissed me *in public*.

In front of his entire family.

And there would be no doubt in any observer's mind—not that anyone around here seemed inclined to doubt anyway—that Webb and I were a couple for *real*.

Webb nodded, like he'd done what he'd intended, then let me go and returned to his seat. "Easy on the chocolate, Aiden," he warned. "I told you this breakfast was a treat, but if you start licking the plate, we're gonna have words."

"But, Dad!" Aiden exclaimed. I could see the excitement in his eyes. "You just kissed Mr. Wil—"

"Drink your milk," Webb said quickly, while Knox

helpfully clapped a hand over Aiden's mouth before he could say anything else. The same excitement danced in Knox's eyes, too. And Gage's... and Drew's... and I was not going to look at anyone else at the table in case I completely lost my ability to process oxygen.

"He was just saying thanks for looking out for you, kiddo," Knox said. "That's all."

Aiden's eyes were big when he nodded. As Knox pulled his hand away, Aiden couldn't help but blurt, "Mr. Williams is the best!"

Gage threw back his head and laughed. "He sure is, buddy. I love this town. I love this diner. And I seriously love this family."

I bit my lip and grinned down at my eggs. I was pretty sure I did, too.

We were nearly finished eating, and I had mostly calmed down, when Helena Fortnum stopped by our table. I'd met her a couple of times—she was teaching royalty in the Hollow and stopped by the school frequently to read to the children—but I'd never actually spoken to her before. She was a little bit intimidating, with her long, gray braid and her way-too-intelligent eyes.

"Where's Hawkins?" she asked without preamble.

"Home," Em said. "Learning way too much about Fogg Peak."

She nodded. "Excellent. I'd hoped he'd sign up for Ernest's committee. We need more young people involved in local politics. Just a few more months until you're old enough to get involved, Emma." Her gaze swung to me. "What about you, Mr. Williams? You seem caring and intelligent."

"See?" Marco said pointedly. "Told you. You'd be good on the mayor's committee."

"Oh, I… don't think so. I'm not much of a political person," I demurred. "I teach and take care of my sheep. That's plenty."

"Your sheep." Her eyes narrowed. "Do you raise them for wool?"

I nodded. "It's just a small flock, and this spring will be my first shearing. But I hope to have enough wool for a few crochet projects next winter."

A slow smile spread across her face. "You need to become a Hooker!"

I blinked. "A… pardon?"

"The Little Pippin Hookers. That's our fiber arts group. I can't believe no one's told you about us yet! We meet the second and fourth Tuesday of the month out at the Apple of My Eye—that's my bed-and-breakfast. You should stop by. We've got a great artisan community in this town, Luke."

"I… I definitely will." My excitement was probably all out of proportion to the event, but I felt like I'd been waiting months for this invitation, even though I hadn't known the group existed until now.

It felt like acceptance. Like an arena where I knew I had something to contribute. And with the taste of Webb's kiss on my lips, it was hard not to feel hopeful.

I beamed at her. "Thank you so much."

And I felt my emotional roller coaster cresting another rise.

"Hey, Mr. Williams? Your phone's vibrating." Aiden tugged on my sleeve. "It says *Mom: FaceTime*."

"Thanks, bud. I'll get it in a minute. So, what kinds of crafts—?" I began asking Ms. Fortnum.

"Or I could get it now," Aiden interrupted with a grin. "So I can meet your mom."

"Aiden," Webb warned, but I snorted and waved him off.

"It's fine, Webb. My mom will love it. Go ahead, Aiden."

"Luke, honey, I only have a minute, but I— Oh, *hello*. Who's this handsome devil?"

"I'm Aiden Sunday," Aiden said proudly.

"No," my mom argued. "Not possible. Luke said Aiden was only seven. You look much too mature to be seven."

Aiden sat up straighter. "Well, I *am* going to be eight in August."

"Ah, that must be it," she agreed. "Sweetheart, is my Lukey there?"

"I'm here," I said, taking the phone. I turned the camera around and showed her everyone at the table. "Mom, these are my friends. That's Drew Sunday, and Marco, and Emma, and Knox, and Gage—" They all waved obediently. "—and this is Ms. Fortnum. Oh, and you already met Aiden and—"

"Well, hey, there, Webb!"

"Hi, Ms. Williams," Webb said, smiling and waving at the phone. My heart let out a little sigh.

"I can't wait to meet all of your friends in person."

"Aw." I turned the camera back around to face me. I wanted that, too. Especially now that I actually had friends for her to meet. "One of these days," I agreed. "Maybe next year. When you're stronger."

"Sooner than that!" Her face was flushed with excitement. "That's why I'm calling. We got the all-clear from my doctor on Friday, and Susie just got the time off work. We're heading up there in three weeks!"

I blinked. Then I blinked some more.

Aaaannd the roller coaster dipped again.

"Lukey? Lukey, did your FaceTime freeze?"

I wheezed out a breath. "I… you… I have school," I said desperately. This couldn't be happening. Not that I wanted her to be too sick to travel, it was just… no. No. It was too soon. There was too much left undone at the house, and she'd be so worried.

My chest felt so tight, I could hardly pull in enough breath to fake a bright smile. "And is your doctor really *sure* it's safe for you to travel? Do we believe her?"

"I'm fine! And don't you worry about us. Susie and I can amuse ourselves while you're at work. Strolling the fields and exploring the attics and whatnot."

"Oh." I was pretty sure the noise came out more like a cross between a gasp and a whimper. "About the attics…" I looked at Webb in panic.

He nodded encouragingly… but I had no idea what he was encouraging me to do.

"I can't wait to meet you," Aiden said. "We can eat chocolate pancakes!"

"It's a date, babydoll! Okay. Off to the movies with Sue. Love to all of you! Talk to you soon, Lukey."

She hung up.

I stared at the phone.

Gage's voice seemed to be coming at me through a tunnel. "Does she know about the handfasting? Because she seems like the kind of person to get a kick out of that."

Knox looked at me with furrowed brows, but his words were for Gage. "Hush, baby. Can't you see he's——"

I shoved back my chair, making a painful screeching noise on the floor that seemed to draw all the eyes in the entire place onto me. My face flamed, and my skin prickled. It was too much. All of this was too much. The townspeople being nice to me and including me in their thoughts and plans, the mayor bringing up the handfasting and trying to interview Aiden, the Sunday family including me in breakfast, my mom springing an unexpected visit on me when I was living in a tangled web of my own lies… and Webb… Webb kissing me full on the lips in front of the entire town as if… as if…

As if we meant something to each other.

I stumbled through the cafe, dodging chairs, nosy stares, Katey's glare, and God knew what other stuff in my desperate attempt to escape.

When the frigid cold air of Vermont took what little breath I had away, I braced my hands against the metal siding.

Mistake. The cold burned my palms and left me shivering.

Real Vermonsters probably knew better than to touch freezing metal with warm bare skin. Yet another way I wasn't cut out to live here in the Hollow.

So I did what my people have done for centuries when faced with an insurmountable challenge.

I closed my eyes and let the tears come.

Chapter Fourteen

WEBB

Ah, shit.

"Wait, what just happened?" Ms. Fortnum demanded as I pushed my chair back to stand. "Is Luke okay?"

"He will be," I assured her. I'd make sure of it. I hesitated before sharing Luke's business, but they needed to understand... some of it, anyway. "Luke's house... Ben Pond let the whole thing practically fall to ruin before he left town, and when Luke won it, it was unlivable. It needs a new roof, plumbing and electrical work, a new kitchen, the whole nine yards. Luke's been living in a camper on the property for eight months because he doesn't have the money to repair it. And his mom doesn't know any of this. She's been sick, and he didn't want to worry her."

"The poor guy," Em said. "That's awful."

"If Ben Pond comes back to town," Ms. Fortum said severely, "I'm going to give him a very *large* piece of my mind."

"And now his mom's coming to visit?" Marco gasped. "Lord."

"Exactly. Just hang tight while I go take care of him, okay?"

"Webb," Knox said, face creased in genuine concern. "If he's having a panic attack, get him to focus on his breathing." He hesitated. "If Gage and I can help…"

"I'll let you know."

"Take him home," Drew advised. "Warm him up. I left a rhubarb pie cooling on the counter. The boy seemed real fond of my pies."

"Or maybe a walk," Em said. "Get him some fresh air."

"Dad, can I help?" Aiden piped up. "Maybe he wants a hug."

I hesitated at that one but shook my head. "Later, okay, bud? I don't want to overwhelm him." I was pretty sure he was already overwhelmed enough.

I barely waited for Aiden's nod before I headed out the door, following Luke into the chilly false-spring morning. It wasn't hard to locate him. He leaned his hands against the cafe's exterior wall, huddled into his oversized sweatshirt, breathing fast and looking very much alone.

"Hey." I didn't think twice before reaching for him and pulling him against my chest. I felt my own anxiety go down the moment he was in my arms. "It's gonna be okay."

Luke immediately wrapped his arms around me and buried his face in the shoulder of my shirt, like he needed the contact as much as I did.

"I'm so sorry. I-I-I'm upset over nothing. So ridiculous."

"No. Hush, baby. It's not nothing. I get it. We're a lot to take." I ran a hand over his cowlicky hair. The strands felt like silk under my fingers. "Seven Sundays was plenty. Maybe too much. Add in that call from your mom and you must feel totally out of control. But we're going to take care of the repairs, and things will be fine. You'll see."

I'd watched Luke's stress level tick up like the pressure gauge on an engine throughout breakfast. The townsfolk all up in his business. My boisterous, teasing family. Ernie and his damn Hand-Fast Watch.

I'd hoped Luke would let me know when he'd had enough. That he'd speak up and call a time-out. But I'd forgotten one crucial detail—Luke had spent the longest time thinking everyone in town didn't care about him. Maybe he didn't feel like he *could* push back. Or maybe he was just so unused to it, he didn't know how.

"I-it's not just that." Luke sucked in an unsteady breath. "I just… *ugh*." His fingers gripped the back of my shirt. "It's fine. I'm being silly. Gosh, everyone must think I'm—"

"Every person at that table wanted to be sure you're okay," I said, leaving no room for misinterpretation. "That's why it took me so long to come after you. Not a single one of them is judging you or upset at you. They only want to help. And if that means telling them all to back off and go jump in a lake—or maybe a very icy pond —that's okay, too."

He pulled back slightly, his gorgeous face a little red and damp. "No, it's not that. They're great. I-I like it! I just have so many *questions*, and my mind started racing, and I couldn't— Oh. Good morning, Mrs. Graber. Yes, it's a lovely day. No, I'm not sure if the groundhog saw his shadow. Maybe Google. Google would know. You too. Take care." He rolled his eyes and huffed out a laugh. "I sometimes don't know if I love this town or it's going to drive me demented."

"The mark of a true Hollowan," I said wryly. "Come on. Let's find a little privacy."

I tugged him down the street and through the town common to where the gazebo stood as the sole, silent sentry over the empty park and nicely shoveled paths.

It really *was* a nice day, especially for March, but I doubted Luke agreed, so instead of sitting him down on the cold gazebo bench, I took a seat, pulled him onto my lap, and settled my arms around him.

He rested his head on my shoulder like he was collecting his thoughts, and I was in no rush. It felt really, *really* good to have him in my arms again, and I savored the feeling.

I wondered idly how many winters he'd have to spend in the Hollow before he got acclimated to the temperature, and selfishly, I hoped it was *a lot*. I liked warming him up. It was a definite silver lining to being fake-handfasted.

"This is nice," he said after a minute.

"It is. I missed you this week."

His body tensed a little. "Yeah? I… I missed you, too. I wasn't sure if you… if you'd want to… again."

I tugged on the ends of his hair so he'd lift his head and look at me. "Was that one of the questions on your mind? Let me clear that up right now. I definitely, definitely do."

He bit his lip. "Yeah, I kinda clued in when you kissed me. In front of everyone."

I winced. I hadn't even factored that into my list of Luke-stressors.

"Right," I said ruefully. "Maybe I should have asked you before I did that, huh?"

"No," he blurted quickly, and then his words began tumbling out like he'd been holding them back. "You should kiss me whenever you want. I just didn't expect it. I didn't know how you were feeling after Saturday, since up to then you considered yourself, you know, *straight*, and then you were busy last week, which I totally, *totally* understood, but then you came and got me for breakfast out of the blue and I… I wondered…" He trailed off.

God, he was gorgeous.

I cupped his cheek, drew his face down to mine, and kissed him with all the pent-up passion of a very long week, my tongue stroking boldly and thoroughly over his. He sighed into my mouth, and I felt the last of his tension bleed away.

"Okay, let's unpack this. I'm not straight." I shrugged. "I don't know how I identify, but I have three gay brothers, so being with a guy isn't a crisis for me. Not at all. I resisted it at first because… I dunno. You think you know yourself, right? And then you find out that actually, you're an ever-changing process. Who I was ten years ago doesn't have to be who I am today. But I'm okay with it. Okay?"

He nodded.

"I told my family I was bringing you for breakfast with us because we're friends… but I think they *might* have seen through that, what with the kissing and all? They're pretty perceptive, so probably."

And I was expecting a ration of teasing as a result, but it had been worth it to see the stunned, happy look on Luke's face.

"And as far as doing it again, I'd really like to keep kissing you," I continued. "And to compare those notes we discussed earlier, if you're good with that."

"Very good with that." He blushed rosily, and I wasn't sure how I'd ever failed to find his blushes sexy. It was the most obvious thing in the universe now.

"So, that's, like, three questions answered," I said once he'd collapsed against my shoulder again. "Look at us, uncomplicating shit left and right. What else is on your mind?"

He laughed, just like I'd expected him to. "When you and I uncomplicate things, they seem to get more complicated, but okay." He blew out a breath. "This is gonna sound weird, but everyone is so... nice. I don't know how to take it. I always wanted to live in a close-knit community, you know? I always wanted a... a big family. And it sucked when I thought everyone didn't like me. But now, they *do*—"

"And it's a little much?"

"No! No, the opposite. I mean, it's overwhelming, yeah, but it's incredible. It's just... how long will it last? What's going to happen when we call off the handfasting? What if I get used to people bringing me soup, and asking how I am, and being a Hooker, and then..." He shook his head. "It was hard enough not having it when I didn't know what I was missing."

I rubbed my chin against the top of his head thoughtfully. "Luke, I know you think no one liked you much before the handfasting. And maybe there *were* some folks who fed off my bad feelings when Aiden went missing. If that's so, I'm sorry for it. But... maybe people just weren't sure how to get to know you."

"What do you mean? I was friendly—"

"Of course you were. But Hollowans tend to show their affection by getting allllll up in your business and solving problems you didn't know you had. If they offered you help and you didn't take it, or asked you to join things and you didn't feel comfortable, they probably backed off because they figured you weren't interested. But that doesn't mean they don't *like* you. They're not just a supportive community; they're like family. You know?"

I felt him frown, and it hit me that he *didn't* know. He was an only child, too. He really had no frame of reference for this place.

"Okay, take me and Knox, for example. He's my brother. I know way too much about him. I know all his admirable qualities—there are a lot—and I also know love *must* be blind in order for Gage to tolerate his grouchy ass."

Luke snorted. "Knox is sweet."

"Sometimes. Most of the time. But sometimes *not*," I said. "The point is, no matter how much shit he gives me, no matter how tempted I am to chuck him off the face of the earth... I would burn the world to keep him safe. He's family. He's *mine*. Kinda like you said about your house. It's yours to take care of, even if it's not perfect. The Hollow is like that. We care about each other, even when we don't agree with or understand each other. Those idiots getting moony-eyed over you *romantically* falling in an icy pond just want you—us—to be happy."

"Oh." His fingers worried the collar of my shirt. "Really?"

"Yup. Once you're in, you're in." I paused. "I'm making it sound like the mafia, aren't I? Or maybe a cult."

He let out a soft laugh, sounding more relaxed than he had all morning.

"The good news," I went on, "is that no one is going to stop being your friend just because we don't complete the handfast. Promise. But it also means you should consider letting people help you once in a while. Trust people to do that for you. Otherwise, how will they feel okay letting you help them when they need it?"

"Wow. That's..."

"Profound?" I asked smugly. "Is profound the word you're looking for?"

"Not quite."

"Convincing and also sexy?" I asked hopefully.

He snickered but then nipped at the side of my neck

and made me groan. "No… but also yes. I'm all in on joining the Pippin Hollow Mafia."

"Awesome. I get a referral bonus," I teased.

"But you should consider taking your own advice."

My grin slid into a confused frown. "What do you mean?"

He shook his head. "Well, you might've noticed that you tend to—"

"Hey, Webb? Luke?" Gage stood on the path, a respectful distance away. "Sorry to interrupt, but I got delegated to come find you. Helena got a great idea about your house, and she called in a bunch of favors and… I think we figured everything out, if you wanna come back to the diner and hear about it. Or if not, that's okay, and Knox said to remind you it's not selfish to focus on your mental health."

"An idea about my house?" Luke looked up at me.

"I told them a little bit of what's going on," I said in a low voice. "Everyone seemed really surprised. You hadn't told anyone about the state of the place, had you?"

"Who would I have told? And I was taking care of things—"

"Yourself. I know. But remember what I said about letting people help a little?"

Luke nodded.

"It's especially true when they're volunteering to help fix up your house in time for your mom's visit."

"Fix up—" His eyes widened. "But that's not a *little*, Webb. That's… that's *huge*. I couldn't possibly—"

"You really could. Because if I know Helena Fortnum, she's called a dozen people, and they're all gonna be thrilled to help. And this visit will put your mom's mind at ease." I paused. "But if you really don't want to, then say so, and I'll back you. I promise. I don't want you to feel pressured."

"Hey, guys?" Gage shifted from foot to foot. "You remember I might be a Vermonter in my heart, but my blood is still Floridian, right? It's freakin' cold out here. What should I tell them?"

"Tell them—" Luke called, then hesitated. "Tell them we're coming to hear the plan. And thank them."

Gage scurried off, and I kissed Luke swiftly before lifting him to his feet.

"Have I mentioned recently how much I like you, Luke Williams?" I demanded. "Because I do. I'm really glad we're... whatever we are."

The unspoken label hung in the air between us, but it didn't seem awkward. It seemed hopeful. Exciting. Full of promise.

"And thanks for getting my kid to see me as a hero, too," I continued. "That was... unexpected." Kind of ironic, too; I'd have thought Aiden would have picked his beloved *Mr. Williams* over me any day of the week.

Luke smiled softly. "I didn't *get* him to do anything, Webb. Aiden's a smart kid. He already knew his dad was great... just like I did."

My face went hot and I cleared my throat. I wanted to kiss that soft smile more than I wanted my next breath.

Luke's eyes were bright, like maybe he was thinking something similar, and I realized if we stayed out here any longer, things were going to turn indecent.

He shot me a teasing grin. "So, would now be the time to talk about the apple tithes you might owe me?" he asked. "You know, as part of Ye Olde Friendship Agreement?"

I slung my arm over his shoulder as we walked back

toward the diner. "I think I might have a better way to repay you. We can discuss it later. *Privately.*"

For the first time in a while, I felt optimistic. My family was whole and happy, things with Amanda were going better than expected, spring was in the air, and I was confident that if the town came together, we could get Luke's problems sorted…

But in our excitement, we forgot the issue that had brought us together in the first place… until Genevieve and Hand-Fast Watch showed up at the house.

With that motherfucking scroll.

Chapter Fifteen

LUKE

You could get a lot of work done in three weeks if you put your mind to it… assuming you also had the entire town of Little Pippin Hollow behind you.

With one day to go until my mom's visit, the work on the house was almost done, from the new slate roof, to the updated kitchen, to the sturdy new front door under the repainted portico. Even Mother Nature seemed to have gotten on board, with forsythia shrubs blooming yellow along one whole side of the long driveway and crocuses poking their fat, purple heads out of the soil.

Today was bright and sunny, warm enough to convince me maybe Little Pippin Hollow was actually going to come out of its winter shell one of these days. Regardless, it was a great day for a final push, and the town had turned out en masse to make it happen.

Jones Bell was here with a crew finishing the exterior painting on the house, several of my students and their parents were here painting the fence around the sheep enclosure, while younger children ran around the patchy grass or petted my very tolerant sheep under Em Sunday's close supervision.

Mary Duarte and daughter-in-law Chrissy were busy directing a crew on cleaning up and staging furniture pulled out of the attics and one of the barns, while I helped Drew set up long folding tables to hold all of the potluck dishes that seemed to be multiplying before my very eyes, ready to feed the hungry crew. Someone—I strongly suspected Jack —had even brought a portable speaker, and eighties rock streamed through the air, giving the afternoon a party vibe.

I was so incredibly thankful that so many people had been genuinely happy to pitch in and help me and that I'd hardly had to dip into the home improvement loan Ellie Walcott had fast-tracked in order to make it happen.

But it had been a *long* three weeks, and God I was ready for this all to be done.

I was ready to have a little bit of peace and quiet in my life again.

And, I thought with a sigh as I watched Webb disappear through the front door carrying a bedside table, I was *really* ready to see my gorgeous, sexy betrothed up close and personal for more than ten minutes at a stretch.

"Luke! Thanks so much for having us!" A Hooker named Estelle kissed me on my cheek. "This is my husband, Ralph. He brought his drill, and I'm ready to clean. Tell me where to put these pies, and we'll get to work!"

"Oh, wow." Had she actually just thanked *me*? "Nice to meet you, Ralph. Thank *you* so much for coming. Pies go anywhere you can find a spot. Drew's got an organization system, I think, but he went to grab some—"

"Cider!" Drew finished, dragging a cooler across the grass. "It's the batch from last fall. Just bottled it up a few weeks ago, so I thought I'd use you all as guinea pigs before I send some over to the Bugle. I'm calling it *Pippin' Good*."

"Always happy to try your cider." Ralph set down his drills and rubbed his hands together eagerly.

But when Drew pulled out the first bottle and uncapped it, he handed it to me. "You look like a man who could use a cool drink, Luke."

I sipped the cold cider gratefully. "Wow. This is delicious. Grown and brewed in the Hollow," I read off the label.

He nodded. "Folks love the hometown connection. See the logo of the apple tree over the well? Emma drew that."

"I love it. Did you—?"

"Luke, which room gets the iron bedstead from the attic?" Hawk called from the front door.

"Second-floor front room, please," I called back. He nodded and disappeared.

"Luke!" Aiden rushed up, dressed in his Nature Scout uniform and brandishing a length of rope, breathless with excitement and panic. "Can you help me with my constrictor knots? *Please*? My mom was s'posed to be here half an hour ago so she could help me practice before Scouts and she didn't come yet, and I asked my dad and he said he would, but then Mr. Avery—not the actual Mr. Avery, but Mr. Avery's son, who's also Mr. Avery, you know? —almost dropped a table going up the stairs, and Dad yelled, 'Holy *sugar*, Anders, be careful or you'll kill yourself!' and Mr. Avery said, 'Holy *sugar*, Webb, you sound like your boyfriend,' and are you and Dad *boyfriends*, like Uncle Knox and Uncle Gage, because Dad said the handfasting was all a misunderstanding, but I think he meant to say *shit* and *didn't*, and do you stop swearing when you have a boyfriend, I wanna know?" he spewed without pausing for air.

"Whoa! Deep breath. How much chocolate have you eaten, kiddo?" I ran my free hand over his head. "Yes, I can practice knots with you, but—" I began.

At the same time, a deep voice said from right behind me, "Aiden Sunday. Language."

My stomach flipped giddily.

"Dad!" Aiden beamed. "You came!"

"Told you I'd only be a minute, then I'd help you with your knots." Webb came to stand beside me, and as he always did these days, as soon as I was within touching distance, he pulled my front against his side and let his big hand caress my hip, erasing every square inch of space between us.

He rested his chin on the top of my head, sucked in a big lungful of air, and made a little noise in my ear halfway between a grumble and a sigh.

So as *I* always did these days, I sank into the firmly muscled, pine-and-clean-flannel-scented warmth of him and tried very hard not to pop wood.

He took the drink from my hand and studied the label. "Drew's new batch of cider?"

His familiar voice made me shiver for reasons completely unrelated to the temperature outside. It was freaking addictive.

I nodded, and he took a sip, putting his mouth right over the spot where I'd drunk earlier. I repressed a lustful groan.

"You doing okay?" he asked.

"Oh, yeah," I said in a strangled voice. "I'm great."

And I was. Not just because my mom was coming and I'd missed her, not just because I'd somehow landed in the middle of a town that cared so much, but because when Webb's arms were around me, I felt like I was actually living the fairy-tale adventure my mom had wanted for me… at least temporarily.

Now if I could just get some time *alone* with the man so my poor cock could stop responding to the slightest whiff of Webb, I'd be perfectly happy. Thanks to my house, and his family, and my job, and his orchard, though we'd seen each other more than ever recently, we hadn't had the chance to do more than kiss and a little handsy exploration.

And for a person who hadn't had sex since moving to Vermont, suddenly going three weeks without seeing Webb naked and knowing we wouldn't be interrupted in the span of ten minutes seemed incredibly difficult.

"So do you?" Aiden prompted. He picked up my wrist and looped the rope around it, frowning in concentration. "Because I think Knox and Gage are doing it wrong."

"Doing what wrong?" Knox demanded from over by the food table. His hair and his sweatshirt were both covered in a fine layer of plaster dust.

"Being a boyfriend," Aiden said matter-of-factly. "You could take lessons from my dad and Luke."

Knox looked from Aiden to me, then settled his gaze on Webb and lifted one eyebrow mockingly. "Is that so, Webb? You offering boyfriend lessons now? *Interesting.*"

Webb flushed. "No. I didn't say—"

"What do you think, Goodman?" Knox interrupted. "Do we need Webb to show us how it's done? Oooh, maybe he could get Genevieve York-Muller out here for a Very Special Episode of Hand-Fast Watch, where my brother shares some tips and tricks on boyfriending. Enlighten us poor idiots who've been half-assing it up to now. Tell me, kids, how many more handfasting require-ments have you knocked off the list in the past three weeks? None?"

The answer *should* have been none, but I'd had an icy patch on my driveway, and when Webb had taken me to Ed's Pippin Pickings to buy some salt on the Orchard discount, Ed had been so excited, he'd contacted the mayor immediately. He and Genevieve had stopped us in the parking lot for an impromptu Scroll-Ticking, where they marked off Part the Fourth.

But that hardly counted, and Knox knew it.

So far, the count stood at *three* tasks completed. And that was plenty.

Gage laughed out loud. He offered Knox a bottle of cold water and grinned around the half a brownie he'd stuffed in his mouth. "I dunno, I think we do an okay job on our own, babe." Then he looked down at Aiden's hand-iwork. "Ooh, constrictor knot? The Nature Scout's best friend? The purpose of it is to tie multiple things together. Like…" He handed Knox his half-eaten brownie, grabbed Webb's wrist to place next to mine, and demonstrated the knot. "There you go. Practice on Luke."

Knox's eyes softened, the way I'd noticed they tended to whenever he looked at Gage… but especially when Gage was with Aiden. "You're right. I have no complaints. Besides, Goodman and I won't be boyfriends for long." He waggled his eyebrows.

Aiden's eyes widened. "You won't?"

Gage blushed beet red. He snatched his brownie back and poked Knox in the solar plexus for good measure. "He means we're going to get engaged eventually, bud, not that we're breaking up. And stop teasing the thing like that, Knox Sunday. Either ask me or don't. Jeez. You keep bringing it up and then… not doing it." He ruffled Knox's dirty hair with the hand that wasn't holding a brownie, sending up a cloud of dust. "Put a ring on it."

"Me? You're the one who wanted to wait some arbitrary amount of time. You told me, 'It's okay, Knox. We've only been dating four months, there's no rush.' Then you said, 'Half a year's probably too fast still, right? Maybe… maybe after a year would be better.'"

"I said that to make myself feel better 'cause you were taking forever!" Gage spluttered. "I thought Sundays were supposed to be efficient."

"Too late for explanations, Goodman," Knox said sadly, but his eyes, which were almost as nice as Webb's, danced. "I feel… *rejected*. And we Sundays are such delicate, sensitive creatures—"

Webb hooted in amusement, and I hid my grin in his biceps. Aiden was still perfecting the knot, and I had to admit to not minding being roped together for a minute.

"—that now I might just have to wait for *you* to ask *me*." He pressed a smiling kiss to Gage's lips, stole the remaining brownie from his hand, and sauntered off toward the house.

"Maybe I will!" Gage yelled after him. "Maybe I just will! And it's going to be so epic, you won't be able to say no! And then I'm gonna husband you so hard. And it'll be all your fault."

"Looking forward to it," Knox called over his shoulder without turning.

Gage huffed out a breath but couldn't stop the brilliant smile that spread over his face as he watched his man walk away. "See that, Aiden?" he demanded before walking off in the opposite direction. "That is ten out of ten boyfriending right there."

I had to agree. And I barely stifled a longing sigh. What Webb and I had was so close to that. Except what they had was real, and I hadn't gotten any signals from Webb so far that he was interested in anything more than temporary.

"Still no sign of your mom, huh, bud?" Webb asked when it was just the three of us.

I knew he was trying to say the words easily, like Amanda's tardiness wasn't ticking him off, but I could hear the annoyance simmering just below the surface.

Apparently, Aiden could, too, because he swallowed hard. "No. Not yet. But she didn't forget, Dad," he said firmly. "Tonight's not just Scouts, it's the *campout*. I'm gonna get my rope-tying badge… I think." He made a frustrated noise as he untied the rope around our wrists and started over. "And Mom was really excited. She said so. She said she never went tent camping before, and she was buying a new sleeping bag and everything. She's coming."

I nodded firmly. "She probably just forgot to come *early*. No big."

"No big," Aiden agreed gratefully.

I felt Webb's body tense against mine.

Over the past three weeks, Amanda had been late for spelling bee practice pickup once because she'd had to stay late at work, and she'd missed a hockey practice due to an issue with her car.

I knew this because Webb had made no secret of his unhappiness both times. He worried that she wasn't taking the judge's warnings seriously and that it was a precursor to more seriously flaky or endangering behavior down the line.

I wasn't sure I agreed.

When Amanda had come to pick Aiden up after practice, her pretty face had been flushed and anxious. She'd gotten a job as an office manager for a Realtor in Keltyville, she'd said, and her boss had needed her to finish a project before she left. She'd apologized profusely.

If I had a nickel for every time a parent had told me a

similar story over the years, I'd have been directing my home repairs from my private Caribbean island. Heck, even Drew Sunday had been late for pickup once. And it was a sad truth that sometimes bad luck hit just when you were trying to make a good impression.

When I'd tried to bring that up to Webb, though, he'd told me I didn't know Amanda. I didn't know their situation. And he was right.

I'd wanted to point out that I'd love for him to *share* that story... but I wasn't sure how much to push. For all that he talked about letting Hollowans help you, he wasn't too great at practicing what he preached. And we weren't actually boyfriends, even if sometimes it felt like—

"Oh, yeah! Turn that speaker up, Murray!" Knox yelled out of a third-floor window.

I blinked... and then chuckled as I recognized the sound of "Sweet Caroline" filling the air.

"Webb, you just feel free to serenade your *boyfriend*, brother!" Knox continued challengingly. "Give him a twirl for us, too, why don't you? Show Luke your dance moves. Give the people what they want."

"Heck yeah! We came for the show!" Helena Fortnum said with a wink, looking up from a bite of pasta salad.

Even Katey Valcourt, the least likely Webb-and-Luke fan on the planet, cupped her hand around her mouth and yelled, "Sing it!"

Webb directed a narrow-eyed glare toward the attic, but when he looked back at me, his mouth twitched into a smile. "Shall we?"

"What?" I frowned. "Shall we what? N-no. You're not gonna—"

Oh, God, but then he did.

And, holy mother of monkeys, there were many, many things Webb did well, but singing was not one.

"Stop," I laughed, trying to cover his mouth with my free hand. "Oh God, hush. You're scarring your son. Aiden, cover your ears. What are you doing with your hips. Oh my stars. Webb!"

Webb pulled my hand away from his face and sang even louder, until Aiden nearly collapsed with giggles.

"Pardon us for a second, bud. I feel like Luke is questioning my dance skills." Webb tugged me away from Aiden, then pulled me into a kind of rhythmless shuffle right there on the gravel driveway, where the primary "moves" seemed to be shaking his shoulders up and down like he was getting ready for a boxing match and then spinning us in a circle. I was dizzy and breathless with laughter while the whole town cheered.

Yeah, there were definitely moments when this relationship felt real.

In fact, I was having a hard time reminding myself that it wasn't.

"You showed him, Webb!" Marco called.

Chrissy Duarte wolf whistled.

Sheriff Carver yelled, "That dance has *got* to be a safety violation of some kind, Sunday! Pretty sure you just struck me blind."

"This is Genevieve York-Muller with Hand-Fast Watch, at the scene of a historic scroll-checking event!"

Webb and I rocked to a stop and stared at each other with wide eyes for a second. "Webb?"

"Yeah, babe."

"Please tell me that Genevieve's cameraman didn't just take a video of us dancing."

"Do you want me to lie?"

I whimpered.

"Just a little to the right, please, Mr. Williams!"

Genevieve said crisply. "Oh, this is so perfect. And just lift the hands a little so we can see the rope."

"The…" I straightened and stared down at my wrist, where Aiden's loosely tied constrictor knots bound my hand to Knox's.

Oh, mother trucker.

"Good Lord, people! Wait for me!" Ernie York slammed his car door and ran over, tightening his tie, with the Scroll of Doom tucked under his arm. "We ready, Gen? Got the house in the background? My hair okay? Okay. *Ahem.* Whereas Thomas Webb Sunday and Luke Guilford Williams were reported to have been repairing this very domicile for future co-habitation, I, Ernest York, as the mayor of Little Pippin Hollow, hereby declare Part the Third—" He unrolled the scroll.

"Uncle Ernie," Genevieve whisper-hissed. "Their *hands.* They're bound by rope."

The mayor gasped. "*And* Part the Eleventh!"

"That is *not* how it happened," I argued. "It was a project for Nature Scouts. Aiden? Tell them."

But when I turned to find Aiden, he'd scampered away.

"They drank sweet water, too!" Ralph announced excitedly.

All heads—which was to say literally every head on the property—swung in his direction.

"Right, Luke? You and Webb both drank Drew's cider out of the same bottle. Cider brewed with water from the Pippin Well. Says so right on the label," he said triumphantly. "We'll count it, won't we, Ernie?"

"But that's—" I began, unsure how to finish.

It was *sweet.* That was what it was.

Ralph clearly thought he was helping us get our tasks completed. Every one of these meddlers—except maybe Genevieve—did. They were enthusiastic the way guests at a wedding were enthusiastic, trying to make the experience as wonderful as possible for the happy couple.

I couldn't bring myself to disappoint them.

Webb squeezed my hand tightly, like maybe he was feeling some of the same things. "I would rather them show a shot of us smiling than a video of me singing."

"True."

"And we're in control, remember? There's no way they're going to get us to blow that bugle the second time."

I wanted to argue precisely because I wanted so badly *not* to argue.

"Trust me?" he asked in that low, deep growl.

My eyes slid shut, and a tremor shook me. "Yeah, okay."

We turned back toward the camera and let Ernie York officially check off three more items from the scroll before rolling it back up and heading over to the food table to sample Drew's cider.

"Thank you, baby," Webb said simply, once the crowd around us had begun to disperse. "You make so many things easier." He cupped my jaw in his big hand and pressed a kiss to my lips, and suddenly I didn't care about how confusing things were getting, I just wanted to throw caution to the wind and—

"Hey! Hi. Excuse me. Sorry to interrupt. Has anyone seen— Oh," Amanda Sunday said, blinking in shock as she pressed through the crowd of people and caught sight of the two of us. "Uh... Webb?"

Webb's whole frame locked down as he stared at his ex-wife. She was picture-pretty, with light brown hair and pixieish features that reminded me of Aiden. She wore a frilly, pretty blouse that was going to get utterly ruined at the campout and a pair of hiking boots that looked so stiff and new, she probably already had blisters.

As far as I was concerned, her picture belonged in the dictionary beside the word *Trying*. But Webb looked at her with wary anger, like she was Godzilla, come to stomp all over the Hollow.

"I'm sorry," she babbled, still staring at us. "I wasn't sure where you'd be, and I was at home waiting. I mean, your home. I mean, at Sunday Orchard. And I wondered why you were so late, but I figured everyone's late sometimes, but then I realized *you* aren't, and then I remembered you said you wouldn't be there, but I couldn't remember where you said you *would* be and you weren't answering your phone, and…" She broke off and swallowed.

It was painfully clear where Aiden inherited his word-spewing.

"Amanda," I said, leaping toward her before Webb could release the angry roar I knew he was working up to. "Hey! I'm Luke Williams, remember? From spelling bee practice."

"You're Aiden's… teacher?" She looked back at the spot where she'd seen us kissing.

"Yes. Yup. I sure am. And Webb's… handfast partner. It's a whole long story. I'm sure Aiden will fill you in. He's been waiting for you! He already practiced his knot tying, so no need to worry about that. And his bag is right there on the porch. Aiden?" I called. "Dude, shake a leg!" To Amanda, I added, "Love this blouse, by the way. But do you have a sweatshirt? Would you like to borrow one?"

"No, I—"

Aiden ran out of the house, grabbed his bag, and ran toward us. "Bye, Luke. Bye, Dad. Love you."

"Aiden," Webb began in a severe tone, crossing his arms over his chest. "I need to speak to your mother. Privately."

"Or maybe not now!" I suggested brightly. "Maybe tomorrow. Maybe after the campout. In fact, I need to speak to *you* privately."

"Luke—" Webb began, but I cut him off, grabbing his bent elbow and pulling him toward my camper.

"Trust *me*?" I demanded softly.

Webb gave in and let me push him into the camper. But when I got inside, he whirled to face me. "What was that? I wanted to talk to Amanda."

"No, you wanted to *yell* at Amanda," I corrected. "And Webb, she's trying."

He shook his head. "You don't know her. She's doing what she's done in the past, Luke. She's got her head in the clouds. She's not focused on her kid or what he needs, she's—"

"*Trying*," I said again. "I don't know the whole story because you haven't shared it, but she's a person who's trying hard and getting a lot of things wrong but not giving up."

He blew out a breath. "Yet. I know where this is going—"

"But you don't. Even you aren't psychic, Webb Sunday."

Webb's shoulders deflated. "I just… don't want anyone to get hurt."

"I know. I know you don't. And neither do I." Not Webb. Not Aiden…

And not me either.

Webb wrapped his arms around me and exhaled a long breath. "You're magic, Luke Williams. You always make things better."

I leaned up to kiss him. Finally, we were alone for more than two seconds. He tasted like Natalie Little's cinnamon swirl cookies, and I realized they tasted ten times better on him than straight from the plate. Just when I was ready to mentally construct a thank-you note to her for her judicious use of cinnamon and sugar, a fist banged on the trailer door, shaking the whole place.

Webb sighed and closed his eyes. "You live in a death trap."

"Coming!" I called out cheerfully before turning to him with a grin. "If we want to get me out of this death trap, we need to get back to work."

He grumbled the entire way out of the trailer. I didn't disagree with his disappointment, but then again, part of the reason I wanted to get back to work was because Aiden was going to be gone for eighteen whole hours... and I would have Webb Sunday all to myself.

I planned on making the most of it.

Naked.

Chapter Sixteen

WEBB

I'd forgotten how good it felt to join with others in service to a neighbor. The fact the neighbor in question was someone as kind and appreciative—and sexy—as Luke Williams made it even better.

There'd been an actual barn raising years ago in Little Pippin Hollow, and I remembered how proud I'd been of my fellow Hollowans for coming together to help the Swansons after a devastating fire. Helping Luke today felt like we were all a part of something bigger than us, a community that looked out for each other.

It made me proud, and it reminded me that there was more to life than focusing on my own family, my orchard, and my never-ending chore list.

What we'd done today was more than work to fix up a house. It was an outpouring of love, and I was grateful to live in a place that valued helping others.

The weather today had been perfect, and I'd seen the difference it had made to Luke's mood. He'd bounced around from person to person, project to project, smiling and laughing, thanking everyone for their contributions.

He'd felt honored and grateful, too, and watching him happily thank everyone for their help, rather than nervously resist, was an indicator of how far he'd come in these three weeks. Not only had he relaxed about accepting help, but he'd also connected with several people outside of work. I could tell he almost felt like one of us now.

"We really only need one napkin per person, bro. What the heck are you doing?"

I glanced up at Em, whose smirk was focused on the mess I was making on the kitchen table. We were back home for dinner, and my only contribution had been setting the table.

So much for that. Apparently, I'd been giving each person their own stack of cloth napkins instead of one.

"Mm," I grunted. "I've seen you eat Marco's chicken before and decided an ounce of prevention would be worth a pound of dirty laundry later."

Knox set a few glasses of ice water down. "Methinks he wants to make a good impression for his Lukey-love."

I snapped my head around. "*Zzzt.* Ix-nay on the uhv-lay."

"There are no little ears around to overhear." Emma laughed. "Aiden's spending the night out, remember?"

My stomach lurched. Of course I remembered. This would be the first time Amanda would have him overnight. Thankfully, it was a Nature Scout group campout, but still. It was hard to leave him in her care for so long when I knew she had a tendency to flake. At least there were several other parents there who knew to keep an eye on him.

Thinking of that reminded me of earlier today when Luke had pulled me inside his trailer to help me get my head on straight before I lost my cool. There was something about him that grounded me, that helped me put things in perspective and not take things so seriously.

I loved that about him.

"Anyway, it's not *love*," I continued, ignoring my mental contradiction. "It's just… the thing with Luke is…"

Uncle Drew snorted under his breath. "Then the dreamy look on your face is just a platonic kind of dreamy. Sure."

"Temporary," I said firmly. "It's not… he's not… we're not…"

"*Why* not?" Gage asked, elbowing me out of the way after yanking the rest of the cloth napkins from my hands.

I was going to tell him why not. It was obvious. "Because."

Knox let out a booming laugh. "Because."

My face burned. Luke was going to arrive any minute and find my family implying we were in a serious relationship. That was a complete falsehood. "We're not in love. We're just engaged," I said stupidly.

Now it was Uncle Drew whose laugh drowned out everyone else's. I sighed. "Please don't embarrass me when he gets here. Okay? I don't know what we are right now, but I like him. And I think he likes me. And I want to see where it goes. Clearly I'm not in a position to enter into anything serious, but…"

"But?" Emma asked before mimicking my voice. "Why aren't you in a position for anything serious?"

I sat down heavily in one of the kitchen chairs. Marco bustled around the kitchen while Drew acted as his sous chef, and Knox and Gage finished preparing the table for dinner.

"Because things finally might be settling down with Amanda. Aiden is happy and secure. The orchard is in good shape. The last thing I need is something fucking it all up."

Drew was the one who pinned me with a glare. "And that sweet man would fuck it up?"

"What? Of course not! He's the kindest human being alive. He could never fuck anything up."

My family stared at me until I realized I'd stood up and poked my index finger on the table to emphasize my point. I sat back down and cleared my throat. "He's awesome. There's no denying that. I just... I can't jump back into the kind of legal mess I had with Amanda. Marriage isn't for me. Not again."

Knox slid into the chair next to mine and straightened the napkin. "How are you doing with the whole... he's a guy thing? Do you have anything you want to talk about there or... I dunno... questions?"

Gage muttered, "Oh God, here we go," under his breath. Knox shot him a look.

"I'm good, thanks," I said, keeping my eyes on my own place mat.

Drew moved closer. "So... you don't want to talk about it?"

I looked up at him. "You guys are gay. I've been around gay men my whole life. I don't have any issues with the fact Luke is gay. It's a little confusing as to why I was never attracted to a man before, but honestly... I think people change. Maybe he's the right person at the right time, and he happens to be a man." I shrugged. "I promise I'm not having second thoughts about that part of it."

"And you understand about safe sex," Drew stated, as if he hadn't lectured us all a million times as teens. "And anal—"

"Can we... not do this right now? Luke is seriously going to be here any minute. Also? I'm not sixteen."

Gage snickered. "Don't worry. I'll send you some links to some videos about bottoming. That'll set you up just right."

Knox sighed. "Don't even think about it, especially if it's the one you tried to get me to watch the other night. That would make him turtle up and never want sex again."

Gage's eyes narrowed. "That was just between you and me. And I'll remember this the next time you imply you want to get a little freaky—"

"Okie-dokie!" Marco snapped, cutting him off with a giant fake smile full of teeth. "Welcome, Luke, we're so glad you're here."

I buried my face in my hands and groaned. It seemed as if Emma was the only one who'd heard the doorbell ring.

"Thanks for having me," Luke said in his friendly, polite voice. I looked up at him and smiled. How could anyone not smile with him around? He was sunshine personified.

"Hey," I said, standing up to give him a hug. "Did everyone finally leave?"

Luke's body relaxed against mine after a beat, and I held him tightly for as long as I could. He smelled like soap, and the ends of his hair were still damp from a shower.

"Yeah," he sighed. "Long day, huh?"

I pulled back and pressed a kiss to the edge of his lips. "Mm. Definitely. But a good one."

His face lit up. "So good. I still can't believe how fast everything has happened. It's like… it's like I have the fairy-tale farmhouse of my dreams. I can't wrap my head around it. Everyone's been so nice and generous with their time."

I nudged him into the chair next to mine and then sat

down beside him. "Everyone seemed happy to help, and the place looks amazing. Your mom's going to love it."

Drew came over and squeezed Luke's shoulder. "Can I get you some beer? Wine? Maybe a little toke to start your night off right?"

Em shook her head. "Not sure Mr. Williams is the weed-smoking type, Uncle Drew."

"Shame," Marco muttered under his breath.

"Wine would be great?" Luke said, looking around. "Unless I'm the only one. Water's fine, too."

Before I could stand up again, Drew waved me off and grabbed the bottle to pour Luke a glass.

Gage apologized for leaving before finishing planting the bulbs he'd brought, and Luke insisted it wasn't a problem.

"After you left, Mr. Avery brought this awesome bulb-planting tool and showed me how to use it. It's got like a hollow shaft that's a blade. You have to really slam it down into the ground hard." He demonstrated with his hands, slamming the heel of his palm against his other hand. The sound of his skin smacking seemed to fill the kitchen with heat. "If you do it right, shove hard enough, it makes a nice channel for your bulb."

I swallowed. When I spoke, my voice cracked. "S-sounds good."

Gage lifted his eyebrows. "I'll bet it does."

Knox nodded. "We need to plant some things now that I think of it."

Emma's forehead crinkled. "We run an orchard and kitchen garden. We plant stuff all the t—"

Marco cut her off. "Dinner's ready. Let's eat."

My mouth watered, but it wasn't for Marco's special chicken.

Dinner was excruciating. Luke had inadvertently

woken my dick up, which wasn't surprising considering how unsatisfying the past three weeks had been sexually. We'd had plenty of stolen moments and even some shared orgasms, but I was beyond ready for more. I didn't need more in the sense of going further than a frot or mutual hand job, but more in the sense of being naked together all night without fear of being interrupted.

For the past several weeks, every time we found each other alone, it seemed like the universe was out to get us. Aiden would come bouncing in, or one of the volunteers at Luke's would need to ask him a question. We both still had to keep our jobs going as well, and Luke had his sheep to care for.

Tonight was the unspoken exception. We'd agreed to a sleepover at my place, in a bed big enough for both of us, when Aiden would be gone and we would no longer have the house projects hanging over our heads.

So why the hell had I included family dinner in the fucking plan?

"I have a lovely turtle cheesecake," Drew began.

"Not hungry," I barked, reaching for Luke's hand and pulling him up.

"Thomas Webb Sunday, you will remember your manners," Drew barked. "We have a guest."

I gritted my teeth and sat back down. "Pardon me, Luke," I said with as much feigned politeness as a deranged serial killer. "Are you hungry for dessert?"

Luke's eyes danced, and he bit his lip against a smile. "Why, yes, actually." I slumped in my chair until he spoke again. His eyes bored into mine. "But not for cheesecake."

I stared at him before looking around at my family members.

"Go," Drew said, waving us off. "Fucking hell. Kids today."

I didn't stick around long enough to hear them all start laughing. I grabbed Luke's hand and pulled him out of the room and up the stairs.

"We should have stayed at your place," I muttered.

"My place smells like paint," he reminded me with a laugh. "And my new mattress doesn't get delivered until tomorrow, remember?"

I led him into my bedroom and closed the door before using my hip to shove my dresser in front of it. "Your trailer would have been better than being under the same roof with my meddling family," I continued.

"You mean my death trap?" he laughed.

His laughter made me so fucking happy. I turned to look at him.

"Are you concerned about our security?" Luke asked, eyeing the dresser in front of the door.

"Yes," I grumbled, taking a step toward him. Then another. "Nothing, and I mean nothing, is going to interfere with the rest of my night with you."

Luke's sparkling eyes stayed on mine while he pulled his shirt off. "Good. I've been waiting three weeks for this."

His confidence surprised me, but it excited me, too. I moved closer and put my hands on his shoulders before moving my palms down the warm skin of his bare chest.

Sometimes I forgot he was so much smaller than me because the impact of his presence was so huge. Whenever he was nearby—hell, even when he wasn't—he was all I could see or think about.

But being with him like this, watching my rough hand stroke along his fine skin, feeling his smaller frame slot against my larger one, the urge to cherish and protect him was hard to resist.

So I didn't.

"You're so fucking beautiful. I could barely sit still at

dinner thinking of all the things I wanted to try with you tonight."

I leaned down and dropped an open-mouthed kiss on his collarbone, his pec, the center of his chest. I laved the area around his nipple with my tongue, avoiding the incredibly tempting, incredibly unexpected, and incredibly fucking hot metal ring that protruded from it until Luke was shuddering, bowing his back, and using my hair like reins to *force* me to suck it.

"Stop teasing!"

My dick thumped against the front of my pants. "Holy fuck, you're killing me," I murmured before taking the ring into my mouth and gently tugging it with my teeth.

Luke sucked in a breath. "Don't die. Please don't die. Not right now. Not before... *Harder*. Please, harder."

I pulled the nub into my mouth with firm suction, and Luke made a noise that was caught between a moan and a sob.

"Oh, yeah," he breathed. "Webb..."

"You taste so good," I murmured against his skin. "Want to lick and nibble every inch of your body."

I moved my hands down to unbutton his jeans. It was still a little foreign encountering the thicker elastic band of boxer briefs rather than dainty panties from years of previous sexual experiences, but that foreign feeling only made me hotter. After several heavy make-out sessions, I knew how incredible it felt palming his hard dick through the cotton of his underwear.

Everything about Luke Williams got me hot. He could meet my eye across a stack of dusty floor tile and I'd imagine getting on my knees for him on that very tile.

"I want to suck you," I said, remembering one of my biggest fantasies from these past weeks.

I dropped to my knees and looked up at him, pausing

before pulling his pants down the way I wanted. "That okay?"

Luke bit his lip and tried not to grin. "Do you think I'm ever going to say no to that? Have you lost your mind?"

I laughed and leaned in to kiss the soft hair below his belly button. The faint musky scent of him made my heart ramp up, and my fingers itched to strip him bare. I worried that if I truly allowed myself free rein, I'd scare the poor guy.

I wanted to attack him and pin him down while I did so many dirty things to his body.

"Your hands are shaking," he said when I forced myself to focus on lowering his zipper without hurting him.

"Want you," I croaked. "S'fuckin bad."

The look he gave me—one of tenderness but unadulterated heat, too—was overwhelming in the best way.

"Take me."

I let out a deep sound from my throat and shoved his pants and underwear down before licking a stripe up his hard cock. Delicate skin over hard steel. The head was flushed pink and sticky wet at the slit. I teased it with my tongue so I could taste him.

My brothers and my best friend, Jack, had never been shy about sharing their love of giving and receiving head, but I'd never in a million years understood how they could like giving it.

Now I did.

Watching and hearing Luke's groans and gasps, feeling the scrape of his fingernails in my hair, and smelling the scent of his sex was... heady. More than heady.

It was addictive.

"Don't stop," Luke urged. His thigh muscles felt lean

and strong under my hands. I reached around to palm his rounded ass while I groaned around his dick.

I didn't want to stop, but I wanted inside him, too. I wanted everything with him.

I pulled off and lunged up to kiss him on the mouth. My hands clasped the back of his head to hold him still while I devoured him. "What do you want, Luke?" I sounded breathless and desperate, which was an accurate depiction of how I felt.

His eyes were glassy, and his chin was pink from my beard stubble. "Would you… do you…" He swallowed. "I would really like you to fuck me. If you're… if you'd like that too."

I closed my eyes and rested my forehead against his. "Baby, I want to be as close as humanly possible to you right now. I would love nothing more than that if you're sure."

His smile was gorgeous as always, even if it was a little shy at the moment. "So super incredibly sure."

For some reason, knowing we were going to have sex and that we had the entire night, helped me calm the fuck down. I still wanted him desperately, but I also wanted to make it good for him.

I moved him over to my bed and pulled the covers back before laying him down. He was completely naked in my bed. I couldn't help but stare at him while I removed my own clothes piece by piece.

The hungry look on his face was almost comical. "You're making me feel like turtle cheesecake," I teased.

He licked his lips. "I've always wanted to devour turtle cheesecake."

I crawled up his body from the foot of the bed, dropping kisses along the way until I could get his cock into my mouth again. Sucking and slurping noises filled the air, enough to make me grateful for the loud attic fan Uncle Drew had insisted on operating tonight.

Smart man.

I forced myself to stop before Luke could come. His stomach muscles were taut, and his toes curled. "Wait right here." I moved over to the side table and grabbed the lube and a condom. When my brothers had left them on the front seat of my truck the other day, I'd wanted to kill them.

Now I wanted to kiss them.

"You have to make sure I'm doing this right," I said, feeling my nerves sneak back in. "I don't want to hurt you."

"I can do it," he said, reaching for the lube. "The prep, I mean. You don't have to—"

I swatted his hand away. "Luke Williams, if you don't grant me the privilege of doing this, I will not be responsible for my actions."

His eyes met mine. "Permission granted," he teased. "But make it quick. I wasn't expecting you to edge me tonight after this danged town has already spent the past three weeks edging both of us."

I lubed up my fingers and reached between his legs to find his hole. He gasped. "Cold... *frick*."

I leaned in to kiss his lips. "You're allowed to curse when we're having sex, baby," I murmured, smiling against his mouth.

"Can't," he said, arching his head back and exposing his throat. "Oh God. If I get... get in the habit, I'll..." He groaned and arched again as my finger breached him and moved deeper inside.

"You'll?"

"Curseinfrontofthekids. Stop talking and *oh my God*."

I kissed him again before moving carefully to insert a

second finger. Luke's chest was red, a tendon stood out on his neck, and his fingers curled into fists around the sheets. He was stunning.

"Stop staring and get inside me," he said breathlessly. "Now."

I tore the condom open and slid it on before slicking it up. "Bossy Luke. I like it."

His eyes met mine. "Please." He said it softly and tenderly, and it made my stomach fly in erratic acrobatic patterns through my gut.

I moved on top of him and settled between his legs. Words of affection and devotion tripped over themselves to escape my mouth, but I bit them back. I knew better than to say something stupid in the heat of passion.

But the words were there anyway, even though they remained unspoken.

I brushed the hair back from his forehead and met his eyes again to make sure we were still on the same page.

"You're incredible," I said softly before kissing his cheek. "So fucking sexy and beautiful. You make me hard. Seeing you every day is like…" Fuck. The words were leaking out past the barricades I'd carefully commanded in place. "Thank you for being who you are and for being here with me right now."

When I started pushing into his body, it was one of the most incredible moments of my life, the kind of moment that would be marked for permanent storage in my memories and come back to the forefront time and time again in the future.

His feelings were plain to see on his face. His responsiveness to my touch, his own affection for me… It was everything.

It took a little while before I was finally fully seated

inside him, and by then, I was a panting, sweaty mess. "Oh God, oh God. Luke. Fuck. Luke. *Christ.*"

I was a babbling fool.

He felt so fucking good, I couldn't even think.

"More," he croaked, wrapping his legs around my waist and arching closer. I began to thrust into him, careful at first, before he convinced me to stop holding back.

What followed was the most exciting and fulfilling sexual experience of my life. I didn't hold back. I held him tight and let myself go. I listened to his body and his words to try and give him as much pleasure as I could before taking my own.

But for the first time in my life, I almost couldn't hold my orgasm off to make sure my partner took their pleasure first. By the time his warm spunk hit the hand I had around his cock, I was coming deep inside his body. My lips were locked onto his neck, and I whimpered under his ear.

We were covered in sweat and semen, practically glued together with it, but I was the happiest I could remember being in a very long time.

And it was all because of the lively, lovely man in my bed and in my arms.

Waking up the following morning still naked and tangled up with Luke was even better than I'd expected. I arched my morning wood into his hip and got a sleepy groan in response.

"Don't tempt me," Luke mumbled.

"Why not? Aiden's not expected home for hours yet, and the dresser is still in front of the door."

The low rumble of his chuckle made me smile. "Barbarian."

I kissed the back of his neck and behind his ear until he woke up a little more and turned around to face me. His cheek was creased and his eyes half closed.

I'd never seen anything better.

"Morning," he said before snuggling into my chest. "God you smell good. I don't ever want to leave this bed."

"Your mom comes today, so unfortunately, we can't stay here forever."

Luke pulled back to give me a mock glare. "Boner killer, thy name is Webb."

I kissed his cheek, his forehead, and his temple while reaching down to stroke him. "Bet I can bring it back to life."

We kissed and stroked each other lazily, teasing and flirting, until we were both hard and ready to come. It didn't take much. I wondered if it would ever take much with this man who seemed to turn me on simply by breathing near me.

We brought each other off with our mouths in a reversed tangle on the bed. As soon as I caught my breath, I grinned up at him proudly.

"First-ever sixty-nine," I admitted. "Five out of five stars. Highly recommend."

Instead of laughing, Luke frowned. "You never did it with Amanda? Ever?"

I thought back to my time with her. "No. Not that I can remember." I moved around until Luke and I were settled back on the pillows face-to-face. "I was obsessed with making sure my partner came first."

"I've noticed," Luke interjected. "And let's be clear, I'm not complaining."

I reached for his hand and threaded our fingers

together. "So I usually focused on her first. And if we came at the same time, it wasn't through oral. Not sure I'd want someone's teeth near my junk while they were losing control during an orgasm."

Luke tilted his head. "But you let me do it."

"That's different," I said without thinking. "I trust you."

The words landed heavily in the room, killing the mood stone dead.

I muttered a curse and an apology. "I didn't mean for her to come up."

Luke reached out and stroked my cheek. "I'm the one who brought her up. And... I've been meaning to ask you about her anyway."

I blew out a breath and turned onto my back. Leave it to Amanda to ruin my morning with Luke. "What do you want to know?"

"I don't want to know anything if it's going to upset you."

I turned my head to face him. "She brings out the worst in me, and I don't necessarily want you to see the worst in me. That's all."

Luke nodded. "That's pretty expected with exes. But I'm curious how things ended with you two to leave such animosity between you. It..." He hesitated.

I reached out to hold his hand again. "Go on," I urged softly.

"It upsets Aiden. He feels like he needs to defend her to you and protect her from you. I'd imagine he does the same with her. Defends you and protects you. That's a lot for a kid his age."

His words were kindly meant, but the blade still cut deeply.

I rolled toward him and buried my face in his neck.

"Thank you for being brave enough to tell me that," I mumbled against his warm skin. "You're right."

We lay like that for several minutes while I processed what he'd said. When I got my thoughts together, I pulled away again. "I married her for the wrong reasons. My dad was sick, and when he passed away… it made me panic a little. With him gone, I realized how short life was. I had the orchard to manage, but I also had young siblings. Em was only eight at the time. I was desperate to keep us together as a 'normal' family, whatever normal means. I guess I thought it meant I needed a wife. I needed to start a family."

"And thank God for that, or you wouldn't have Aiden," Luke added with a smile.

I pulled his hand to my lips to press a kiss on it. "Absolutely. I have zero regrets about that. But… in hindsight, the marriage itself wasn't fair to Amanda or me. I rushed us both into something out of fear instead of love."

I thought about it for another minute before continuing. "Because I'd married her for stability, I noticed right away when she started being unreliable. I think that's what makes me so angry. She's unreliable. I can't trust her to show up when she's supposed to. She doesn't stick around when things get tough, and raising a kid is tough."

As soon as the words were out of my mouth, I realized Luke was the opposite of unreliable. He was the opposite of flaky. When Luke promised to show up, he was always there. When faced with the nightmare of Ben Pond's dilapidated farmhouse, Luke didn't bolt back south. He stayed and persevered.

I opened my mouth to say something about it, but he spoke first. "She's here now. She has a job, and Deb Reinhardt at the Hookers meeting said she's doing great at it. Deb's brother Joey is a real estate agent in Keltyville.

Amanda has also been to a spelling bee practice even though she had to leave work early to make it on time. She brought the kids a batch of cookies decorated like bees. And she's shown up for every visitation with Aiden."

"She's been late for every visitation," I amended.

Luke nodded. "You know her better than I do, obviously. All I'm saying is… people change. Do I know whether she's going to run again? Of course not. But it seems to me she's trying. And if that's true, it could be a good thing for Aiden. If nothing else, her trying to be here for him sends him the message that she cares about him."

"I don't appreciate you being so levelheaded and kind," I muttered, pulling him in for another snuggle. "It's annoying as fuck."

"You're not as grumpy as you pretend to be," he said with a laugh.

"Don't kid yourself. The only thing keeping me from full-on grizzly bear status is large quantities of coffee."

"Then maybe we should slide the dresser over and go in search of some," Luke suggested, crawling out of bed. "We'll grab coffee and then come back up here for a lesson on soapy shower hand jobs."

After we slipped on pajama pants from my dresser, we moved it away from the door and made our way downstairs.

It wasn't until we were halfway to the coffee maker that I realized we weren't alone.

"Hi, Dad! Hi, Mr. Williams! Did you…" Aiden's face wrinkled adorably from his spot at the kitchen table. "Did you have a sleepover? Oh, wait! You did that thing Mayor York was talking about. Bed bundling! Part Nine of the handfast! Oh my gosh, you're really getting married. This is the best thing ever!"

My face ignited. *Shit.* Technically, he wasn't wrong. If I

remembered correctly, Luke had even said, "Oh, God," a number of times, and that was pretty close to a prayer.

Luke let out a helpless sound under his breath, and Amanda set down her coffee mug. Uncle Drew's lips stayed closed, but his nostrils flared in laughter.

Amanda looked down at her coffee. "So, it's true? You're getting married?"

Her voice was curious, not judgmental, but still I panicked.

"No! Of course not. Not really. Don't be ridiculous. This is just... it's..." I glanced at Drew for help, but there was none to be found. I glanced at Emma, who'd just stumbled in, but she was obviously still half asleep. "It's nothing. Right, Luke?"

I glanced at Luke.

And realized I'd fucked everything up. Again.

Only worse. Because this time I had so much more to lose.

Chapter Seventeen

LUKE

I was stuck in a 1950s sitcom. If 1950s sitcoms had been about a family of hippie gay lumberjacks, my mom, and Aunt Susan.

"This pie looks incredible, Laura," Drew Sunday said as my mom set a slice in front of him on the Sundays' big kitchen table. "Thank you so much for bringing it."

"Aw. No trouble at all! Least I could do after you and Marco so generously invited us to dinner," my mom said in her soft, musical voice. "I hope y'all like it. It's one of Luke's favorites."

My eyes moved back and forth from one polite comment to the next. This was excruciating. If Marco and Drew hadn't extended the invitation directly to my mom, I would have insisted on declining. The last thing I wanted was to force my family upon Webb.

To force *myself* on him.

When he'd told Amanda things between us were "nothing," it had been a cold bucket of water to the face. A *necessary* cold bucket of water. I absolutely did not want to get in the way of Aiden's stability, the Sunday family

unit, or… or… Webb's existing mountain of responsibilities.

And it was great to have gotten that reminder before
any… feelings were involved. Because there weren't any.

No feelings.

None whatsoever.

And thank gosh for that, right? Whew.

"I bet we will." Gage gave me a friendly wink. "Since
we like Luke."

"Yeah we do," Aiden said, leaning over to rest his head
on my arm for a beat… before attacking his own slice of
pie like a school of hungry piranha in a feeding frenzy.

I smiled down at him. Was there anything better than
enjoying a meal with the people you loved? I didn't think
so. And in my case, it was the cherry on the sundae of my
life, which was pretty close to perfect these days. Per-fect.

Just… just really, unbelievably *perfect*.

My mom and Aunt Sue had been here in Little Pippin
Hollow for several days already. My mom looked healthier
and more hopeful than she had in a long while, and she
was making a point to introduce herself to all the people
and places in my new hometown.

My newly renovated farmhouse was absolutely
gorgeous—not to mention warm and solid, which were
two qualities I'd never take for granted again.

Spring had arrived, and my sheep spent every day frol-
icking in the fields… which, yes, were mostly mud swamps,
but the girls didn't seem to mind. In fact, I was thinking it
might be time to expand the herd.

Aiden had gotten his Nature Scout badge for knot
tying, he was going to kick butt in the spelling bee this
week (though I was impartially rooting for all the kids,
obviously), and I'd even sat in the stands with Amanda the
other night when Aiden's Mites hockey team had made the

playoffs. We'd been cordial to each other, which had been a relief.

Work was going well. Principal Oliver had reversed direction and thrown her support behind the Pick-a-Book drive, even offering to take a shift working the fundraising booth at the Spring Fling.

The Sundays were my friends now—and not just neighbor-friends across the orchards, like the original lie I'd told my mom, but honest to goodness friends who brought me to Jack's for breakfast and invited my mother to dinner.

In short, I was living the freaking fairy tale I'd written about in Old Ben Pond's essay contest and then some.

Happily Ever After? *Pfft*. Lame.

Try *Happiest* Ever After.

Try *Ecstatically* Ever After.

Try… try *Wholly and Completely Satisfied, Without Requiring A Single Other Thing or Person or Relationship*, Ever After.

Of course, before tonight, I hadn't actually *seen* Webb since Sunday morning, but that was fine. Better than fine! Friends didn't live in each other's pockets, after all, and it was important to remember that was what we were.

Friends, friends, friends.

Friends who used to have occasional benefits but were absolutely not going to do *that* anymore because those benefits were *confusing*. And addictively sexy. And could actually have been really hurtful, if I'd gone and done something foolish like, say, falling in love with my gorgeous, kindhearted, steadfast, lumberjacky neighbor, when he'd made it abundantly clear that he wasn't interested in anything more than a casual… *nothing*.

Thank goodness I'd saved myself from that, right?

It wasn't like there was any tension between me and Webb. Gosh, no.

I mean, yes, I'd dressed and left the farmhouse immediately after the conversation with Amanda on Sunday—the one where Webb had so clearly said the handfasting meant *nothing*—but that was only because my mom had been on her way, not because I'd been upset or, like, brokenhearted.

And Webb had been busy, too, doing damage control with Aiden, who'd burst into tears at the idea that we weren't getting married, and with Amanda, who was the one person in the greater Hollow area who didn't know all the details of ye olde handfasting, and with Em, who'd been ready to challenge Webb to a duel on my behalf for "denying Luke a second time, for fuck's sake, *Judas* Webb Sunday"—which was kind of funny, or at least I'd chosen to think so.

And then I'd been incredibly, genuinely busy this week —nearly as busy as I'd been the week before, really—with school, and showing my mom around, and making final preparations for the Pick-a-Book fundraiser and the spelling bee.

Webb was probably busy, too, but he wasn't upset either… or so it seemed from reading between the lines of the riveting, deeply personal texts he'd sent this week: "*Muriel's pins have dropped. She could calve any day.*" and "*Weather looks good for the Spring Fling on Saturday.*" and "*Found a striped sock under my bed. Might be yours?*"

He hadn't apologized for what he'd said on Sunday, but then… why would he if what he'd said was true?

I just needed to remind myself that it didn't matter.

Did not matter.

Because I had the fairy tale, and only a greedy idiot would want to keep the handsome prince, too.

"Lukey, honey, if you don't like the pie, just say so." The scent of my mom's White Diamonds perfume got stronger as she leaned over to whisper in my ear.

"Hmm?" I looked up to find her—and my Aunt Sue,

and most of the Sunday family—watching in concern as I hacked my dessert to smithereens.

My face got hot, and I hunched over my plate. "Oh, gosh, I'm so sorry. No, the pie's great. One of your best, Mom!" I scooped an enthusiastic bite into my mouth in demonstration. "I was just thinking about, uh… nothing? You know how it goes. Long day."

"Understandable," Knox agreed smoothly. "Many's the time this week when I've found Webb chopping at something while he thinks about nothing. Isn't that right, Webb?"

Webb ignored his brother. "Ms. Williams, this really is delicious. I don't like pie, but this one's got something different about it. Something… flowery."

"Yes! It's lavender! Not just a gorgeous face and a fine set of shoulders, is he, Lukey?" My mother elbowed me in the side, and though I refused to look toward the other end of the table, I could picture Webb blushing at the compliment. "Your *betrothed* is a smarty-pants, too."

I forced a smile. "Isn't he, though?"

Smarter than me, that was for sure.

Webb would never come as dangerously close to catching real feelings as I had. Webb was smart enough to cut himself off from the possibility entirely.

"Really, though, who doesn't like pie?" I demanded of no one in particular. "That's just… odd. Isn't it? Because pie… It's a pretty broad flipping category of food. Just because a person doesn't like onion tart doesn't mean they won't like strawberry refrigerator pie, does it? And just because you had a bad experience with an apple pie one time doesn't mean you won't enjoy a crustless bacon quiche! Nothing is wrong with *pie*, okay? Pie is… pie is great. Pie can be *amazing*."

I ended my tirade and noticed silence had fallen

around the table. I felt the weight of ten heavy stares. "And this pie here... it's yummy. Really, Mama. So yummy."

"I *said* it was good," Webb insisted defensively. "I said it was delicious."

For the first time since we'd sat down to dinner, I looked up the length of the table and let my eyes drink their fill of Webb Sunday. Somehow, he was even sexier than I remembered him being half an hour ago, which was annoying.

"Yes, I heard what you said. It's nothing personal, Webb. I'm simply saying that if a person goes around telling himself and everyone else that he doesn't like pie, then maybe someday he won't be offered pie anymore. And that would be a tragedy. Because you just admitted that *this* pie is delicious." I shoveled another huge bite in my mouth and swallowed it as he watched. "So maybe you should open your mind, okay?"

Webb tilted his head in confusion. "I... suppose?"

I nodded once, firmly.

"Well." My mom clapped her hands once. "That was... a great reminder for all of us, thank you, Lukey. But you know, now I'm just *dying* to hear the whole story of how y'all came to be handfasted. Such a charming town tradition!"

"I still wanna know what handfasting *is*," Aunt Sue added.

"I already explained it," I reminded her. "The other day when you arrived."

"You gave us the CliffsNotes," she argued. "We want the whole thing. How'd you go from blowing a trumpet to having your names on refrigerator magnets and commemorative scrolls at the gift shop in town?"

"It's a *bugle*," Webb corrected. "Not a—wait, they have commemorative scrolls with our names?"

"Yep. And the mayor's giving 'em away free to anyone who helps you and Luke check off your list," Marco said happily. "I'm angling to get one."

Webb shot him a dirty look.

"You know, Ms. Williams—*Laura*—makes an excellent point," Knox said, leaning his elbows on the table and resting his chin on his hands. "I still haven't heard the whole bugle story myself, just a bunch of rumors. I think this might be… *enlightening*."

"I agree." Drew raised an eyebrow in Webb's direction.

Webb's shoulders slumped.

"I agree, too!" Aiden said eagerly, brandishing his pie spoon. "Tell the story."

"Aiden, I think it's homework time." Webb's voice was uncompromising.

"But I don't have any," Aiden informed him with clear satisfaction. "Mr. Williams didn't give us any this week, because the Spring Fling is coming up." He looked up at me. "Right?"

Webb lifted a judgy eyebrow, like I really should have foreseen this eventuality.

"But you could still practice for the spelling bee Friday," I said mildly. "Go do that, and I'll come quiz you in half an hour, okay? Promise."

"And read me a chapter of my book?" the pint-sized negotiator challenged.

My heart flipped. It was nice to be wanted. "Agreed."

"Okay, then," Aiden sighed. He put his plate in the sink and clomped up the stairs.

When he was gone, Webb spread his hands flat on the table. "Look, I know it's gotten all blown out of proportion, but it's not really a funny story," he began. "Luke and I had a couple of drinks, and we thought it would be fun—"

"No, no, no. If you're going to tell it, start it in the right place." I pushed my empty pie plate away. "See, for the longest while, Webb hated me—"

My mom's expression fell, and she looked back and forth between Webb and me suspiciously. "Hated you?"

"What?" Webb scowled. "I did not!"

"Okay, you disliked me, then," I amended agreeably. "The point is, we were not friends at that time—"

"I didn't hate you, Luke," Webb insisted hotly. "If anything, I didn't let myself—"

I paused and waited for him to finish, but he pressed his lips together and folded his hands on the table. "Never mind."

"Right, okay," I resumed. "So, as I was saying, I was at the Bugle—our local bar—having a couple drinks, because I'd had a *day*. The ceiling in my living room—" I broke off and darted a look at my mom. "Uh. I found a minor repair was needed. Nothing to worry about. Just an inconvenience."

"Wait, that was the day your ceiling—uh, had that *minor inconvenience*?" Webb's forehead furrowed. "I didn't know that."

"Well, no, how would you?" I shrugged. "We weren't friends, as I said."

He frowned harder, and I had to force myself to look away.

"Anyway, I was sitting there drinking, and Webb—who didn't hate me but also didn't like me—came over and called me an apple thief." I chuckled, because it all seemed so long ago. Like a whole different Luke, living a whole different life. A Luke who had no clue just how much Webb Sunday would come to mean to him. "Remember that?"

Webb nodded. "Luke's attorney said part of my land—

my orchard—might actually be Luke's because of issues with property laws from two hundred years ago—"

"Don't forget the apple tithes," Em interjected. "And the friendship agreement."

"Or the spongy moths," Hawk supplied. "And the fruitful harvests."

"Yes, thank you," Webb agreed. "Suffice it to say, I was annoyed that something from that long ago could possibly impact my life today—"

Knox grinned. "That's what we call irony."

"—and I blamed Luke."

I snorted. "Webb's the most protective person ever when it comes to someone or something he loves," I told my mom. "Whether it's Aiden, or his family, or his land, he'll fight tooth and nail to make sure the things he cares about are safe." I couldn't help smiling a little. "It's one of his best features."

"Yeah, I don't know about that. I yelled at Luke," Webb admitted softly, his eyes on me. "Which I was ashamed of almost as soon as it happened. So I sat down with him to buy him a drink, and after maybe two minutes…" His mouth tipped up on one side. "I realized that he was impossible not to like. He's a good person. The best. Loyal and fun."

"Aw." I forced a smile. He made me sound like a golden retriever. "That's sweet. Anyway, it turned out Van the bartender had told Webb the story of the town's lucky charm—the Unity Bugle that hangs in the bar—which involved a pretty girl and…" It was my turn to frown. "You know, you never actually told me the whole story."

"Because I don't remember the whole thing," he admitted. "Something about star-crossed lovers and the spirit of friendship and unity. And the bugle, obviously."

I raised one eyebrow. "You didn't mention the star-crossed lovers at the time."

"Didn't I?"

"*That* I would have remembered," I said with a lightness I did not feel. I finished up my tale quickly. "So, we took the bugle off the wall, went outside, and blew it, thinking it was for *unity*. I can't even imagine how ridiculous we must've looked! And then the next day, the mayor—"

"Hey!" Webb complained. "Now who's telling the story wrong? Let me tell it. So, it was my idea to get the bugle down," he informed my mom. "But Luke was the one who convinced Van to let us take it, using his obey-me teacher voice. It was the funniest, sweetest thing. His cheeks were all pink, and he had these cute freckles—"

"Stop." I clapped a hand to my nose, embarrassed. "My freckles are not pertinent to this story."

"I beg to differ. And then we ran outside. It was dark and cold and clear, and there must've been a billion stars in the sky—"

"It was February," I told my mom with a shrug. "It was nothing special."

"And then we held hands right there on the common—"

"More like, we each held up a hand to recite this silly pledge Van told us to say. It wasn't like we actually intended to hold hands," I explained a little desperately. "Because we didn't."

"Didn't we?" Webb stared at me and stroked a finger over his bottom lip pensively. "I dunno. I sort of remember that I did it on purpose. Your hand was cold, and I—"

"You were being a good friend," I said with something like rising panic, because he was making the whole thing sound so *romantic*, and what the heckity was that about when he'd said we were *nothing?* "So we said the stupid pledge—"

"Come *on*! It wasn't stupid," he argued. "Dude. It was… special. It was meaningful."

"We were drunk," I scoffed.

"It was beautiful."

"I guarantee you can't even remember the words!" I nearly yelled. "Webb, for pity's sake, stop making it sound like… like…"

"The specific words don't matter, Luke! What matters is what's in your heart, and I…" He swallowed hard and glanced around the table, then back down at his hands. "I felt united with you."

"United in *friendship*," I gritted out. I swallowed and turned toward my mom. "That's what's so annoying about this Hand-Fast Watch thing. People are getting confused."

I was getting confused.

I cleared my throat and stood up. "And that's the story. Now, if you'll excuse me, I have a date with an impatient first grader who needs to practice some spelling."

"You don't have to." Webb pushed to his feet. "I can take care of him while you—"

But I was already halfway to the hall. "Stay there. Be back in a bit."

I practically raced up the stairs, in case anyone thought to follow me, but then I paused before heading to Aiden's room and took a deep breath. Tears pricked the back of my eyes, which was so foolish, but I pushed them back.

I knocked on the frame of Aiden's open door and found him sitting on his bed, holding a cell phone in his hand. "Hey. How's it going with the practicing?"

I expected him to look guilty because I'd caught him playing a game, but when he glanced up, his lower lip quivered.

"My mom just called. She said she's not sure she'll make it to the Spring Fling. She might have to do mandatory overtime. Mandatory means she has to do it. And she's trying to get out of it, but she doesn't think she can."

"Oh, dang." I picked my way through the toy cars scattered on the floor and sat on the twin bed beside him. "Dude, that stinks. So disappointing for both of you. I know she really wanted to be there. Maybe we can video chat part of it for her, you know? It won't be the same, but—"

"Do you think my mom loves me?" Aiden asked suddenly. "Because my dad says…"

I ground my back teeth together, fighting the urge to snap something about Webb.

"I think your dad cares so much about you, he doesn't always look at things clearly. He goes into protection mode, and his brain starts thinking, 'Must. Keep. Safe.' Like a robot." I moved my hands up and down in a terrible robot impression, and he gave me a watery grin. I continued. "Your mom definitely loves you. Not a doubt in my mind."

"Dad says love isn't a thing you say, it's a thing you do. He says love means showing up for people when you say you will."

"There are a lot of ways to love, Aiden. That's your dad's way, for sure. And that's real love, for sure. But love can also mean your mom working hard so she has money to take care of you. To take you to the movies. To buy sleeping bags for campouts."

"But if she loves me, then why did she leave? My dad stayed, so why couldn't she?"

Oh, Lord.

I hesitated. "Because… because your dad is like a tree. Like… like an apple tree! No, really," I said when Aiden wrinkled his nose. "Go with me here, okay? Your dad is a tree, and he's stretched down roots. He's happiest staying in one place forever. He gets strength from consistency. But your mom... she's more like a butterfly, isn't she? You remember when we studied them in class? Butterflies can't stay in one place too long. That's not what they're designed to do. They can't root themselves to the soil. They'd die if they tried. But they do come back, over and over, season after season, to visit the places they love." I shrugged. "I mean, that's not a hundred percent accurate, but——"

Aiden threw himself into my lap and wrapped his baby-soft arms around my neck. "Thank you, Mr. Williams. That makes me feel better."

"Oh." I hugged him back, so very tightly. One of the things I loved about teaching children this age was that they constantly teetered between the babies they'd been and the grown-ups they were becoming. It was easy to forget they still needed snuggles and reassurance to feel safe. "I'm glad, sweetheart. I know for sure that your mom and dad don't want you to be upset, okay? They both love you, and they're doing the best they can for you."

"And you."

"Hmm?"

Aiden pulled back. "You do the best you can for me. I love you."

"I love you, too," I told him, trying not to show just how overwhelmed I was at his simple, innocent declaration.

It *should* be simple to tell someone you loved them. I wasn't sure why adults made it so dang complicated.

Aiden sniffled, then scooted away to grab his spelling flash cards.

"So, which are you?" he asked over his shoulder. "A tree or a butterfly?"

"I..." I paused to think about it, even after Aiden

dumped the stack of flash cards in my lap. "I dunno. Maybe a bird? A squirrel. I haven't thought about it."

"Nah. You're more like…" He twisted up his mouth in thought. "I know! You're like the branches my dad grafts onto the trees in the orchard."

"So basically I'm a stick?" I poked him in the ribs. "Thanks bunches."

He giggled. "No, Dad gets these tree branches from other places and then kinda sticks 'em to the trees that are already there."

"Oh, right. He grafts them." Webb had explained that too, sort of, the day I'd fallen in the pond.

"The trees bring the sticks back to life, kinda. And they make flowers and apples again. But the sticks make the trees stronger, too, so they make *more* apples. Better apples. That's you."

"Wow. That's…"

"I know kind of a lot about apple trees," he said modestly.

"You sure do. And that might just be the nicest thing anyone ever said to me. Thank you, Aiden."

"Sure." Aiden grinned, showing his teeth that still hadn't grown all the way back in. "I'm a black bear, by the way. I eat food and make messes."

I snorted. "Let's get this spelling practice done, black bear," I said lightly, telling myself not to dwell on life lessons from a seven-year-old.

But that night when I went home, Aiden's words… and his father's… were all I could think about.

Chapter Eighteen

WEBB

It had been nearly a week since I'd fucked things up royally. A week of regretting, of wanting to apologize and not knowing how.

Of missing him.

Luke had been busy with his mom, and I'd been busy feeling sorry for myself. So, when my attorney had suggested an update meeting Friday afternoon, I'd agreed immediately, desperate for anything to distract me.

It hadn't worked quite the way I'd intended.

"Hey, Katey. Jack around?" I asked as I walked into Panini Jack's. The lunch rush had ended, but the after-school rush hadn't quite begun, which I knew from experience was Jack's favorite time to concoct new recipes.

Coincidentally, it was also my favorite time to visit him.

"Webb, honey! I haven't seen you in weeks." Katey gave me a flirtatious little smile, tucked a strand of blonde hair behind her ear, and leaned her forearms against the hostess stand. "How're things?"

I had no idea how to answer that. "Good, I guess. Busy."

"Anything I can help with?"

"Not really. It's mostly, um…" I pondered the things that had occupied my time for the past month. Figuring out I was bisexual, getting accidentally handfasted, sorting out Aiden's custody situation. "Muriel's getting ready to calve," I said out loud.

"Ah." She gave me a bewildered look. "Well, I don't know much about cows, but if I can help with anything—"

"That's sweet," I began, moving toward the swinging door that led to the kitchen. "But I don't—" I stopped short and turned back to her as a thought occurred to me. "Oh! Actually, you know what? There *is* one thing."

"Name it!"

"Maybe you could listen a little more closely when Luke orders breakfast from now on."

"Huh?"

"I know, he's really tough to understand with his North Carolina accent," I said sympathetically, lying through my teeth since the only time I'd ever heard Luke speak with any discernible accent had been the morning he'd defended Aiden… and that had been so freakin' hot, I'd've loved for him to "y'all" me all day long. "He's real sensitive about it," I continued. "About being an outsider. And I know you're such a sweet person, you'd hate to think he was feeling that way."

"I… I would," she agreed. "Does he really feel that way?"

I nodded sadly. "Sometimes, I'm afraid. But anyway, now I know you'll help, at least."

She bit her lip and nodded. "I'll… I'll do that, Webb. And I hope I haven't made him feel bad in the past when I, uh… didn't understand him. I've always sorta really liked Luke."

I grinned. "I bet you have. He's a great guy, Katey."

One who deserved to be treated well... especially since his fake betrothed kept trampling all over his feelings.

I pushed through the double door into the kitchen area and found Jack standing alone by the gleaming metal prep table, chopping something green, with a black cap pulled over his fair hair.

"Hey," I called softly. I grabbed the backless stool he kept in the corner so I could sit and watch him cook—the stool he unofficially called "the Sunday stool," since as far as I knew, Hawk and I were the only ones he allowed back here while he was experimenting—and carried it closer to the table.

Jack didn't look up, and the blade of his knife continued to rock through a pile of herbs, turning them to... well, mush.

"Uh. Jack?" I demanded.

"Huh?" He sucked in a startled breath and set down his knife. "Oh, shit. Hey. I didn't hear you."

I looked from the herbs to Jack, then from Jack to the herbs. I imagined I'd just discovered Jack's version of my ax and chopping block.

I thought about what made *me* chop furiously and wondered if it were possible...

"Did you, um..." I cleared my throat uncomfortably. "Were you having any... Do you want to... talk? About... Fuck, I don't know." I felt my face go hot. "Relationships or anything?"

"A *relationship*?" Jack scoffed. "Me? *Pfft*. With who? For what?" He shuddered. "A mutual distrust of relationships is the cornerstone of our friendship, Webb Sunday. That's why you and I have never become the Hollow's most scorching power couple."

I laughed. "That... and the fact that I thought I was

straight until two weeks ago," I reminded him. "Oh, and that we're not attracted to each other in any way."

"Well, okay, yes, all those things, too," he conceded with a smirk. "But Jesus. Friends don't accuse friends of having relationship drama out of a clear blue sky. That's cold."

"Alright, alright." I held up a hand for peace. "I'm just starting to recognize uncontrolled chopping as a sign of distress, that's all. I thought I'd see if I could, you know… listen. As a friend."

Jack pressed his lips together. "Wow. That's a sign of true friendship, right there, because you'd rather give me a kidney than talk feelings, wouldn't you?"

His wall oven beeped, and he grabbed a kitchen towel to remove a pan of something delicious-smelling.

"No! I'm not the Sunday who hates talking about feelings," I argued. "That's Knox."

"Ah, right. Silly me. In that case… how are things between you and Luke?" Jack set his dish on a counter.

"That's… We…" I cleared my throat and fell silent.

"Mmm. Obviously. Well said," Jack teased. He grabbed a plate and began filling it with mashed potatoes and a portion of something from the pan, then garnished it with some of the herbs he'd chopped and slid it in front of me, along with a fork. "Taste this for me. If you die, I won't put it on the menu next week."

I snorted. It smelled even better up close, and I hadn't had lunch yet. But instead of taking a bite, I pushed my fork through the potatoes distractedly. "I talked to Curt just now."

Jack folded his arms over his chest and leaned a hip back against the counter. "And?"

"And…" I blew out a breath. "I asked him to look into some shit about Amanda. She had Luke convinced that she'd turned over a new leaf, you know? That she was *trying*. She kept showing up late to things because her boss supposedly kept her after hours or canceling at the last minute, claiming she had car trouble. It was the same shit she pulled back in the day, when she had one foot out the door."

"Mmhmm. And now you don't know how to tell Aiden his mom's been lying."

I winced. "Actually, no. It all checks out. She just got a promotion at work. And the auto shop halfway between here and Keltyville says she's a regular there—they've towed her car twice. And… she voluntarily submitted her financial records to the court, including a fucking retirement account and a pre-approval letter from her bank for a mortgage. It's like they're talking about a whole different person than the one I know… *knew*."

This information was so inconsistent with the woman who'd run off several years ago—heck, even with the woman I'd been married to, for the last few years of our marriage—I couldn't even wrap my head around it.

"I dunno, Webb," he said dubiously. "People don't just become responsible overnight."

"My thought exactly, but…" I heaved a sigh. "Then he told me she actually has a confirmed employment history for almost the entire time she was away. He was all, 'Is it possible she wasn't quite as flighty as you thought, Webb?' And now… shit. I don't know what to think. I can't deny it when the evidence is right there."

"Where was she, then, for the past couple of years? What was she doing?"

"Investing in a cosmetics company in Arizona, at least part of the time. Curt's exact words were 'It failed spectacularly.' But… then she started working two jobs to stay on her feet. And she didn't do very well at any of them. She moved around from job to job with the seasons. She kept going, though. Curt said, 'I imagine she learned a lot from that experience. Maybe she's grown and changed.'"

"Damn."

"Yeah. The judge is almost definitely going to allow her to take him on unsupervised visits."

Jack watched me carefully. "And are you good with that?"

"No… but also yes. Aiden really wants it. And Luke…" I trailed off and shook my head.

"Luke," he prompted.

"Last night at bedtime, Aiden told me he finally understood why Amanda hadn't stayed. That it wasn't because she didn't love him." I looked up at Jack bleakly. "I had no idea he'd been struggling with that."

"Webb," he said gently. "You're one person. And you're a great dad—"

"Luke knew, though," I interrupted. "And he explained to Aiden that Amanda is like a butterfly. She can't stay put because it's not in her nature. 'But that doesn't make her bad, Dad. She's just not like you.'"

"Ohhh, fuck," Jack groaned. "That's seriously deep, and…"

"Special?" I supplied. "Yeah, I know." I dragged my fork through the potatoes again. "And, as if that weren't enough to make my mind explode, Curt also told me that the Pond Orchard isn't actually in dispute. He got a clean title for me. Which I guess means Luke gets a title for his land also." I struggled to make this not sound like a sign of the apocalypse.

"Those are good things, right? Best outcome for both of you."

I hesitated. "Yes. Except Curt said something like, 'Possession is nine-tenths of the law,' and 'If his lawyer had wanted to fight it, he might have been able to get some kind of settlement, but the man's incompetent,' and now…"

"Now you're thinking that you've treated Luke unfairly? That his attorney should have fought and made you pay after all?" Jack surmised, laughing a little. "Dude, weren't you the one who told me Luke invited you to *have* the orchard? To take as much land as you wanted?"

My mouth tilted up at one corner. "Yeah." He was generous that way.

I still needed to tell him about this development, though. I wanted him to hear the news from me and not because he got a formal letter from Curt.

I felt like I owed him that.

In fact, I owed him a whole lot more than that.

"And aren't you the guy who just paid for the roof on his house with the sale of your tractor? I think you're probably even."

"Yeah, I know. That's the problem!" God, the words sounded so stupid, even to my own ears. "It's like we've had this *real* issue with the property line, right? And this *real* issue with his death trap of a house. And now those things are gone, and all we have left is…" An accidental handfasting. A pretend betrothal.

"You know, maybe Amanda's not the only one who grew and changed," Jack said thoughtfully. "Maybe it's time you, you know… reconsider your stance on relationships."

He said this with the same enthusiasm with which he'd discuss recreational root canals.

"Not you, though, huh?" I asked, amused.

"No." He looked uncharacteristically serious, and maybe even a little sad. "No, I can't see that changing for me."

Before I could ask him what his problem was, though, he forced a smile and tapped the edge of my plate. "Are you gonna eat this or play with it?"

Oh, right.

I took a large bite and savored it. "Holy shit. This is phenomenal." I swallowed and immediately took another. "Is that biscuits on top of chicken? The herbs are fucking delicious."

He beamed. "Excellent. Chicken biscuit pot pie is going on the menu for next week."

I coughed on my mouthful of chicken. "This is pie?"

He narrowed his eyes. "Ye-es? Why?"

"No reason." I pushed my plate away and stood. "Put me down for an entire pie for next week, okay? And you and I are gonna eat it and drink some beer, and you'll tell me whatever the fuck you're angsting over."

Jack's eyes widened in horror. "Ohhhh, no. Hold the phone, buddy. Go have deep convos with your betrothed. And don't you have four billion brothers to meddle with? What's Reed up to down in DC, huh? He never calls, he never writes. And Porter. He's at such a crucial age. You should check in——"

"I do have concerns about Hawk," I admitted.

"H-hawk? What's, um… what's wrong with Hawk?" Jack wiped an imaginary speck off the counter.

"Oh, just this whole business with Fogg Peak." I waved a hand. "You know how he is. Ninety percent of the time, he's the most easygoing guy in the world, but once he gets an idea in his head…"

"Yeah. Tell me about it," he said faintly.

"Anyway. I'm really glad he's got you looking out for him." I patted him on the shoulder. "As a boss and as an honorary big brother. Just knowing he's got you to hike with and talk to… You're the best friend I could ask for."

The smile Jack gave me could only be described as…
pained.

"Dude, seriously. Take the compliment." I rolled my
eyes. The man was way worse at discussing his emotions
than I was. "Look, I gotta go. I'm going to tell Luke
about the land. I just… I need to make sure he
understands."

It wasn't at all that I was absolutely dying to see him, to
talk to him, to reassure myself that I hadn't fucked things
up too badly.

I jogged out of the restaurant and drove straight to
Luke's place. The more I thought about it, the more
desperate I was to let him know about the land situation, to
tell him I would never want to take advantage of him
under any circumstances. I was starting to believe I'd give
him any amount of Sunday land, if that's what it took to
make him happy.

And that scared the crap out of me.

But when I knocked on the front door, it wasn't Luke
who answered. It was his mom.

"Hi, Ms. Williams," I said, a little out of breath from
jogging across the yard and up the front steps. "Is Luke
around?"

"Oh, no, honey. I'm afraid he's not. He said he was
going to a dance recital this afternoon that a couple of his
students are performing in. He took his aunt with him
since she used to teach dance classes a million years ago. Is
there something I can help you with?"

She must have seen the disappointment on my face
because she ushered me inside. "Come, come. I'm just
making some tea, and I'd love the company if you don't
mind."

I followed her into the newly renovated kitchen. It was
Luke's dream kitchen, so it made me smile every time I saw

it. Today, I noticed he'd put some of his students' drawings on the big side-by-side fridge.

"Those are pretty flowers," I said, nodding toward the overflowing vase.

Ms. Williams moved over to the kettle already steaming on the stove. "Aren't they? Some man sent those to him. I can't remember his name now for the life of me."

"A man sent him those?" I asked. My voice sounded harsher than I'd intended. What man was sending Luke, *my* Luke, flowers? We were practically married, for fuck's sake.

Ms. Williams let out a laugh. "Pretty sure it was an older man thanking him for taking an ewe and her lamb off his hands. My new grandlammy is the cutest thing you ever saw. She's out in the nearest enclosure if you want to see her."

I let out a breath and a huff of laughter. "I'm an idiot. He got a lamb? How? He must be over the moon." Why hadn't he told me? This was a big deal.

"Someone rescued them and couldn't keep them. Knew Lukey was set up for taking them in. I'm just grateful he was able to give them such a good home." She eyed me for a moment. "Since the farm wasn't in such great shape until recently."

I opened my mouth to respond but realized I was walking into dangerous territory. Ms. Williams hadn't known about the sad state of the farm, so when did she get this information? And how?

She poured water into two mugs and continued. "It seems like we owe you and your family a heapload of thanks."

I swallowed. "Luke's been working hard."

"Mm. He has. I can see that. I would imagine that taking a… how did she describe it? *Hovel* and making it

253

into this…" She waved a hand around, indicating the sparkling new kitchen. "Had to have taken quite a bit of effort."

"Who called it a hovel?"

She bobbed the tea bags up and down in the water. "A lady from the knitting group stopped by to pick up some yarn Luke wanted her to have. She said she couldn't believe he'd had time to even think of her considering he'd been working on the house from sunup to sundown every day in preparation for my visit. She told me the last time she'd been out to the place, Ben Pond had run it into the ground. Even the roof had a hole in it that, quote, a vee-dubya hippie bus, unquote, could fit through."

Her eyes never left mine.

"It wasn't that big," I muttered. "Valerie Tippington is a busybody known for exaggeration."

"What I want to know, Webb Sunday, is why Lukey didn't feel like he could tell me the truth." She picked up the mugs and nodded toward the farmhouse table. Once we took our seats, I bought myself a little time by blowing on my tea. "Stop stalling," she said with a soft chuckle.

"Ms. Williams," I began.

"Laura, please," she corrected. "Since I'm practically your mother-in-law, I believe we can dispense with the formalities."

My face burned, and I stared at my tea again. "Laura. Yes, ma'am."

What was I supposed to say? And would Luke get mad at me if I corroborated Valerie's story? I took a sip of tea even though it was still too hot.

"Is this thing between you and my son real?"

I choked on the tea, nearly snorting it all over myself in an effort not to drown. Laura calmly handed me a napkin but continued to look at me with a knowing smirk.

Once I got control of myself, I met her eyes. "I have real feelings for him, yes. But…"

"But."

I ran a hand through my hair and thought about the but. What exactly was the hesitation here?

"He's upset with me. Justifiably so. And I received some information today that might make him even more upset. So I came over here to talk to him about it."

She sipped her tea carefully and pondered my words. It seemed like the more agitated I got, the calmer and *slower* she got.

"I see."

"Has he said anything?" I blurted. "About me? About us? About the handfasting thing?"

Fuck it. I needed to know, and this was my best chance at gathering intel.

Even if I sounded like a fourteen-year-old lovesick loser.

There was something about Laura's kind face that made me feel like she'd accept me, loser and all, the same way her son accepted everyone he'd ever met.

She smiled. "He said you have a lot going on right now. Aiden and his mom, the orchard, your other family members. It sounds like you carry a lot of responsibilities on your shoulders."

I nodded. "He does, too, though."

She dipped her chin. "True. He takes his job very seriously. Always has."

"He loves those kids," I said. "More than anything. He's the most dedicated teacher I've ever seen. And the Hollow is lucky to have him. Hell, he ramped up this whole Pick-a-Book thing in the middle of the big house renovations because he didn't want to miss out on a chance to publicize it during the Spring Fling. He's been working day and night to make sure the children's book charity gets plenty of support at the festival."

I stopped to take a breath. "He's one of the best humans I've ever met," I added softly.

"You're falling in love with him, aren't you?"

I blinked up at her. Was she nuts? Love? *Pfft.* But how did I tell Luke's mother, of all people, that...

I stopped when my brain—and heart—caught up with her words.

"I..." My throat felt lumpy and weird. "I... he..."

Laura reached across to pat my hand. "Kinda makes you feel like puking, doesn't it?"

"Oh God. I love him. I want this to be real. Not a town joke."

Was it suffocating in here, or was it just me?

"Good. But be sure, Webb. Because if you're not ready for this, you need to tell him. Luke is sensitive, and he needs someone who's going to be there for him. Someone who won't run when the going gets tough. A man who won't flake out on him. He deserves someone reliable."

Her words made my head swim. I felt like fate was playing a cruel trick on me. Since when was *I* the unreliable one in any situation?

But she was right. I wasn't being consistent with Luke.

I'd let my fear get the better of me.

The back door slammed open, making me jump out of my skin. "Mom, help! The baby got out, and I need help getting her before the cows do. Stella somehow broke through—" He stepped far enough into the kitchen to notice me. "Oh. Webb. Hi."

I stood up and raced toward him. "What happened? Stella's out?" That cow was going to be the death of me. We'd put her and the others in a different area to keep them away from Muriel while she was calving, but she must have found a way out of her pasture.

We hustled outside and across the yard to the sheep enclosure.

"I got a lamb," he said over his shoulder. "And she's tiny." I could hear the fear in his voice.

"We'll get her, baby," I said, rushing ahead of him. "I promise."

When we got past the enclosure to the other side, I saw my brother Knox headed our way on the 4x4 with Marco in the passenger seat.

I also saw Stella and Diana munching sweet spring grass next to a fat ewe and an adorable baby lamb, who looked like a collection of cotton balls on Q-tip legs. Everyone was chilling as if it was no big deal.

Thank God we didn't have a bull.

"I'll get Stella and Diana heading back in the right direction if you grab the baby," I said to Luke.

He agreed and headed toward the sheep while I made my way to the cows. What followed included a comical amount of mud, manure, Luke's special brand of non-cursing, my ear-curling brand of actual cursing, and Marco's colorful commentary while taking video with his iPhone to post on the Pippin Peeps Facebook page.

Once we'd gotten the sheep back in their enclosure, we herded Stella and Diana back onto my family's property and into a pasture with better fencing. Knox offered to run Luke and me back to Luke's place in the 4x4 since my car was still there.

Before we took off, Marco looked up from his phone with a grin. "Lookie there. I just earned myself a commemorative scroll."

Dread pooled in my gut. "What do you mean?"

"I'm the one who documented Part the Sixth. You

commingled yon flocks or some shit. Well done, kids."

He returned to the house while still belly laughing.

The ride back to Luke's was awkward as hell. None of us spoke until it seemed Knox finally couldn't stand it anymore.

"How'd it go at Curt's office, Webb? Any news about the custody stuff with Amanda?"

The reminder of the orchard deed sat heavy on my heart. I wanted to tell Luke about it so he could hear it from me, but I was due to pick up Aiden in twenty minutes from Olin's house. Now wasn't the time.

"We're going to allow unsupervised overnights," I said numbly. "But Curt's going to try and make sure there are some parameters in place."

Luke didn't contribute to the conversation or ask any questions. His lack of involvement made me feel even worse.

Knox tried to include him. "Luke, how was your day?"

"Good. Spelling bee was this afternoon. I won't tell you how Aiden did, since I know he'll want to tell you himself, but I was really proud of him."

"He won?" Knox demanded.

I cuffed him lightly on the head. "He just said he wasn't gonna tell. Jesus."

"No, but let's just say I was even more impressed with his attitude than with his performance. It's a hard thing not to get everything you want," he said softly. "It's even harder to do it gracefully."

That was the damn truth.

Silence fell again.

When Knox dropped us off, he shot me a look I couldn't interpret. I followed Luke back to the kitchen door. I needed him to know I wanted to talk even though I didn't have time to do it now.

"Listen," I began. "I have some things I need to say about the land—"

"Thanks for helping me get the animals sorted," he said quickly before I could continue. "I was freaked out when I got home and saw them all mixed in there together. I was worried about the lamb because she's too small to protect herself. But don't worry about staying. I know you're busy. I ran into Maryanne at the school pickup, and she said you and Aiden and a bunch of other families were meeting up tonight to make posters for the Spring Fling Scout booth. So that's awesome. I know Aiden's really excited. And if you need any poster supplies, let me know! I have a ton. Well, you've seen them. In my trailer. That's where I still keep them. I'm kind of using it as a Pick-a-Book office right now. The trailer, I mean."

I stepped forward to grab him and slam my mouth against his to shut him up and stop his nervous babbling, but before I got close enough, the door opened, revealing his mom and aunt.

"There you are! Everything all settled?"

The look on Laura's face was hopeful and clearly indicated an interest in more than the animal mix-up. I shook my head.

Luke plastered on a fake smile. "Definitely. But Webb has to run. He's got a thing with Aiden tonight. Have fun! Tell Aiden I said I can't wait to see how the posters turn out."

Before I knew what was happening, I was in my car, headed down the long driveway.

Alone.

Much later that night, after my fingers were stained with marker ink, my knees were sore from crawling around on the school gym floor, and my talkative son was finally

259

silently sleeping, I slumped into a kitchen chair and let Uncle Drew pour me a beer.

"Long day?" he asked.

I took a deep glug of the cold beer. It tasted amazing. After I swallowed, I took a breath. "Do you have any idea how many people cracked a joke tonight about me commingling my flock?"

Drew smiled and shook his head. "Marco was pretty desperate for one of those scrolls."

"It's one thing for the other folks in town to be all up in my business about it, but family? C'mon."

Drew's smile dropped. "Hey. Watch it. Marco loves you, and he cares about Luke very much. It's not *his* fault you managed to stick your foot in your mouth *and* have your head up your ass at the same time where Luke Williams is concerned. That little pretzel of dumbfuckery is of your own making. Marco happens to believe you and Luke are perfect for one another just like I do, so don't blame him for helping that along."

I sighed. "I'm sorry. It's just been a long day. And... I..."

Why was this so freaking hard to say out loud? I took another sip of beer.

Drew's patience outlasted me.

"I miss Luke," I admitted softly.

Drew pulled a slow, knowing smile. "Thank fuck you admitted it. So go see him."

I let out a laugh. "It's late."

"Tomorrow's Saturday. You can sleep in."

"The Spring Fling is tomorrow, remember? And I have an excited child. There's no such thing as sleeping in."

Drew pierced me with a look. "I can manage Aiden. You know that."

It was tempting, but the last thing I wanted to do was

show up late at night while Luke's mom and aunt were there. If there was one thing this town didn't need, it was footage of Webb Sunday climbing the trellis to his hand-fasting partner's bedroom.

"Maybe I'll take him some breakfast in the morning," I said.

Drew nodded. "Suit yourself. But know if I don't see you at this table in the morning, I'll get Aiden ready for the fair."

I stood up and kissed his cheek before washing my beer glass and setting it in the dish drainer by the sink.

It took two hours of tossing and turning before I realized Drew's words had wormed their way inside and taken hold of me. I needed to see Luke.

And I wasn't willing to wait another minute.

Thankfully, the 4x4 was quiet enough to get close without disturbing his animals or the house. My plan was to text him when I got close if I didn't get lucky enough to find a door unlocked.

But when I made my way onto the property, I noticed a dim light on in the trailer. Had he left it on by accident, or was he up this late working on his book stuff for the Spring Fling?

I opened the door to the trailer and peeked in. He was curled up in a ball, asleep on the bed, surrounded by stacks of books.

My heart squeezed with affection for him. He was everything kind and good. How would I ever do enough to deserve him?

I moved across the space and began pulling the books off the bed until it was clear. He was already dressed in an old T-shirt and pajama pants. I moved him under the covers before sliding in next to him and pulling him into my arms.

His eyes blinked open and met mine. There was a confused look but not a single ounce of resistance.

We didn't speak. The time for words wasn't now. Now was the time for action.

I kissed him tenderly, relishing the now familiar taste of him and reveling in the feel of his lithe body in my embrace.

My hands roamed over his body, under his shirt, down his pants. After a while, our hot breaths ramped up and filled the small space around us. We pulled each other's clothes off and moved against each other with patience and reverence.

This was no longer simply sex.

It was hope and promise, a window into a lifetime of possibilities. It was an answer to a question I'd been avoiding, but one so critical to my future happiness, it made me almost dizzy.

He was here with me now, in my arms, in my heart, in every hope and dream I had for the days and years to come.

Somehow, he managed to come up with the supplies we needed, but for the first time, I fantasized about a time in the future we wouldn't need the condom between us anymore.

If he was willing. If he would be mine for real.

When I entered his body, my eyes were on his. Not a word was spoken out loud, but I heard everything in his touch and the sounds he made, the way he welcomed me inside his body and held me tight.

This was it. It was everything.

All the pain and heartache I'd gone through to get me to this place were worth it in the end.

Because I was here now with Luke Williams.

And I wasn't going to let him go.

Chapter Nineteen

LUKE

I woke up with such divergent thoughts, it was almost nauseating.

On the one hand, I'd never felt so loved, so adored, so incredibly overwhelmed with the soul-presence of another human. Webb had taken me over completely last night, and it was an experience I'd never forget.

On the other hand, something about the silent intensity of the experience had seemed final. Definitive. And I couldn't help worrying that it had been a goodbye.

My first instinct was, as usual, to put a sunshiny face on it. To try to convince myself that I was fine with us being friends and that my life was perfectly great as it was.

But I'd been trying that all week, and it hadn't worked. Not even a little.

It turned out, forcing yourself to be positive and optimistic as a means of protecting yourself was approximately the least positive, optimistic thing a person could do.

The truth was, I was in love with Webb Sunday. Full-on, hard-core in love, in a way that I hadn't believed I could love someone. And Webb was too important to me to let him go if there was any possibility we could be together.

After the way he'd touched me, *loved* me, last night, I wasn't willing to slink away without fighting for him. Without being sure.

"Webb," I said, reaching out to run a hand over his prickly cheek. "Wake up."

For a split second, when he opened his eyes and saw me there, his face softened into an affectionate smile. But then it disappeared.

"Fuck. The Spring Fling! What time is it?" He jumped off the bed and scrambled for his clothes. "I told Aiden we could get over to the festival early."

I sat up and pulled the blanket around me. Clearly this wasn't the best time to suggest we have a serious discussion about our feelings, but when was I going to see him again?

Don't be an idiot, Luke. He lives next door. And you'll see him at the festival.

Still. I hated to let him go without saying *something*.

"Thank you for the sex!" I blurted.

Webb froze before looking up at me in slow motion. "Uh… you're welcome?"

I squeezed my eyes closed. "That's not what I meant."

"You didn't want to thank me for the sex?"

I opened my eyes to see a teasing glint in his. God, he was beautiful.

I let out a breath. "Just go. I'll see you later."

He stepped past a stack of books on the floor and pressed a kiss to the top of my head, and I had to restrain myself from grabbing his shirt and holding him close for another few minutes… or maybe forever.

Fortunately, I had plenty of commitments of my own this morning and no time to waste. I finished loading the last few boxes of books into my car and ran inside the farmhouse for a quick shower, which was how I ran nearly headlong into my mom as she was trotting down the stairs.

I couldn't remember the last time I'd seen her move that quickly.

"Hey! Why are you running? Is Aunt Sue okay?" I darted a look upstairs. "Did she take a fall?"

"Lukey Lou," she said reprovingly. "Since when do you assume the worst in a situation? Sue's in the kitchen drinking coffee and getting ready for Drew and Marco to come pick us up in a bit. She's fine. And so am I. I'm just excited for your town festival. See?"

She did a pirouette in the front hall, showing off her jeans and the purple-and-yellow Pick-a-Book T-shirt she wore under her hoodie. Then she jammed a baseball hat on her cropped white hair that read "I Scrolled For Love In Little Pippin Hollow."

"Oh, Mom," I groaned.

"Oh Mom what? I think this scroll business is the cutest excuse for two humans to fall in love that anyone ever invented," she said firmly. "People meet their match in all kinds of ways—through internet dates, and reality TV shows, or because they happened to be on the same airplane at the same time—so why can't fate operate through a scroll and some centuries-old laws?"

She had a point, but I shook my head resolutely anyway. "Don't buy in to the hype. Whatever Webb and I are… it's not what Hand-Fast Watch makes it seem like we are. It's not real."

Her voice lost its usual sweetness. "Don't tell me what's real and what's not, son. My lungs might not be the greatest, but my vision is just fine. You might need *your* eyes checked, though. Because as far as I can tell, Hand-Fast Watch is only saying you and Webb are two idiots in love… and I think that's pretty accurate."

My face went red, and I grimaced. She was half right, anyway.

"Please don't overdo it today, okay?" I pleaded. "I know you're feeling better, and maybe I'm a little overprotective, but you seemed tired last night. And… it doesn't feel like that long ago that you were really sick."

"I know what I can handle, kiddo."

Outside, a horn beeped, and when I glanced out the window, I saw Drew and Marco pulling up in a gigantic old Ford convertible with the top down. Marco was sitting in the middle of the front seat, and Drew had an arm over his shoulders.

"What in the world?" I said, bewildered. "Where's he been hiding that beast? That thing is *not* eco-friendly. Frankly, it looks like it might collapse halfway to town. You know what, why don't I drive you—"

"Nonsense. Sue!" Mom called excitedly. "Hurry it up. Our dates are here!" She pressed a kiss to my cheek. "I don't know why you never told us just how amazing this town was, honey. I would've visited a long time ago." She walked out the front door with no hesitation.

"Maybe grab a warmer sweater!" I called. "It's not nearly as warm as it looks out there!"

She ignored me, and I could've sworn I heard Aunt Sue snicker as she ran out the door after her.

I shook my head as I watched my mother and aunt climb into the back seat of the car before the car went careening down the driveway.

I wondered if this was what parents felt like when their kids went off without them. But gosh, how much worse must it be for someone like Webb, who had at least half a dozen people he must worry about like that?

I'd known from the beginning that Webb was responsible for a lot of things and people, but it hadn't occurred to me until that moment just how heavy that responsibility must feel. No wonder he wasn't eager to jump into another relationship, especially with a person he'd only really gotten to know a few weeks ago, and *a man*, at that.

My fear of rejection was making me impatient, but it didn't have to be all or nothing. Not right now anyway. I could be patient for Webb. I could show him how good we could be together. And once the time ran out on this hand-fasting business, once his custody situation was nailed down… well, then we would see.

I was in a much better frame of mind when I got to the town common than I'd been when I woke up, but it would've been impossible not to be cheerful anyway, once I saw how transformed the usually empty park was.

It looked like a traveling flower festival and the Las Vegas Strip had a baby… but in the best possible way.

White festival tents were set up across the center of the grass in neat lines like regiments of soldiers, each deco-rated with a giant numbered flower hanging above the opening, and volunteers were already buzzing around like honeybees, setting up their booths. One whole corner of the parking lot had been roped off, and someone had laid down straw for a petting zoo area. Even though there were hours to go until the fair opened, when I opened my car door, I found the air already redolent with the scents of coffee and sugary fried things.

"Morning, Luke!" Em Sunday called before I'd even had a chance to orient myself. "Need some help unloading?"

"Hey! No, I think I…" Before I could finish my denial, a couple of teenagers were already opening my back doors and lifting out my boxes. "Oh. Well. Okay, then. Thanks."

"Coordinating the festival is our senior service project," Em explained with a wink. "You're kind of obligated to let us help, or we won't be able to graduate." To the teens, she added, "Luke's in booth fourteen, the Pick-a-Book tent. I assigned you one of the best booths in the place, right across from the elementary school's PTA splash booth. Gets lots of traffic, so hopefully you should be able to give out lots of books and get lots of donations."

"Aw, thanks! Do I want to know what a splash booth is?"

"Oh, it's like a dunk tank, sort of? People—usually little kids—buy a couple dollars' worth of beanbags to throw at a target, and if they manage to hit it, a bucket of water falls on the head of the person—usually a volunteer parent—who's sitting underneath."

"But… it's way too cold for that! I want to help the PTA as much as the next guy, but I'm not willing to risk hypothermia for it. Maybe in July…"

"Eh." She shrugged. "Feels pretty warm out here to me. Besides, it's a small bucket of water, and most kids are shit at throwing. There's hardly any actual splashing happening."

"Ahhh, I see."

"Every once in a while, you see an adult step up to the booth to settle a grievance, though, and that's always fun." Her smile turned a little evil. "I might convince Webb to take a turn later, just FYI…"

"I'll have my dollars ready," I promised.

She bumped her arm into mine, and I grinned as she waved and walked off.

The setup hours passed really quickly. I hadn't thought I had much to do—hanging up the decorative posters my kids had done for the Pick-a-Book stall, making sure the mayor had the names of the spelling bee winners, and arranging some books—but before too long, Phillip Vincent, one of the Little Pippin Hookers, had brought me over some fresh sour cream donuts his wife was selling. We'd started chatting about my sheep, who were due to be sheared the following week, and brainstorming all the projects I could do with the wool and how I could involve my students... and before I knew it, I'd promised Phil some yarn, and Mayor York was already taking the stage near the gazebo to officially open the Spring Fling.

It quickly became clear that Em had not been joking about me getting a prime spot for my booth. It seemed like every student in my class came by at some point to give me a hug and show off their contributions to the posters, before ruthlessly attempting to soak one of their family members or teachers.

Olin and Maryanne came by, and I was able to meet his dog "in person finally, Mr. Williams." I also had a fair number of people I didn't recognize at all who asked me to autograph their commemorative scrolls, which was bizarre... but kind of funny... the kind of funny I knew I needed to share with Webb.

Me: (picture of autographed scroll) *FYI, last night you slept with a celebrity*

"Is that right?"

I glanced up and found the man I'd been thinking about standing a few feet in front of my booth wearing a Nature Scouts T-shirt, his eyes crinkled with a smile and his lips twisted in a smirk. He was so gorgeous, I wanted to throw myself at him.

Aiden, on the other hand, didn't hesitate to show his affection. As soon as he saw me look his way, he launched himself toward me at a run, hugging me around my waist like we'd been apart for months and not hours.

"Luke! I have so much to tell you this morning!" he announced. "I officially got my knot-tying badge today, and Dad took pictures so you can see later. And? All the spelling bee winners get to be on the stage this afternoon with the mayor to get trophies, and I'm getting a silver one and Olin's getting gold, and Dad said he'd FaceTime my mom so she can watch on her break. And? Dad said I can stay with you while he helps out with the Touch-a-Goat. And! Dad says I should call you Mr. Williams while we're in public, because you're my teacher, and only call you Luke when it's just us, because then you're like my friend. But only if that's okay with you, so is it? And can I stay here at the Pick-a-Book with you while Dad goes? Because I know almost as much about books as I do about apple trees."

"Wow. Of course you can stay and help me, if your dad says it's okay." I looked up at Webb, but he just tilted his head as if to say *Of course.*

I felt that look to the tips of my toes, and suddenly, I remembered something else Aiden had said the night before. That Webb believed loving someone wasn't about words but about deeds.

If I ever needed a sign that Webb could someday be open to a relationship with me, the fact that he'd trusted me with this sweet boy in his Nature Scout uniform—a boy who'd been too excited about his best friend winning first place in the spelling bee to care that he'd come in second —was it.

"I'll be back in a couple hours," Webb said. "Aiden, do not attempt to convince Luke that you're starving. Try not to talk his ear off. And do what Luke tells you, okay?"

"Of course," Aiden agreed piously, kicking his legs against the chair. "I always listen to Mr. Williams."

And he did. Especially when Jason McEnany came by to take a shift at the booth a little while later, and I told Aiden we could go buy some sour cream donuts together.

Walking up and down the aisles of the fair—seeing the

carnival games and the flashing lights, hearing the music and the constant cheering of people winning prizes—was way more fun with Aiden in tow. His innocent enthusiasm and talkative nature were a joy to be around.

It didn't even bother me when Mrs. Graber, the worst gossip in a town *full* of gossips, met us outside the Pippin Floralscapes booth and started asking about Hand-Fast Watch.

"A little birdie told me that all of the requirements have been filled," she said coyly. "Well, except the final one, of course. But it won't be long until you two are blowing that bugle and saying your vows!"

I bit back an impatient retort. Thankfully, she was wrong. By my count, there were at least two other items left to check off, and since I couldn't imagine Webb declaring his intentions to my mom—*the very idea was laughable!*—and neither of us had any call to bestow garments on the other, we were probably safe.

I wasn't going to tell her that, though. Otherwise, I could envision folks intentionally throwing us into mud puddles so we'd be forced to exchange clothes or claiming Webb told my mom he "intended" to buy me a coffee and Mayor York deciding that counted.

"We're taking our time with it," I informed her. "There's no rush."

Mrs. Graber frowned. "Except doesn't the time run out tomorrow night at sundown?"

Nerves roiled in my gut. After tomorrow, there'd be no more fake relationship tying us together. I had to trust that there were real feelings there, instead.

"We're capable of taking care of completing the tasks on our own, Mrs. Graber. *If* we decide to."

No reason not to throw that in there, right? Let her

spread *that* information, and maybe the Hollowans would get an idea of what was coming.

I expected her to be surprised by my statement. Maybe even disappointed.

I did *not* expect for her to laugh out loud.

"Oh, sweetheart. It's not a matter of being capable of completing them; it's a matter of getting out of your own way and letting it happen. And nothing I've seen over the past half a year has suggested either one of you is capable of *that*."

I stared at her, part confused and part insulted. "Nonsense. It's only been a few weeks—" *that we were even together*, I started to say, but I stopped myself, caught up in my own lies. Surely we were supposed to have been dating before our betrothal.

"Maybe officially, but we've watched you and Webb dance around each other for months. Even when he wasn't speaking to you, he knew exactly where you were whenever you walked in a room. And the harder he fought it, the harder it gripped him." She sighed exultantly. "He's needed someone like you for years, and it's a real satisfaction to all of us to know he's found you."

I blinked at her, and then I blinked some more. *What?*

"Well! I'm off to go see my grandbabies at the petting zoo. Congratulate your mother for me on winning that commemorative scroll!"

She bustled off, and I stared after her. My mother? How would my mother have won a commemorative scroll?

"Luke?" Aiden tugged on my shirt worriedly, recalling my attention to him. "Are you and Dad really not gonna blow the bugle?"

I winced. "You know we're not," I said softly. "Your dad told you it was all a big misunderstanding. And then the other day, when you came home from the campout and your mom asked, he told you again——" I broke off as I saw a familiar woman in a hot pink T-shirt standing by one of the booths toward the end of the row. "Aiden, didn't you say your mom couldn't make it?"

"Yeah. She has mandatory work time," he said impatiently. "I'm gonna tell her all about it later. But you and Dad... you finished almost all the steps on the scroll——"

Right. "We didn't mean to get handfasted," I reminded him, "and we haven't set out to complete those steps intentionally. For example, you know we didn't *choose* to get our hands tied together, did we?" I raised an eyebrow. "We were helping you practice your knots."

"Well, yeah, but you were together all the time. And Dad kissed you a *lot*. And you make him laugh," he accused.

"I know. I know we did. And I'm sorry we confused you. But——"

"Do you love my dad?" he interrupted, point-blank, staring me down with a serious look in those Sunday green eyes, cutting to the heart of the matter.

I swallowed hard, my heart beating way too fast. I couldn't, wouldn't, lie about this. "I do, yeah. And I... I think he cares about me, too. Getting married for real, though... it takes more than just caring about someone. You remember me talking about how your dad gets into his protective mode?" I reprised my robot dance from the other night.

Liz Avery wolf whistled from the Hollow Fire and Rescue tent and called, "You gonna show off those moves in the talent show later, Mr. Williams?"

Good Lord. "Not this year, Liz. Still perfecting them," I called back.

I hurried Aiden back toward the Pick-a-Book tent. "What I'm trying to say is, your dad's got lots of worries on his mind that are more important than our handfasting. He's not ready to be married. So no," I said, fighting not to let my own unreasonable disappointment bleed into my words. "No bugle blowing. But we're still friends! And we'll just… take things slow and see how it goes."

"But what if he never decides he's ready? Why does it have to be this hard? Wouldn't it be better if you just—"

"Aiden, listen to me." I crouched down next to my booth so I could get on his level. "I promise you this much: I love you, always. You can always call me Luke, when we're not in class. You can always talk to me if you need a friend, and I will always help you with your craft projects and your Nature Scouts badges. I'm right next door. Whatever else changes, that won't. I'm going to be there for you, no matter what, okay?"

His little mouth twisted in disappointment, but he nodded. I ruffled his hair before pulling him in for a quick hug.

"I'm going to be there for you, too," he whispered.

Honestly. He was the most adorable child alive.

"Thank you," I said solemnly. "Now. How about if we wash down those donuts with a smoothie from the—"

I broke off as the same pink T-shirt appeared and then disappeared into the crowd again. It was Amanda, I was almost positive. Why hadn't she come over to say hi?

"Mr. Williams!" Principal Oliver's strident voice always made me feel like I was a student getting called into her office for something. "Finally. I've been looking all over for you."

I couldn't see how that was true. I'd hardly been hiding.

I stood up and laid a protective hand on Aiden's shoulder. "Good morning, Principal Oliver. Are you enjoying the, uh… the fair?"

Unlike the rest of the folks in town, who were wearing jeans and T-shirts or even shorts, Principal Oliver was dressed in the same pantsuit combo she wore to work, right down to her shiny, sensible black flats. Her blonde, chin-length bob did not move in the breeze. I wasn't sure she understood the concept of enjoyment.

"I might have enjoyed it," she barked, "if people could do their jobs appropriately. Two of the three parent volunteers who were supposed to be running the splash bucket booth have gotten delayed due to a minor stampede over at the petting zoo. I need you."

"You… need me for what?"

"I need you… to come with me… to the splash bucket," she said insultingly slowly, pointing to the PTA booth like I was being obtuse.

"To… sell tickets?" I asked hopefully.

She threw back her head and brayed like a donkey. It took me a second to realize the rusty sound was her laughter. "Oh, no, Mr. Williams. You'll be sitting under the bucket."

Ugh.

"Ohhhh, yeah, no, I'm afraid I couldn't possibly," I argued. "I don't have a change of clothes—"

"No one has gotten splashed yet this morning. Besides, it's only a cup of water. Don't be dramatic." She turned around like my agreement was guaranteed.

"Sorry, still no. I need to watch Aiden," I said with false regret. "Webb left him with me. So."

"Aiden will stay with me. I'm the school principal. *And* I'll man the Pick-a-Book booth," she said, taking away my final excuse.

I was going to insist that I still couldn't—maybe even take my life in my hands and suggest that she and her

pantsuit should take a turn under the bucket instead—
when Aiden unexpectedly threw me to the wolves.

"That sounds great, Principal Oliver!" he said sweetly.
He stepped toward her and took her hand, which seemed
to surprise her as much as it did me. "Luke, you're the best.
I hope you have so much fun. I can't wait to see!"

Damn it.

"Fine, then. Same rules your dad gave you earlier apply
with Ms. Oliver, okay?"

"Sure."

I sighed. At least Em had said that hardly anyone ever
got splashed.

Still, I gave Aiden my cell phone and my keys to put
back in my booth, just in case.

But after I'd taken my seat on the folding chair under
the bucket of water—which was ginormous, and I was *not*
being dramatic—I realized I'd underestimated just how
badly the kids wanted to splash one of their teachers.

They clustered around the booth, laughing and
cheering as, one after another, they tried and failed to hit
the target. Above the sea of faces, I could see Aiden and
Olin, both standing on a chair in the Pick-a-Book booth,
getting a bird's-eye view of the spectacle and laughing their
heads off, and I found myself laughing, too.

"Jasmine," I said as one of my students paid her dollar
and collected her beanbags. "Dude. You don't wanna
splash me, do you? We're friends."

"No, I don't." Jasmine giggled. "My aunt Katey might,
though."

My eyes widened as I recognized the adult standing
behind her. None other than Webb's favorite server at
Jack's. The woman who had a huge crush on him. The
woman who'd once told me she was the best softball
pitcher in Hollow Swingers history.

"Katey!" I said a little nervously. "H-hey. Don't you look nice today?"

"Thanks." Katey grinned and tucked her blonde hair behind her ears. "I want you to know, Luke, I really like you. And I hope we can be friends."

Then she proceeded to slam the beanbag into the target.

Oh, sweet merciful muffins.

"Ahhhh!" I screamed as the chilly bucket of water splashed down, plastering my hair to my head and soaking through my T-shirt. I jumped to my feet and squeegeed the water away from my eyes with both hands. "Oh, God. You got me! Wow. You weren't kidding about being a great pitcher, huh? Awesome job. Well. Who's the next splash victim?"

I pulled my soaked T-shirt away from my chest and looked around... but no one appeared.

Katey smiled again... a little evilly and held up her remaining beanbags. "It's still you, Luke. I paid for six."

Six?

"N-no, but. But—"

Janice, the other PTA parent working the booth, shrugged as she refilled the bucket with water from a cooler. "You and I are the only ones here. I guess we could both get wet..."

What the duck? There was no one else coming?

"No," I groaned. "I'm already soaked. How much wetter can I get, right?"

It turned out the answer was much, much wetter.

I'd barely gotten my behind back in the seat when Katey hit the target with her second beanbag and I got doused again—with even *colder* water. And then she immediately landed her third shot.

By that point, I was coughing and spluttering water. I

was soaked all the way to my shoes, and the back of my legs was the only dry spot on my body.

"Okay, then! Fun is fun, but now it's done," I said, standing up and clapping my hands like the entire crowd was my first grade class... since many of them *were*. "I'm getting cold, so you guys will have to wait for the next volunteer!"

Fortunately—for me, anyway—one of the volunteer dads ran up at exactly that moment, all apologies, and took the splash seat... wearing shorts, flip-flops, and a heavy waterproof rain poncho like the prepared person he was.

I snicker-snorted at my own soaked state. If I was going to continue living in Little Pippin Hollow—which I was—I was going to start carrying a change of clothes and a rain-coat in my car.

I squelched my way through the crowd, receiving several back pats of support, and ended up back at my booth—which was nearly deserted for the first time all day.

"What happened to you?" Principal Oliver asked.

"What do you *think*?" I shot back. I glanced around the empty booth. "Where's Aiden? I need to go home and get changed, so I'm going to drop him off with Webb."

"Aiden?" She blinked in confusion. "Oh! Umm." She darted a guilty glance around also, even looking under the folding table and behind a pile of boxes. "He... he must've wandered off! *Tsk*."

Was she kidding?

"He's *seven*." I narrowed my eyes. "Seven-year-olds wander, which is why they need adult supervision. What happened to 'I'm the principal, you can entrust him to my care'?"

I stood on my tiptoes, trying to see above the crowd, and when that didn't work, I stood on the chair the boys had been using.

"Well, I *was* watching him. But then someone came in and asked a question about donations… and Maryanne and Olin Kopra were here talking about hamburgers, and Aiden said he was hungry also…" She set her chin. "And I could hardly do two things at once."

"So he went with the Kopras, then?"

"I… yes. Yes, he did."

I rolled my eyes, mildly relieved and still wildly annoyed. It amazed me that she'd actually been a teacher at one point. She liked the bureaucracy so much more than the kids.

I stopped myself from screaming at her, barely, by scouring the crowd. Fortunately, Maryanne was a redhead just like Murray, and I spotted her pretty easily just a few booths down.

Without saying another word to Principal Oliver, I jostled my way through the crowd to where I'd spotted Maryanne. But when I found her and Olin eating burgers at one of the high-top tables someone had set up, there was no one with them.

"Hey. Where's Aiden?" I asked, a little breathless and extremely wet.

"Aiden?" Maryanne blinked at the state of me but quickly shook her head. "He's not at the Pick-a-Book? He was there when we left. I figured he'd be chatting with Amanda."

"A-Amanda," I repeated. "She's here for real?"

"I think so? I saw someone who looked just like her heading toward the Pick-a-Book when we were in the burger line." Her eyes narrowed. "Problem?"

"Maybe? I don't know. Amanda wasn't supposed to be here at all. I mean, she *was*, but then she said she had to work, so Webb wasn't expecting her. But I thought I saw her earlier, too. And now Aiden's gone, and I really don't think he would have randomly *strolled* off all by himself, which means—" I couldn't make myself complete the sentence.

I didn't notice I was close to hyperventilating until Maryanne laid her hand on my arm. "Don't panic. Even if he's with her, they probably just ran to grab some food," she said soothingly. "He was complaining that he was starving."

"Right. You're right. I'm jumping to conclusions." I reminded myself that I trusted Amanda. That I had no reason not to. "I'm going to go look—"

God, where should I even begin? He—they?—could be literally anywhere. I ran both hands through my hair.

"We'll look, too," Maryanne said. "Come on."

But ten minutes later, though I would have sworn we'd covered most of the stalls, we hadn't found him, nor any sign of Amanda. This was starting to feel horribly familiar.

"Where could he be?" I demanded, close to panic.

My brain was spiraling, imagining the worst, because it was literally impossible to stay positive when a child you loved could be in danger. I remembered Webb telling me time and time again that he'd known her better and longer than me, and me encouraging him to trust her, giving her the benefit of every doubt.

Maryanne held her hand over her eyes to block out the glare of the sun. "Okay, he's not here in the booth area, but he could be out on the grass by the gazebo, where the mayor's got the stage set up. He could be in the portable restrooms. He could be over in the picnic area. He could be over by the petting zoo, even."

"Right. Okay. We need more people to look. Em! Emma Sunday!" I yelled when I saw her pass by with her clipboard. "Have you seen Aiden?"

She shook her head. "No. Shit, what happened to you? You're—"

"Splash booth," I said shortly. "But that doesn't matter. Aiden is missing."

She frowned. "Have you checked with my brothers? Hang on. Gage!" she shouted, waving an arm. "Get over here."

"No. And I left my cell back in my booth," I said as Gage ran over. "I haven't called anyone. I checked with Maryanne and Olin. Oh, and Principal Oliver." God, I was so disorganized. Panic was making me run around like a chicken with my head cut off.

But I knew what I needed to do.

"Call Webb." My throat went tight. "Call him, okay? Tell him Aiden's missing, and… and Amanda might be here at the fair."

Em's eyes widened. "You don't think—"

"No, I—" I shook my head. "God, I don't know what I think, Em. Just tell Webb. And tell him… tell him I'm so freakin' sorry, okay?" My eyes filled with scalding tears, though this was not remotely the time for them. "I did it again. Like, jeez Louise, what are the chances that I could lose Aiden *twice*? Webb is never going to forgive me for this." I was never going to forgive myself.

"Luke," Gage began, putting an arm around my shoulder. "Whatever happened, I know it couldn't have been your fault. You—"

I shrugged him off. "It doesn't matter. We just need to find him. I'm going to get my cell. *And* I'm going to talk to Principal Oliver again," I said menacingly. "She seems to always be around when he goes missing."

"Whoa." Gage's eyes flared. "Dude. I'll come with you."

"I don't need help. Go look for—"

Gage shook his head. "I'm not coming to help you, Luke, I'm going to help Principal Oliver, because you look like a very wet avenging angel right now."

When we got back to the booth, Principal Oliver was sitting precisely where I'd left her, not helping look for Aiden at all, and it took all my willpower not to turn her upside down and shake her by her sensible shoes. I was *not* a violent person or even an angry one, but for Aiden, there wasn't much I wouldn't do.

"Where's Aiden?" I demanded, slapping my palm on the table beside her. "Is he with Amanda?"

Principal Oliver lifted her chin. She didn't bother trying to lie. "No, I… I don't know where he is. I assumed he was with the Kopras. I *did* know Amanda was coming to surprise Aiden," she admitted. "Her boss let her out of work early. But I haven't seen her. If she'd tried to leave the booth with Aiden, I would have encouraged her to… to inform someone beforehand."

"But the truth is, you have no clue whether she was here or not because you weren't paying attention," I fumed. "You are the worst kind of—"

Gage grabbed me by the wrist and dragged me out of the booth.

"Let me go!" I insisted.

"I know," he soothed. "I get it. But that's not helping. She probably doesn't know where they are, and she wouldn't tell you if she did, especially if you threaten her. Let's wait for Webb, and we can all organize a search, okay? We'll find him. Luke, we *will*."

"Don't you get it? Webb's not going to want me to search for Aiden. God, Gage, he's not going to want to lay eyes on me. No wonder he doesn't want a relationship. No freakin' wonder he has trust issues! The woman he married probably just took his kid, and I let it happen. *Again*."

If one hair on Aiden's head got hurt, I knew I'd only have myself to blame.

Which was why, when I saw Webb striding across the grass a moment later, his face contorted in anger and his eyes spitting fire, I forced myself to stand exactly where I was and take what was coming to me.

Even though I could barely see him through the tears.

Chapter Twenty

WEBB

When I saw Luke standing outside the Pick-a-Book booth looking like a drowned rat, stuck halfway between murder and tears, I was pretty sure I knew exactly what had happened to cause this situation...

And I was *not* fucking pleased.

"Luke needs you," Em had said when she'd called, worry and anger bleeding into her voice. "Principal Oliver sent him to the splash booth, and now he can't find Aiden. Amanda might have been involved. Luke looks ready to rip someone's head off, starting with Principal Oliver. And Webb? He said to tell you he's sorry."

Sorry? Fuck that.

I'd started running across the town common before I'd hung up the phone.

I knew the moment Luke saw me coming, because he visibly braced, like he was ready for me to scream at him—or maybe to go back to disliking him and cut him out of my life again.

And fuck that, too.

Gage watched me warily as I stalked closer. "Webb," he

said cautiously, holding out a restraining hand like he might try to hold me back. "Dude, maybe chill —"

But I couldn't chill. I didn't pause or hesitate, because this whole fucking situation was unacceptable, and I wouldn't tolerate it for another second.

I grabbed Luke around the back of the neck, and he let out a little grunt of surprise.

Then I pulled him in for a single hard kiss that left him gasping.

"We're going to find him," I said decisively. "It's going to be okay."

Luke's stiff posture melted like candle wax, and he shuddered against me, burying his face against my sweatshirt. "But you don't understand—"

I cut him off. "I do. I get it. I— First things first. Baby, you've gotta be freezing." His shirt was so sodden, water was seeping into my sweatshirt as I held him. "Here, come on." I pulled him out of the crowded walkway and into the Pick-a-Book tent, shooting Principal Oliver the most scathing look I could fathom. And without preamble, I stripped off Luke's T-shirt, tossed it to the ground with a *plop*, and removed my sweatshirt so I could pull it over his head.

My shirt was still warm from my body, and Luke shivered as he burrowed into it.

"I lost him," he said bleakly. "You left him with me and I got distracted and I *lost* him. God."

"It's not your fault."

I wasn't sure whether he even heard me.

"You knew," he said softly, pulling away from me. "You knew something like this would happen, didn't you? That's why you didn't trust Amanda. And you were right—"

"No, Luke. Listen to me. I *didn't* trust Amanda. But you were right to call me on it. *You* were right. I didn't get a chance to tell you this yesterday, but I talked to my attorney. Amanda's been holding down a job. She's been showing up, despite her bad luck. Which is why I'm not freaking out. Believe me, if she took Aiden away from the fair without telling anyone, I'm going to be *pissed*. But I'm going to be pissed mostly because she worried us all and made you fucking cry. She won't let any harm come to him. I know that now."

He took a deep, quavering breath. "How are you so calm? I thought—"

"That I'd be losing my mind? I'll save that for when he's back safe and sound." I wrapped my hand around the back of his neck again. Touching him grounded me and kept me focused. "We're going to find him. Right now."

Luke nodded, like he'd only needed that reassurance in order to regain his natural optimism. He amazed me. "Okay. What do we do?"

"I'm going to call Amanda, first off." I pulled out my phone to do just that. "And you're gonna figure out a way to get everyone's attention." I waved my hand in a circle to indicate the booths and all the areas beyond. "The whole crowd."

"But what if he's with Amanda and they already left? What if they're halfway to the highway? Should we call the police?"

"We'll let Sheriff Carver know, but they can't have left. The parking lot's been shut for over an hour because someone left the door to the pig enclosure open, and two of the pigs escaped." I rolled my eyes. "One of them was Donna McKeown's sow Peppa, and she started farrowing."

"Farrowing?"

"Giving birth," I explained. "Right there in the parking lot."

Luke sucked in a breath. "Donna did?"

"No, honey. The pig."

"Oh." His jaw dropped, and he gaped at me for a long moment before he recovered. "I have so many questions."

"Later. Right now, we have a mission. Amanda's not answering, but that doesn't mean anything. They're either still here, or someone's seen them walk off. We need to get everyone's attention and find out."

"Webb, what's going on?" Drew hurried up, breath heaving.

I spoke loudly so at least the people around us could hear. "We need to get everyone's attention. Aiden's gone missing."

A murmur of concern spread quickly.

"The mayor has his microphone set up for announcements," Drew reminded us.

"Good. But—" Someone nearby won a game, and a chorus of cheers and ringing bells filled the air. "—that won't be enough. See if the mayor or anyone has a bullhorn. Something we can use to spread the message all the way back to the picnic area."

"Mayor York's got the bugle over at the gazebo!" a childish voice piped up. "That could be loud… if you blew it."

Luke tilted his head in mild reproof. "Olin, sweetie, is now the time to bring up that bugle?"

But I blinked, because actually, when I thought about it…

"Luke. What's the one thing that will make this whole town stop and take notice?"

"Uh. I dunno."

"Yes you do. What makes every patron of Panini Jack's stop eating their breakfast? What *one* subject is so popular, my freakin' family is selling us out to win commemorative scrolls?"

MAY ARCHER

Luke's lips parted in horror. "No. No, there are other ways. Skywriters. Fireworks. Air raid sirens."

"Do you have an air raid siren handy, baby?"

His shoulders slumped. "No, but—"

"Love, it's gonna be fine. Trust me?"

Luke's eyes softened, and despite the worry still in them, he nodded without hesitation. Despite all the things left unsaid between us—all the things I hadn't told him last night about land deeds, and Amanda, and the fact that *I was in love with him*—he still said yes.

And I vowed to myself right then and there that I would work hard every single day for the rest of our lives to be worthy of that instant trust.

I grabbed his hand, and together we ran toward the table by the stage in the center of the common by the gazebo. The mayor wasn't there, but Dora York was, holding down the fort for her husband.

"Dora, Luke and I need the bugle. Right away. And we're gonna need to use the stage."

Dora gasped and fluttered her hands excitedly, like she wasn't sure whether she should find her husband, text her friends, contact Genevieve with an exclusive story, or hand over the bugle first.

I made that decision for her by reaching over and snatching the bugle off the temporary plaque that some kind and overly invested soul had erected on the table.

"Thanks so much, Ms. York," Luke called over his shoulder as he let me tow him up the makeshift stairs to the stage.

We stepped up to the microphone stand, and I stared down at the brass instrument in my hand. It still looked a little dented and tarnished and old but somehow seemed more intimidating than it had all those weeks ago. Maybe because I knew just how powerful it was.

I put it to my lips and blew… and, yep, my drunkenness had not distorted my memory of that noise one little bit, but it seemed to have the desired effect.

People near us stopped talking and laughing, and the silence spread outward like ripples in a pond. Game bells stopped jangling. The music slowly died.

The silence didn't come quickly enough for the man at my side, though. He grabbed the bugle from my hand impatiently and blew it once again, even louder than I had.

"Holy crap," someone in the crowd muttered, covering their ears.

"Oh mah gahd, they're doing their vows," someone else said.

"Webb *bestowed* Luke his sweatshirt! Part the Fifth is complete! This is really happening!"

"Lukey! Oh, Sue, it's Lukey and Webb. I told you they'd work things out. Didn't I tell you?" Ms. Williams yelled from somewhere nearby.

"Heck, yeah, Luke!" Alan Laroche yelled, wiping his misty eyes with his Habs jersey. "Couldn'ta happened to a nicer guy!"

"We're looking for a missing child," Luke said into the microphone, and the cheering cut off as quickly as the carnival sounds had. His voice wobbled a little with worry and unmistakable love. "My—uh. Webb Sunday's boy Aiden's gone missing, and we need help finding him. For those of you who don't live here and maybe don't know him, he's seven years old. Four and a half feet tall. He's got dark hair and big green eyes. He's wearing a Nature Scout uniform with a brand-new knot-tying badge on it—" Luke sniffled a little and tried to cover it with a cough, and I wrapped my arm around his waist.

There was a reason why, once I'd stopped irrationally

disliking Luke Williams, I hadn't been able to erect any barriers or defenses against him.

Luke continued. "And, uh… his front teeth haven't grown in yet—"

There was a reason why, even when I'd tried to tell myself I didn't trust him, *I had*.

"Aiden's sweet and talkative and smart, and—"

There was a reason why falling for this man had been as easy as… as falling off a damn roof. How could I *not* fall in love with a man who was gorgeous and warm as sunshine? Who was smart enough to know what was most important in the world and had a heart big enough to treasure it?

"—and if you've seen him, please just tell someone. Nobody needs to be in trouble, okay? We just want to know he's safe—"

"Webb?" Amanda pushed through the crowd toward the stage, towing a not-particularly-pleased-looking Aiden behind her. "He's okay, you guys."

Oh, holy shit.

Luke covered his face with both hands. A single, low sob emerged, like he'd finally let himself fall apart now that he knew he could. "Thank God," he whispered into my shoulder. "Oh, Webb, thank God."

"I wanted to surprise you all when my boss let me out early," Amanda continued. "But when I was on my way to the Pick-a-Book tent, I saw Aiden dart out, and I followed him to the playground."

"Aiden," I said severely. "Is that true? Why in the world would you do that? Why would you worry us—"

Amanda set a hand on his shoulder. "Tell them what you told me."

"I didn't want to worry you, Dad, I wanted you to blow the bugle!" Aiden cried, the words rushing out of him in a torrent. "I wanted you guys to get married, and I wanted Luke to be in our family. So I left the tent, and I told Olin to tell you to blow the bugle, and you *did*, and I'm not sorry!"

"We're going to discuss your behavior at home, young man," I said.

His defiant stance faltered a little, but he forced himself to rally. "I don't care! You blew the bugle, and now you're married! And that's all that matters."

"*Jesus*," I whispered under my breath.

Ernie York heaved himself through the crowd. "Not so fast, kiddo." He smoothed his hair with one hand. "They haven't said their vows yet. And they'd better not either," he added, "until Genevieve gets here. She was planning to do a live broadcast tomorrow, but this'll be better."

Aiden looked from Ernie to Luke to me, clearly crest-fallen. "Vows? They gotta do vows, too?"

Amanda squeezed his little shoulders gently.

"Yep," Ernie said. "They've gotta pledge their love and declare their desire to be together."

Aiden's eyes went wide. "Okay, but… but you *do* love each other. Mr. Williams! Luke! You love my dad. You said so!"

Wait, what?

I turned to look at Luke. His face was bright red beneath his freckles, and he looked up at me shyly. "I… I know," he said, turning back to Aiden. "But…"

"You do?" I asked in surprise. I knew he cared about me and Aiden—it was there in everything he did for us, the way he put his trust in me so completely—but was it possible he'd fallen for me as hard as I'd fallen for him?

"Of course I do," Luke said softly and maybe a little sadly. "You're… gosh, Webb. You're everything. You're so strong and protective. You love so devotedly. You make me feel like nothing is impossible. How could I not love you?"

His words reminded me of my exact thoughts from a moment before, and I couldn't help my short huff of amusement.

Luke's next words sobered me instantly. "But I don't want you to say it back! I know you're not ready for a relationship right now, and that's okay. I can feel how much you care for me, and that's way more important than you saying—"

"I love you," I said emphatically. "I love you so damn much."

"What? No! You can't," Luke blurted, stepping all over my romantic declaration, and I laughed out loud, just like I did every damn day that this man was in my life.

I took his hand and held it up, twining mine around it so we were palm to palm. The moment felt just as right, just as fated, in the stone-sober bright light of day as it had on that cold, dark February night.

"You brought me hope. I didn't realize I'd lost it until you found it and brought it back to me. You helped me trust in people again. To believe that life can be as full of good things as bad. And I'm keeping you. If you need me to blow that bugle all day every day to prove it—"

"Oh, God, please don't," Knox said. "That thing sounds like the bellow of a constipated elephant."

"Hey!" Van the bartender appeared out of nowhere and smacked Knox on the back of the head. "Respect the damn bugle, Sunday. That thing is good luck."

I laughed. I was definitely going to respect it from now on, but the bugle wasn't lucky. The only luck I'd needed was the man in my arms, the starry-eyed flatlander I'd fallen in love with.

"Good enough for me," Ernie York said, sniffling and

drying his eyes. "That was... beautiful." His wife patted him on the back gently. "I hereby declare, by the power vested in me by the Town of Little Pippin Hollow, that the articles outlined in the Little Pippin Hollow Handfast Act of 1762, that Thomas Webb Sunday and Luke Guilford Williams are hereby..."

He paused dramatically, as if giving me and Luke one final chance to back out.

The two of us looked at each other and grinned; then Luke wrapped his arms around my neck and kissed the hell out of me—or as my *husband* would say, the heckity out of me—right in front of all the people we loved best.

"...married!" he concluded happily. "What the bugle has joined together, let no man put asunder."

Epilogue

LUKE

August

"Where are you taking me? I was supposed to be at a Hook-Up twenty minutes ago," I said, hoping Webb didn't accidentally walk me into a tree branch.

"Surely there must be a better term for your knitting club meetings," he sighed. "And no, I already told Phillip you were missing it because you had plans. With your *husband*."

I grinned under my blindfold.

If you had told me six months ago, when Webb and I first blew the unity bugle, that Webb Sunday would one day refer to me as his *husband*, I'd have assumed you, too, had partaken of one too many Rusty Spikes, because such a thing could never happen.

Even if you'd told me back in April, on the day Webb and I officially pledged ourselves as husbands to one another in front of the whole town, I wouldn't have believed the man who hated relationships could be so damn comfortable with the word.

But four months had passed since that day. Four

chaotic, heart-squeezingly wonderful months. And now I knew better.

Because over those four months, I'd sat many a night in a chilly hockey arena, cheering myself hoarse, screaming, "Two hands on the stick, Aiden!" and "Hey! Dirty hit, ref!" while Webb told the other parents, "What can you do? *My husband* is kind of a hockey fanatic, especially when our kid's in the playoffs."

Over those four months, Webb had proudly bragged to every tourist who came through Sunday Orchard—and there was a metric *ton* of them after Hand-Fast Watch went viral on YouTube, much to Ernie York's delight—that all the hand-woven textiles in the gift shop were *his husband's* designs.

Over those four months, my mom and Sue had simply extended their visit longer and longer until they were officially living in the fixed-up farmhouse, helping me with plans for the Hollow Fiber Arts Center that I hoped to get off the ground the following year, and Webb introduced them to everyone he knew as "the women who helped make *my husband* so amazing."

And over those four months, every time Aiden's new collie puppy, Black Bear, sat on my lap while I read a chapter book to Aiden—even when she grew way, way too big to fit there—Webb would turn to Amanda, who was at our house more often than not these days, and say, "That's *my husband*," in this tone of quiet satisfaction that made it clear he wouldn't have done a dang thing differently, even down to the bugles and the commemorative scrolls… and she'd smile and say, "I know."

"Okay, *now*. You can take off your blindfold."

I pulled off the bandana and blinked at the late-summer sun streaming through the full branches of the nearest apple trees.

"We're in the orchard," I said, stating the obvious.

"Yes," Webb said excitedly. "But not just any orchard. The Pond Orchard. *Our* orchard."

I got the feeling he was trying to make a big sentimental point about how it had been the contentious disagreement about this parcel of land that had brought us together, but... it hadn't been. Not really. Not any more than the Rusty Spikes or the Unity Bugle had.

Webb Sunday and I had been meant for each other all along. It had just taken us a little while to figure it out.

"So it is," I agreed. "Oooh! Did you bring me up here to see the Black Oxford?" I gestured toward the nearby dwarf tree. Since Webb's favorite activity—well, his favorite *family-friendly* activity—was walking the trees with me and Aiden, it was safe to say I was becoming as much of a tree expert as Aiden was. "I know you were worried about the leaf spots, baby, but it looks like it's really improv —*ooof!*"

"I did not bring you up here to talk about leaf spots." Webb hauled me over to stand against one of his prized Gravensteins. Then he stood back, pulled something from his back pocket, and cleared his throat.

"Oh my God. Tell me that isn't a historical scroll," I said with a laugh. "I thought you were allergic."

"Hey. We're about to have a very sentimental moment here, okay?" He pressed a firm kiss to my lips, which was enough to get me to stop laughing... at least temporarily.

Then he unrolled the scroll and began to read. "At a private affembly... I mean, *assembly*, held at the parcel of land borderethed on one side by a natural waterway of some notability and on another by a stone wall commemorating the Great Spongy Moth Plague, on this the twenty-fourth day of August, be it here Enacted that Partners who are hereby enjoined together in Matrimony, be it through Historical Handfasting or—"

I couldn't hold back my laugh. "I get it. We're married. It seems to be something you enjoy reminding people of." And something I'd never get tired of hearing.

Webb's answering smile was so sexy, it made me want to jump his bones. I looked around. We were actually plenty far away from both farmhouses. The Sundays wouldn't be able to see us from the Sunday side, and Aunt Susan and my mom wouldn't be able to see us from the Williams side.

"Hush, baby," he warned, leaning over to drop another quick kiss on my lips. "This is important. And if you were married to someone as sexy and kind as my husband, you'd want everyone to know, too. Now, where was I? *Ahem*… Be it through Historical handfasting or one of those Quickie Vegas Deals—"

"It does not say that."

"It does! Let's see… blabity-blah about commingled family members and such… okay, this is the important part. Let it be Known that Thomas Webb Sunday, by this Extremely Legal Decree which He Did Not Order off the Internet, hereby Disclaims, Proclaims, and Exclaims that the Land Parcel so nameth-ed doth belong In Perpetuity to one Lukey Guilford Williams Sunday in a gesture of Unity, Commitment, Appreciation, and *Uncomplicated* Love—see what I did there?"

"I see," I agreed, though I was pretty sure our love was the only uncomplicated part of this.

"—And also as a Marriage Portion symbolic of his Everlasting Gratitude to the Williams Family. According to the agreement here signed, Let It Be Known that the Land Parcel, henceforth to be known as Hand-Fast Hill—"

"No!" I sputtered in amusement. "Hand-Fast Hill?"

"—will remain a Celebratory Prominence upon which the Sunday and Williams family may congregate, and from which Lukey should probably pay Apple Tithes, at a Rate to be Determined Later, but since it's Legally His Land, He May or May Not So Chooseth—"

"Wait," I said as the oldie-worldie words translated in my head. "Is this… are you… You're joking, right? You're not actually giving me your orchard."

Webb frowned and squinted at the scroll. "I could have sworn this says it's *your* orchard. Hmm."

I grabbed the scroll, rolled it back up, and placed it safely on the 4x4 seat before returning to stand in front of him. "You're giving me this land?" I asked again, bewildered.

Webb's face relaxed into a smile. "Yep. I mean, we're married, so things are a little murky. This protects the land for your descendants and keeps it separate from the Sunday Orchard properties in case you ever decide you want to do something else with it. It is legally part of the Williams Farm now. Or, well, I guess you could separate it out and—"

I took his hands in mine. "I don't want to separate anything out. That's the point. I want the Williams Farm and the Sunday Orchard to be one big happy family… estate." My face heated. "That sounded fancier than I intended. I mean, I want my descendants to be your descendants, Webb."

Webb stepped closer and wrapped his arms around me. "I want that, too. And now that your mom and Aunt Sue are moving into your farmhouse and you're at our place, and Knox and Gage are up the hill in the Pumpkin House, it feels like a family estate already. But… I need you to always know you're worth more to me than any parcel of land, Luke. You and our family… there's nothing more important."

I laughed and nestled closer to him, kissing the side of his neck. "You've been watching Hallmark movies with Marco again, haven't you?"

The breeze blew apple scent around us. Webb had once described it as the scent of his childhood, and I wondered if there would be any future Williams-Sunday children to join Aiden in experiencing the same magical memories one day. I hoped so.

"You might be right," he admitted. "But so am I."

I pulled back and gazed up at him. "Thank you. For the land… Hand-Fast Hill… and the love. And the family. And for being part of my happy ever after. You're my dream come true in real life."

"Fucking Christ. Now who's been watching Hall-mark?" he teased.

"Have you *seen* Betty White in *The Lost Valentine?* I can't help it if every time Marco plays it, I happen to be folding laundry in the same room."

Webb leaned in and kissed me. Even though we'd been living together full-time as a married couple all summer now, his kisses still took my breath away. It only took seconds before I was hard and desperate, having dirty fantasies about getting naked on Hand-Fast Hill.

"You drive me fuckin' crazy," Webb said against my ear. His hands were down the back of my pants, and his hard dick was jabbing me in the gut.

"Lonnie Duncan warned me the bloom would fall off the rose pretty fast now that we're truly married," I said, gasping when Webb's teeth clamped lightly around my earlobe. "Seems like he didn't know what the freak he was talking about."

The rumble of Webb's laughter made my dick even

harder. "Mrs. Duncan's bloom has been solidly planted in Mrs. Graber's rose garden for years."

"Ew!" I laughed until Webb's fingers wandered under my shirt, found my nipple ring, and tugged. "Oh God. More of that, please."

Webb pulled back just long enough to yank my T-shirt over my head before lowering his mouth to suck on my other nipple while he continued to toy with the piercing. He knew exactly how to drive me wild.

The warm sun hit my skin, adding to the heat Webb was already building up inside of me. I threaded my fingers through his hair and looked around. He was right. There was no way anyone from either side of our properties would see us unless they'd gone out of their way to find us.

"I told everyone to stay away," he said as if reading my mind. "Aiden's at the movies with Amanda, and everyone else knows to avoid this area unless they want a free show. We're alone, I promise."

"You told them that?"

"Can we stop talking about our family? I have half a mind to build a little hideaway house just for us. Something over past the river on the northern edge of the property. But we can talk about it later."

His voice took on a gravelly, growly tone when he was turned on, and it drove me wild. He knew it, too. I swore he did it on purpose.

"My pants," I squeaked. "Too tight."

His hands moved down to make quick work of removing them. As soon as he palmed my dick through the cotton of my boxer briefs, I let out a loud, desperate groan that would have been embarrassing if I was lucid enough to care.

I wasn't.

And now I was fantasizing about a sex cabin, a place we could be as loud and debauched as we wanted. Now that Webb had fully embraced the male side of his bisexuality, he'd been an eager student insistent on trying all kinds of things.

I'd never been a complainer, and I wasn't about to start now. Even if it meant I was getting naked in broad daylight among the heritage varietals on our family land.

"Take off... clothes," I said through heaving breaths. "Naked... Webb."

His grin was sexy as heck, especially when it had that hint of devilry in it. It promised very good things for me and my body. I knew this from experience. Lots and lots of experience. Our dresser had carved a groove in the wood floor in front of our bedroom door until one day a simple hook-and-loop latch had appeared on the doorframe.

Uncle Drew had rolled his eyes at us that day and muttered something under his breath about the dresser being louder than the sex. Maybe he was right, but that was only because Webb had gotten excited about using his T-shirt as a gag that week.

Within moments, Webb and I were naked like freaking Adam and Steve, up against an apple tree, and I was too drunk on desire to even make a joke about it. His fingers had gotten magic slick from somewhere and were already dancing across my gland. One of my legs was hitched up over his hip, and the rough bark of the tree dug into my overheated back.

I was too far gone to help keep my leg up, and it kept slipping down. Finally, Webb spat out a curse and spun me around, shoving me face-first against the trunk. Apple trees weren't, in general, very tall, but thankfully, this was one of the old heirloom ones from a million years ago before they...

"Fuhhhh-freaking freak!" I cried when he slid his fingers back home. "Freak. Right there. Babe. No-oh-oh, *yes.*"

His fingers were little miracle-makers, and I needed them to stay right there forever and ever amen.

Instead of doing that, he pulled them out and replaced them with his bare cock. I groaned against the trunk. One of Webb's hands clutched the back of my neck and held my face against the tree as his other held me spread open for him. I focused on relaxing.

"Good boy," he teased affectionately. Even though it had started off as a joke the first time he'd said it, it made me hot when he said it during sex. Very hot.

"Shut up," I argued weakly. We both knew I didn't mean it.

"Have I told you lately how grateful I am that you prefer to bottom?" he hissed in my ear from behind me. "Because the clench of your body around me like this is the fucking best thing in the fucking world."

We'd tried switching things up. Webb had been super open to bottoming and had actually handled it well, but afterward, we'd both admitted to preferring it the other way.

Thank God. Thank all the gods. Thank the god of bottoming specifically.

"Move," I groaned. "I'm good. Go."

His soft lips grazed the back of my ear even as his hand held my neck in its firm grip. "Don't want to hurt you, love."

I squeezed my eyes closed and focused on the feel of him. "I love you," I breathed.

"Thank fuck for that because I can't live without you, Luke. I love you so damned much."

His arms wrapped around me, and his clever, callused

fingers toyed with my piercings as he thrust into me. I was sandwiched between the rough bark of the tree and the warm strength of my husband, whose cock lit me up inside until my usual babbling pleas spewed forth.

"Need to come," I cried. "Please. Webb. Please. Need. You. *Please.*"

He murmured endearments into my ear as he reached down to jack me off and continued pounding into me. Sweat pooled between us where the sun broke through the thick, leafy branches above. The scent of apples surrounded us, and the sound of fat, lazy bees nearby echoed the sex buzz taking over my brain.

When my orgasm hit, it all slammed together in one big, sensuous moment. "Fucking *fuck*," I screamed. Two birds shot from a nearby tree, and the bees disappeared.

Webb grunted through his own release before letting out a belated chuckle. "Would you listen to that? My precious angel husband just cursed a blue streak."

"Fuck," I said again as aftershocks continued to course through me. "Fucking fuck."

Webb kissed down my neck and across to my shoulder while I floated back down to earth. When I was finally lucid again, he pulled out and moved over to the 4x4, where he pulled out a package of wet wipes.

"You really did plan this," I said.

He used the wipes to clean off his hands before tending to me with gentle, affectionate attention. "Duh."

His hair was a mess, dotted with a few glossy green leaves, and his nose was red from being pressed against my skin. He was gorgeous as always.

"Got any food in there? I'm suddenly starving," I admitted.

Webb finished cleaning us both up and handed me my clothes before finding his own. "Nah, but I thought we could head over to Panini Jack's for an early dinner. He said he's making your favorite avocado ranch sandwich today. And then I happen to know Drew's planning Sunday Sundaes for later… with Boston Cream Pie ice cream."

I shot him a look. "You're really pulling out all the stops today. Expert-level romancing."

Webb reached for my hand and kissed it. "I don't ever want you to doubt how much I love you, Luke. How grateful I am to be your best friend and partner for life. How humbled I am that you love Aiden and that you look out for the rest of my family just like I do. I… *we*… are so lucky you're part of us now. And you deserve the world."

I fought against sappy tears of happiness by cracking our new favorite joke. "That was bugle-worthy right there."

Webb groaned as he led me to the 4x4 and helped me into the passenger seat. "Speaking of, did you hear about the tourists who tried blowing the bugle last night?"

He hopped in and started us back toward the house so we could switch the 4x4 out for his truck.

"No, but that has to be like the tenth one this summer, right?"

He shrugged. "I can't decide if Ernie York is excited because of the booming tourist traffic it's brought in or if he's annoyed at how many scrolls he has to carry around now."

We both laughed, but I was pretty sure the answer was the first one. It turned out Ernie York was a romantic at heart, and to this day, he got misty-eyed when he saw me and Webb.

When we arrived at Panini Jack's, we realized the Sundays, my mom, and my Aunt Sue were already there with the same idea. They waved us over to the huge table they'd commandeered. "Join us!" Gage called. "We were just talking about you two."

Hawk came over to set two glasses of water down in front of us, but when he got a closer look at Webb, his face turned stormy.

"You look like you just had sex in the orchard," he accused.

My face lit on fire, and I pretty much died right there on the spot. Webb's face turned crimson, but his was anger rather than embarrassment. He opened his mouth to call his brother out for his rude behavior when Hawk turned and glared at Jack, who was standing a few feet away, delivering someone's bill.

"Everyone in this town is having sex except me! I'm going to be a virgin until I die old and alone. I'm living with a damned cherry that will *never be picked*!"

He yanked off the denim half-apron around his waist and threw it down on the floor. "I quit." Then he stormed out the front door.

Everyone in the entire restaurant turned to Jack, who looked like he'd eaten last week's fish. His eyes shot to Webb with a pleading look. "I didn't do anything, I promise."

Webb's face scrunched up in confusion. "Do anything about what? What was that all about?"

If my sweet husband had a blind spot, it was that he still thought of Hawk as a child like Aiden instead of an adult almost the same age as Gage. By the look on Jack's face, it was pretty clear not everyone had trouble seeing Hawk as the fully grown, handsome man he was.

Jack's nostrils widened before he looked around the restaurant and realized everyone was gawping at him. "Nothing to see here, people. Please respect Hawk's privacy and allow him to have a bad day without spreading it around town. Understood?"

Several people gave him reluctant nods, but not a soul in the place expected this outburst to remain out of the Pippin gossip mill, including Jack. He sighed and suddenly looked tired and hopeless. "Back to work," he muttered to no one in particular. Maybe he was talking to himself.

After he returned to the kitchen, I nudged Webb. "Go talk to him. He needs his best friend."

"Yeah, okay. I can't imagine what Hawk was thinking with that outburst," he hissed in a low voice. "Jack doesn't think of him that way. They're friends."

I opened my mouth to remind him that he and I had been friends, too… for about ten minutes before we started having sex, but quickly shut it again. "They'll sort their relationship themselves, baby. Just let him know you care."

Once Webb had followed Jack to the back, Katey bounced up with her order pad and a big smile. "Hey, Luke! Jack's making your favorite avocado sandwich today. Do you want waffle fries with it or fruit?"

Seemed like when Katey had paid a king's ransom to dunk me at the Spring Fling, she'd worked something out of her system, because after that, she'd decided we were BFFs. I supposed now that Webb was fully, legally mine, she no longer had cause for jealousy.

"Fries, please," I said politely.

"He's already had plenty of fruit today," Knox added under his breath. "Considering he smells like our orchard."

I sank lower in my chair, but Knox reached over to ruffle my hair. And then pulled a small stick out of it.

When Webb returned from the kitchen, he took the seat next to mine and leaned over to press a kiss to my cheek. "Love you," he whispered.

"He okay?" I asked in a low voice.

Webb shrugged. "He wouldn't talk. But I told him I'm here if he needs me."

The door to the café opened, and Aiden came running in, followed by Amanda.

"Dad! Luke! Guess what we saw? The new Dreampest movie! It was so freaking cool."

He nudged himself between the two of us and climbed onto my lap. He was getting big, all knees and elbows, but I loved every chance I got to give him hugs while he was still young enough to let us.

He faced Webb and started rattling off details about the movie. When Amanda approached, my mom reached out to wave her into an empty chair at the table. "I was hoping you'd come, honey! We need a gossip update about your Realtor and the cute mortgage broker."

Amanda grinned, but before she sat down, she glanced at Webb as she sometimes did when someone invited her to stay for a cookout, or to meet us at Jack's for breakfast, or to come for a campout at the Orchard to celebrate Aiden's birthday. Her look said, *This okay?*

Webb rolled his eyes and nodded, which was lumberjack code for "You're very welcome, of course, Amanda, please sit down," and that's exactly what she did, pulling up a chair beside my mom and launching into her story.

Webb and Amanda had made a real effort to heal their relationship over those first few weeks after the Spring Fling. They'd had several long talks—more than they'd had in their entire marriage, according to Webb—and while things hadn't been perfect, they were both committed to getting along for Aiden's sake.

Aiden was thriving, and that was what mattered the most.

That and the love we all had for each other.

Because there were a few major elements of my fairy-tale happy ending that I hadn't realized were missing from my fantasies.

Good things happened as often as bad—I still believed that.

But a person's good fortune didn't come from the Unity Bugle, just like his farmhouse didn't come complete with a fairy-tale happily ever after, his legacy wasn't a parcel of land, and his home had very little to do with geography.

Real good fortune was being surrounded by people you loved—people who loved you, too, and who'd work beside you every day to make your dreams come true—and I'd found mine in this large, nosy family… and in Little Pippin Hollow.

Need more Sundays in your life? Get ready for Hawk's story, CHERRY PICKED, which is coming soon!

And don't forget to check out Pick Me, Knox and Gage's story, as well as the free short story Pick One!

Acknowledgments

A huge thank you (as always) to Lucy for being the world's best alpha reader and friend.

Thanks to my daughter, for helping me brainstorm the most fun (but ridiculous, but *fun*) list of handfasting demands.

Thanks to Carlie Marie for the hockey mom lingo!!

Thanks to my army of amazing Canadians - Sandra, who always says "we'll make it work," Cate who is endlessly talented and encouraging, Leslie who is an incredible beta and kitten herder, and Chelsea who brings sunshine wherever she goes.

And thanks to YOU, reader, for spending your precious reading time with me. <3

Also by May Archer

Licking Thicket series (with Lucy Lennox)

Sunday Brothers series

Love in O'Leary series

Whispering Key series

The Way Home series

M/F Romance written as Maisy Archer

About May

May lives outside Boston. She spends her days raising three incredibly sarcastic children, finding inventive ways to drive her husband crazy, planning beach vacations, avoiding the gym, reading M/M romance, and occasionally writing it. She's also published several M/F romance titles as Maisy Archer.

For free content and the latest info on new releases, sign up for her newsletter at: https://www.subscribepage.com/MayArcher_News

Want to know what projects May has coming up? Check out her Facebook reader group Club May for giveaways, first-look cover reveals, and more.

You can also catch her on Bookbub, and check out her recommended reads!

Printed in Great Britain
by Amazon

84374592R00181